W9-ATK-946

BY AMELIA GREY

The Heirs' Club of Scoundrels Series
The Duke in My Bed
The Earl Claims a Bride
Wedding Night with the Earl

The Rakes of St. James Series
Last Night with the Duke
To the Duke, with Love
It's All About the Duke

First Comes Love Series
The Earl Next Door
Gone with the Rogue
How to Train Your Earl

Say I Do Series
Yours Truly, The Duke
Sincerely, The Duke

Anthologies
The Heirs' Club of Scoundrels
Kissing Under the Mistletoe

SINCERELY, THE DUKE

AMELIA GREY

St. Martin's Paperbacks

First published in the United States by St. Martin's Paperbacks, an imprint of St. Martin's Publishing Group.

SINCERELY, THE DUKE

Copyright © 2024 by Amelia Grey.

All rights reserved.

For information, address St. Martin's Publishing Group, 120 Broadway, New York, NY 10271.

www.stmartins.com

ISBN: 978-1-250-85043-0

Our books may be purchased in bulk for promotional, educational, or business use. Please contact your local bookseller or the Macmillan Corporate and Premium Sales Department at 1-800-221-7945, ext. 5442, or by email at MacmillanSpecialMarkets@macmillan.com.

Printed in the United States of America

St. Martin's Paperbacks edition / April 2024

10 9 8 7 6 5 4 3 2 1

CHAPTER 1

"She had a son."

Roderick Cosworth, the Duke of Stonerick, considered his mother's frown as he bent to place a hello kiss onto her cheek. "Oh?" Ignoring the fatigue in his body and throbbing in his head, he managed to smile as he straightened. "I don't remember you mentioning Peg was in the family way again."

"Not your sister." The dowager duchess sighed wistfully and lightly brushed him away with her lace-trimmed handkerchief. "Your cousin's wife. Hildegard just gave her husband an heir, and you still haven't bothered to marry."

So that was the reason his maman sent a second note insisting he must come to her London town house after he'd declined her first invitation because he was feeling so hellish. A fever had come upon him during his late afternoon card game. It was a fierce one and the second he'd had in as many months. Grousing with her, however lightheartedly, about his cousin's good fortune or anything else wasn't something he was up to tonight.

Rick stepped back and digested his younger cousin's news while the palatable aromas of cooked fruit and baking pastry dough wafted up into the drawing room from the kitchen. Smells that would have enticed him to stay for dinner on any other evening.

"I trust mother and child are well?" he offered, doing his best to steady his weak knees, appear normal, and ignore the wretched way he felt.

"Perfectly, it seems." The dowager pretended to adjust a three-buttoned cuff on her puce-colored sleeve. "The rather long letter from Shubert arrived earlier today and, as you can imagine, it's had me in a tizzy of a mood. They didn't want to tell anyone she was in the family way until after the birth and they knew all was well. No doubt that is why they had excused themselves from your invitation to join us in London for Christmastide."

"That sounds reasonable. This is a happy occasion."

Her full brows rose with skepticism as she fiddled with her other sleeve. "I'm sure it is for him. Only twenty-two, married less than a year, and already a father."

His maman didn't sound bitter or cynical, just perturbed. "He has many reasons to crow," Rick answered, careful not to move his upper body too much while making himself comfortable on the plush velvet settee opposite his mother's chair. The fever had brought on a raging ache in his head and an uncommon weakness in his limbs that wouldn't pass. "Let him do so in peace."

"Of course, I will," she answered in her softly spoken voice. "I'll only complain to you. It's quite refreshing to hear about sons who please their mamans and give them grandsons."

Rick grunted more from the way he felt than from

his mother's thinly veiled grievance. His lack of a wife had been her favorite topic of conversation for as long as he could remember. Though he was nearing thirty, there was nothing she relished more than reminding him he was late to the altar. Truth to tell, Rick usually enjoyed their contending discussions and looked forward to them, but with being chilled one moment and then in the next feeling so hot as to think the devil himself was after his soul, he wasn't up to sparring with his mother.

"Are we back to that?"

"We are always back to that, my dear," she admitted, a gentle scolding in her tone but a twitch of good humor on her lips. "You leave me no choice. You know my constant fear is that you'll end up not having an heir and the title will go to Shubert and his son instead of your father's lineage. That would have him spinning in his grave through all eternity. And me too."

"You're not dead yet, Maman," he countered her doom-sounding prediction. "And not likely to be anytime soon." That new ladies' society she'd joined a few months ago was obviously plying her with nonsense again.

"I'm getting old," she insisted without a smidgen of complaint or conviction in her voice. "I have no way of knowing how much longer I'll live. It's not for us to say."

"Many years. You are fifty and in perfect health."

"Well, not that age quite yet," she corrected with a hushed breath and appreciative smile while smoothing one side of her slightly graying, tawny-brown hair. "Though it won't be long. Nonetheless, if you'd married as young as your cousin, you'd have one heir bouncing on your knee, and I'd be running through the meadow at Stonerick with—" She paused. Her eyes narrowed and searched his face. "You seem a little flushed. Do you feel all right?"

Rick clenched his teeth a moment before speaking. No, he didn't, but he'd manage for his maman. He should have known she was too astute not to notice something. "We had a rough cricket match this morning."

"I do wish you'd give up your sporting club as Wyatt did last year."

He rolled his shoulders and took a deep breath. "You used to be delighted I was in the club because I spent too much time alone. You are looking for more to worry about."

She inclined her head cheekily and leaned against the arm of her chair in a rare, relaxed way. "Your father always said I worry so well."

Indeed she did, and considered it an admirable asset.

Alberta Fellows Cosworth, Dowager Duchess of Stonerick, was a classic beauty in every sense of the word. A lovely face with a determined chin, and blue eyes that sparkled no matter her temperament. The soft lines that feathered from her eyes and upper lip spoke of a genteel and easy life. Rick didn't know of any other lady who had aged as gracefully as his mother. Part of her charm among the bevy of Polite Society matrons was her characteristic expression of contentment no matter what might be going on around her.

Always exemplary in manners and faultless in appearance, she was graceful and the epitome of all a dowager should be. Quietly regal, strong as oak, and in control. It was only with her son that she relaxed her public persona and spoke the true emotions she felt.

"Father was right. You worry sweeter than anyone I know." He managed to smile despite his weariness. "I have dinner with you most every Sunday and attend church with you Christmas and Easter. How can you imply I don't try to make you happy?"

"Suffice it to say I'm feeling more melancholy than usual because of Shubert's gift of a son."

"You've been fretting over me not having an heir since the duke passed away when I was barely three years old."

"True. I should have ignored all the solicitors and betrothed you to someone then," she admitted with all confidence, no shame, and only a hint of teasing glimmer in her eyes. "It was a little more acceptable and would have been much easier to accomplish such an agreement back then. My error at the time." She finished with a dispassionate lift of her chin.

Rick blew out a short laugh and immediately took a deep breath to keep from wincing. He should have gone home and drank a cup of willow bark tea before coming over, but her second note appeared urgent. He'd splashed water in his face and downed another brandy instead. The aftereffects of it were hitting him hard. That, along with a haze of exhaustion settling over him, caused a wave of renewed concern about the return of the fever so quickly.

"You frivolously pass off your obligation now," she added, "but I daresay one day you will be sorry you haven't married, and instead have chosen only to amuse yourself with actresses, opera singers and dancers, mistresses, and only God knows who else."

"They keep me out of trouble, Maman."

"No, they keep you from marrying," she corrected without condemnation. "If women were not so easily accessible for your enjoyment whenever you wished, you might decide you could revel in the pleasures of a lady living with you and find a wife from the abundance of lovelies available."

Rick grimaced at the thought of someone sharing his home night and day. He'd rather continue visiting his mistresses in their homes. Suddenly having a hard time focusing on the matter at hand because of the continued weakness flowing through his limbs, he rubbed his temples. Shubert's news had unsettled his mother more than he would have thought. "You don't care who I marry, do you?"

"Of course not, if the lady is suitable in all ways," she replied honestly. "Many are. As it happens, I asked my new assistant to make you a list of all the ones making their entrance into Society this Season. You might want to have a glance at it while you are here. Perhaps it has a name or two you've heard mentioned at one of your clubs as a young lady who's arousing all the bachelors' interest."

"You say only names of the current belles are on your list? That surprises me."

"There's obviously no use in considering the ones who've made their debut and haven't married. If you'd been interested, you would have asked one of them to marry you by now."

If he'd felt better, he would have chuckled at her accurate deduction. Since there was no emergency, he needed to end this conversation and go home.

"I don't need your help deciding on a bride," he assured her, fighting the debilitating consequences of the fever.

"No, you don't," the duchess continued in a guileless manner. "I need your help picking my daughter-in-law. Now, be a dear and pour me a sip of brandy, will you, Your Grace? It's on my desk."

Gladly, he thought, rising gingerly from the sofa. His pulse was pounding in his ears, and his head was getting heavier. He managed to walk a straight line to her desk. Another shot might dull the smoldering pain long enough to say his goodbyes and leave without his mother's eagle eye detecting his true condition.

When he looked down to pull the stopper out of the brandy decanter, he saw the list his mother had referred to conspicuously placed where he was sure to see it. His brow furrowed as he picked it up and tried to concentrate on the page that wouldn't stay still in his hand, making it near impossible to focus.

His mother rose and walked over to stand near him. Rick dropped the page back onto the desk, picked up the decanter, and added a splash to each glass.

"I don't recognize any of the names," he noted, giving her one of the drinks.

"Good." Her voice sounded especially pleased. "That means their fathers kept them out of Society's sight so they'd be much sought-after at their debut. It never turns out good for a young lady who's already been seen by bachelors before her debut, considered, and discarded as if a dried weed on a shelf."

Rick downed half the brandy in his glass in one swallow. The sting of it caused his face to flush with more heat. A roar throbbed in his ears, and a deeper weakening ran along his limbs. What the hell was wrong with him? Suddenly, he didn't feel invincible. He felt as if a thousand hot needles were pricking his skin. The fever was the same as he'd had before, but he had weathered it. Now, for the first time he was beginning to worry about his mortality.

He had to leave while he still had enough wits about himself to do so.

The easiest way to do that was to agree with his mother. Nothing made her happier, and he was beginning to think it *was* time he married. That the fever had returned and with such ferocity was reason to worry. It *was* his responsibility to have an heir to the title. Not Shubert's or anyone else's. For once, his mother's meddling couldn't have come at a better time. He needed to make use of it and pick a bride fast.

"Perhaps you are right, Maman," he said, feeling beyond the point of caring what might happen and only eager to get home to his bed. "It's time I do my duty, marry, and have a son."

Without thinking about the repercussions of his actions, he closed his eyes and ran his forefinger down the names until he felt like stopping. Opening his eyes, he wondered what the hell he was doing. There were better ways to pick a bride.

Somehow tonight this seemed the sensible way, even though it was most irrational. He lifted his finger, bent down, and looked closely at the name.

Miss Edwina Fine.

With a surname such as that, how could he go wrong? Rick was a connoisseur of life's finer things. He enjoyed the taste of fine wine, the feel of fine silk, the warmth of fine wool, and the speed of fine horses. He could think of more fine things if he wasn't so fuzzy headed. She would be perfect.

Breathing heavily, he slipped a sheet of un-monogrammed parchment from his mother's stack, pulled the quill from its stand, and dipped it into the inkpot. The devil take it, he thought, and proceeded to write:

Dear Miss Edwina Fine,
    Will you marry me?

                                        Sincerely,
                                The Duke of Stonerick

Rick plopped the quill back into its holder and handed the sheet over to his mother. It wasn't as praiseworthy as the proposal he'd helped Wyatt write last year, but it would get the job done.

"This should do it, Maman. Let me know when she accepts."

CHAPTER 2

THE ART OF BEING A FINE GENTLEMAN
SIR DUDLEY SAMSON PEMBERTON FINE

*When necessary, a gentleman will step into
the fray to help avoid a fight.*

After several days of drinking the concoctions of willow bark and other remedies the apothecary had given him, the high fevers, body-rattling pain, and weakness were gone. His strength had returned but the mysterious bouts that came on suddenly and ravaged him left Rick with the gnawing concern it truly was time to shake off his bachelor leanings, and to marry and produce an heir. But not today. He was back at his desk and handling a typical morning routine of reading correspondence, signing documents, and checking over the account books delivered for his review. He would be meeting with his solicitor, account managers, and several others later in the day to catch up on all his duties as duke so that he could return to his social schedule tomorrow.

His friend Wyatt had an early fencing match, and later, the two of them planned to meet Hurst at his stables to admire the new thoroughbred he'd purchased a few days ago and perhaps see him run. After that, the three of them were riding to the outskirts of Town to an area referred to as The Field for Rick's shooting match. Some young men who'd recently come to London to enjoy a romp or two before the Season started were itching to test their skills against him.

But before his busy day started, there was much to do today. Having been waylaid because of the ailment that had plagued him, Rick's stack of correspondence was enormous.

Hurrying through his responsibilities wasn't something he liked to do. He always attended to the business of his estates before all else. He had an innate distrust of people. That wariness was especially true of solicitors, accountants, and overseers. The same type of man who failed to realize his father's best friend was in cahoots with one of the dukedom's trustees and hadn't caught on to their practices of embezzling monies from Rick's funds while he was still under the man's guardianship.

Ever since that treachery was discovered, Rick diligently checked behind everyone in a studious way and kept up with the entailed holdings and all other properties and businesses he owned by inheritances. Only after important matters were taken care of would he concentrate on his sporting club, entertainment, and games. And then he did so with relish.

On occasion, he dabbled in the political affairs surrounding Parliament, but not with much frequency. He found doing so made him more friends and enemies than he wanted. Frankly, he had enough of both.

"I'm sorry to interrupt, Your Grace."

Rick glanced up at his butler before returning his attention to the document he was about to sign. "Yes, Palmer."

"Mrs. Pauline Castleton is here and wishes to speak to you. She says she is related to Lord Quintingham's family by marriage."

"Probably true, but I don't know the viscount or any-one by her name." Rick added his signature to the document.

"The young lady who accompanies her insists it's quite urgent they speak to you."

"It always is and not surprising considering the Season is starting in a matter of days." Rick placed the quill back in its stand. "I don't have time to see anyone today, no matter the reason. Send anyone who calls on me over to see Mr. Wrightmyer."

"Yes, Your Grace."

Rick impatiently dug back into his paperwork, but a nagging worry crossing his mind caused him to pause. Neither the physician nor the apothecary could promise Rick's recent illness wouldn't return and there might come a time when the powders and tonics wouldn't keep the fevers at bay. There was no way of knowing. Everyone agreed intermittent fevers could be dangerous.

In his many years of attending the Season, Rick had never given serious consideration to any of the young ladies. Now he had to. Not because of his mother's wishes, or because his cousin beat him to the nursery. Neither of which bothered him. It was his duty to the title that had him now returning to the idea it was time to settle on a bride.

But if he met with every mother and father who wanted to talk about their daughter's virtues in hopes of making a match with him, he'd never have time for anything else. Besides, he would meet all the young ladies making their debuts at the first ball of the Season. That wasn't far away and was soon enough to begin a dedicated search.

He pulled the next document from the pile and started reading, but moments later, sounds of raised voices coming from the front of the house disturbed his concentration. He looked up and listened. A young lady's voice. And Palmer's. It was unlike his butler to speak in such an authoritative tone. The big bear of a man never had, that Rick remembered. Although he couldn't distinguish the words, it was apparent they were having a set-to. Rick felt a twinge between his shoulder blades. Whatever was going on, something didn't feel right about it.

It wasn't uncommon for people from various walks of life to arrive at his door saddled with all manner of questions and propositions in hopes of gaining an audience with him. That had been the case for as long as he could remember and was one of the reasons why Rick didn't take well to others. Customarily, if someone came to see him without the benefit of an invitation, it was because they wanted something, be it money, a favor, or influence. However, they usually didn't start an argument with his butler when told to be on their way.

More than a little interested by now, Rick strained to hear what was being said, but was too far away. Curious and a little suspicious too, he laid the papers aside.

Shoving back from his desk, he rose, sauntered to the door to look down the corridor. Palmer was holding the front door open with one hand and pointing outside with the other. An older lady, Mrs. Castleton, Rick presumed, stood in front of the open doorway, wearing a wide black bonnet with extremely long pheasant feathers shooting out of it. She urgently motioned for the other, younger female to come with her. Clearly, the belle wasn't budging.

With her back to him, Rick couldn't see much of her but sufficient to know she was above-average height, a slender build, straight back, and had softly rounded shoulders. Her hair was completely covered by a black bonnet. The matching pelisse she wore cinched at the back of her waist just enough to give her an attractively feminine shape.

"I'll not tell you my private affairs concerning the duke, sir," the young lady said. "That would be most improper of me to disclose. Nor will I leave until I speak to him."

"As I said, you will not see him today, Miss. Allow me to direct you to his secretary, Mr. Wrightmyer. He will be more than happy to help you."

"That won't do. My aunt and I will sit quietly and not bother anyone, including you, while we wait, but we must stay here until the duke's available."

"You'll see Mr. Wrightmyer or no one," Palmer said in a firm tone that would have sent the staff or anyone else scurrying away to do his bidding.

Her shoulders seemed to stiffen. "I don't know what else I might say to assure you this matter is of utmost importance, and the duke wants to see me."

That last statement was uncommonly bold. Insisting he wanted to see someone he'd never met. Where would she have gotten such an idea?

It hadn't taken Rick long to figure out this young lady was not going to listen to Palmer. And Rick didn't expect his butler to show her any mercy either. Intrigued, he leaned a little farther out the door. Her voice was determined, but not harsh, her stance sturdy, but not rigid. She appeared quite fearless and headstrong talking to a man of authority twice her size. That took fortitude in spades, but what could be her reason for not wanting to leave when repeatedly asked to do so?

"He will not see you." Palmer remained adamant. "You'll take your leave immediately, or I'll summon a footman to carry you out."

"You best bring half a dozen of them, sir, for I feel sure it will take that many to remove me from this spot."

She tossed the words out to Palmer as if she issued such challenges every day. Rick smiled at her comment. He'd never been a friendly sort and, apparently, she wasn't either. She certainly wasn't trying to win the butler over with the usual feminine wiles and ways of talking softly, smiling sweetly, and pretending to be helpless. There had been no tears or whimpering yet, and Rick had a good feeling that those would not be forthcoming from this maiden.

However, the brazen remark of Palmer needing six footmen warranted an astonished gasp, a loud sniffle, and scorching frown from her companion, who remained quietly in the doorway.

"My dearest, please, let's go," she pleaded anxiously. "We can do no more than write for an appointment or perchance we may come back tomorrow. Let's behave properly today and do as the man says."

"Propriety is not getting through to him, Auntie, and you know how important this is. He's quite set but so am I. We stay until we get this matter with the duke settled."

There was an air of unyielding purpose in her tone that her companion wasn't sharing as she continued to timidly cajole the younger lady to join her so they could depart. It struck Rick as odd that the miss was the one taking the lead and refusing to go. Usually, it was the pushy mamans, aunts, or fathers who were so bold as to insist on seeing him. If young misses accompanied their guardian, they usually stood by without making a peep. It was only natural her boldness attracted his attention.

The miss turned back to Palmer. "And you, sir, would do well to have a copy of my father's book on manners so you could refer to it at times like this. You are lacking in knowing the proper way to talk to a lady who has come to the door."

Palmer's back bowed and his chest pushed forward quickly. "I need no instructions on deportment from anyone."

"Apparently, you do. I will gladly have a copy sent over to you."

He set her with a rigid grimace. "You will not."

"Suit yourself on that, but I'm merely asking to wait here quietly and not disturb anyone, including you, until the duke is available."

She had pluck, Rick would give her that. But suggesting Palmer needed training in manners from someone else was going a bit too far for a man of his experience and impeccable qualities. He'd written and published his own book of rules for butlers, housekeepers, and all other household staff.

Rick was sure Palmer wouldn't take kindly to her insinuation that he needed tutoring. However, Palmer's answer to the young lady was spoken so low Rick couldn't make out the words. That didn't matter. His butler's wide eyes and red face left no doubt about his meaning. The six footmen would be called.

The way Rick saw it, he had two choices. Go back into his book room and close the door so he couldn't hear the scuffle the young lady promised would happen—and he didn't doubt her for a moment. Or stop that from happening and see what the ladies wanted.

Normally, he would have taken the first choice. And should today. Every minute mattered if he was going to finish the paperwork and meetings so tomorrow he could make the fencing match that would be the start to his first enjoyable day in over a week. He had more pressing things to do than settle this argument, but his male stirrings of interest in the outspoken belle had Rick looking back at the clock behind him.

He might as well take this situation into his own hands. The sooner it was handled, the better so he could peacefully get on with what he had to do. Besides, he was more than a bit curious as to what the two had up their sleeves. He was undeniably drawn to the younger lady's mettle. Not to mention that manly interest had him wanting to see her face before she left his home.

Rick strode down the corridor. When sounds of his boots hitting the wood floor reached her, she turned. His gaze met hers across the distance. An unexpected, instant spark of attraction flashed through him at the sight of her lovely face. A sudden warmth curled deep inside him. Her bonnet, simply adorned with only a small, dried nosegay poking out of one side of the satin band, gave her an innocently wholesome quality that immediately appealed to him.

Rick glanced at Palmer, who opened his mouth as if to inform the lady who was approaching, but Rick lightly shook his head. As his steps brought him closer, he studied her more carefully. Her complexion looked delicate and smooth as polished ivory, except for the flush on her cheeks. She had a small, attractively shaped nose, full, sculpted lips, and sparkling, almond-shaped eyes the color of deep summer green. Clearly her beauty matched her strength.

"What's all the commotion going on out here?" he asked, not trying to hide his genuine interest or the touch of irritation the ruckus had caused.

"There is none, sir," she responded quickly and

confidently, dismissing him with no more than a half-hearted side glance, returning her attention to Palmer. "I'm waiting for someone and feel sure you can't help me with this private matter. My business is with the duke. I'm quite sure His Grace wouldn't appreciate me talking to anyone, including his secretary, until I've spoken to him."

Her gloved hands were clasped together tightly in front of her. A black velvet reticule dangled from one of her wrists. Whatever the reason she wanted to see him, she was intense about it. Not only that, but she was also either fearless, adventurous, or mischievous enough to invade a duke's home and make demands. He hadn't decided which. Maybe all three.

When Rick stopped in front of her, she offered him another quick glance. He realized at once from her staunchly searching expression that she was more than determined. She was resolute, and he couldn't let her leave until he knew why.

"I am Stonerick."

Mrs. Castleton gasped loudly from the doorway. The belle sucked in a startled breath, as both women immediately curtsied and whispered, "Your Grace."

Keeping his gaze firmly on the young lady as that was where his interest rested, he nodded casually.

She didn't shrink away from him, but her spine stiffened as she stared at him with an uncensored steady gaze that seemed to want to look into his soul. There was a connection between them. Of that he was sure. His loins tightened in response to their eye contact and she blinked rapidly as if something unexpectedly wonderful had passed through her.

Recovering from that quickly, an embarrassed flush eased up her neck to settle in her already pink cheeks.

He watched her swallow hard. It was one thing to remain bold when talking to a butler or secretary, but quite another to confront a duke face-to-face. Often his title caused panic in ladies and gentlemen alike. She was undoubtedly surprised by his appearance, but *she* wasn't backing down an inch.

Mrs. Castleton stepped into the vestibule again. Rick nodded for Palmer to close the door. The matron looked as unsure of herself as a newborn foal taking her first steps. "Your Grace, I—that is, we—do humbly apologize for not recognizing you. It's not every day a lady gets to see a duke, is it? Especially with you being so busy."

He nodded to the woman and then noticed he didn't see any expression of regret in her companion's face, but it was enough that he had taken the young lady unawares. What he saw was a prideful vitality that drew him instantly. He was willing to wait before passing further judgment on what she had in mind.

"What can I do for you, Mrs. Castleton?"

The woman wearily cleared her throat as her attention swept indecisively back and forth between him and the spritely maiden. "Well, you see, Your Grace, I'd like to—that is, with your permission, I'd like to present my niece."

Rick took note of the young belle again. Her features were beautifully feminine, but he sensed a willful strength inside her that wasn't common in most men, and he hadn't detected it in any other lady he'd ever met. He liked the way she held a long, deep breath and remained silent, accepting his scrutiny of her without hesitation or offense, and all the while, somehow managing to give him the once-over too. He never minded a beautiful woman taking a long look at him. Especially when he could see she had cautious interest in him too.

Odd as this situation was, and his timeframe pressing, he was still intrigued. "Proceed."

Mrs. Castleton smiled nervously but proudly tilted her chin up, and said, "Your Grace, I present Miss Edwina Fine."

An unanticipated flash of memory surged through Rick's mind. *Fine.* Her name was familiar. He didn't remember having ever seen the green-eyed beauty but knew he'd recently seen her name somewhere, or maybe he'd been told about her by someone, but couldn't immediately place where or why he knew it.

He had a lot of documents to wade through and sign before his meetings started, but right now it was this lady who held his attention. He wanted the mystery of who she was and how he knew her name settled so found himself saying, "I recognize your name."

Her arched brows lifted quickly as did her shoulders, chin, and whole body seemed to lift slightly. She stared at him with vigilant indignation. "I should hope so."

"Edwina, dearest, no," her aunt cautioned as she held up her hands to silence her niece. "It's not proper for you to speak to the duke in such a manner or about such an important matter. That's why I'm here. I'll take care of this for you, dearie."

Rick could see she was hesitant to acquiesce to her aunt's plea and eager to take care of this matter in the way she wanted it handled. She clutched tightly on the strings of her reticule and pressed her lips closed for a moment.

"You know silence is not my best virtue, Auntie."

"But let it be today," she prodded earnestly, anxiously pulling a handkerchief from beneath her sleeve and lightly patting the center of her forehead. "The viscount charged me with taking care of this."

Her niece looked as if she was itching to say more but, whether out of respect for her elder, or simply forcing herself to be prudent for a change, she remained quiet and turned her unyielding attention back to Rick.

The aunt braved another smile from trembly lips and watery eyes. "We had many discussions about what to do and how to do it after your proposal arrived."

Proposal?

CHAPTER 3

THE ART OF BEING A FINE GENTLEMAN
SIR DUDLEY SAMSON PEMBERTON FINE

*A gentleman of refined deportment should
never disappoint a lady.*

Rick's jaw tightened and the hair at the back of his neck prickled. What the devil was she talking about?

"We . . . we didn't know whether Edwina should accept, and if so," Mrs. Castleton continued breathlessly and as nervously as an unseasoned tightrope walker. "We worried, or, er, that is, wondered—well, we worried too—if we should answer by mail or come in person."

"Wait, madam." A good amount of suspicion rolled through him. Rick pushed his coat aside and propped his hands on his hips. This had gone far enough. "Where is Miss Fine's father? I should speak to him. Not you."

The trembling woman patted her forehead again. "Oh, well, of course, w-we assumed that you . . . you would know since you offered—"

"Since I offered what?"

"Well, your, ah, letter—"

Miss Fine took hold of Mrs. Castleton's arm as if to help steady her, and said gently, "Let me handle this, Auntie. I can see you are getting flustered, and I know you are tired."

"Perhaps it is best, dearie. I can't seem to keep my thoughts straight on what I'm to say, and I know how important this is."

Settling her guarded gaze on Rick, Miss Fine continued softly, "My father passed early last winter, Your Grace. His cousin, Viscount Quintingham, is my guardian."

"And why is he not here?" Rick asked a little more brusquely than he'd intended.

Mrs. Castleton made a sighing sound, catching Rick's attention again. She was pale as a ghost and her bottom lip quivered. She looked to be on the verge of fainting while her niece was solid as a rock. "Palmer, show Mrs. Castleton into the drawing room. Give her a cup of tea and a vinaigrette if necessary."

"No, no. I beg your pardon, Your Grace. I don't want to . . . to be of any trouble. I'm going to be all right. A bit lightheaded perhaps and winded. It's all a bit overwhelming, you know, talking to a duke about such matters." She blinked rapidly. "Not only that, but it's not proper that I leave Edwina alone with you. I assured the viscount I could manage this quite efficiently." She stopped abruptly.

Rick narrowed distrusting eyes on the intriguing Miss Fine as he shifted his stance. It could be possible she was out to catch him in a parson's mousetrap, but he didn't think so. Women who tried such devious tactics to snare an unsuspecting gentleman were usually more accommodating and approachable than Miss Fine seemed to be. She'd not made the first move to entice him with soft, sweet-sounding sighs, or tempting, pouty lips moving ever closer to his. All of which he would enjoy if she were so inclined.

"No need to concern yourself with thoughts of impropriety, Mrs. Castleton," he answered in an obliging tone.

"I assure you I'm not going to ravish your niece in the vestibule of my home."

The elder lady gasped. Determination remained settled in the younger lady's lovely features. Her glittery green eyes held steady on his and her self-confidence seemed unshaken. He hadn't truly riled her yet, as Palmer had, but perhaps he was close.

"I ask your pardon," Rick said. He typically didn't think twice about what he said or to whom. For as long as he could remember his position in life had safeguarded him from much of the usual civility of Polite Society. His internal need for privacy fed that and most people accepted it without question or rancor.

"She's safe," he amended what he'd said moments before and then took a deep, short impatient breath. "You'll only be twenty feet away. I have no doubt she'll call if she needs you."

"True, Your Grace." Miss Fine gave him a pointed stare before looking at her aunt. "Please go sit down, Auntie. You've been tired and worried for days now and you do look peaked. I'm capable of keeping the duke in line."

Rick's brows drew together tightly. She said that as if she believed it to be true.

Mrs. Castleton looked from her niece to Rick before stammering, "I am feeling . . . a touch weak. It's . . . it was a long and tiring journey to London without much rest since we arrived."

Miss Fine smiled affectionately at her aunt. "Please accept the duke's hospitality and rest for a few minutes. I'll take care of this for you."

Suspicion concerning Miss Fine seeped into Rick's bones once again as Palmer showed her aunt down the corridor toward the drawing room. Rick ran a hand through his hair and slightly shook his head. His impatience was growing but his interest in the young lady hadn't deteriorated. He didn't know what kind of nonsense she was trying to accomplish, or how she could do it while looking completely innocent of any subterfuge. He was still attracted to her, and that stirred thoughts of wanting to know more.

The second Mrs. Castleton's back disappeared around the corner and into the drawing room, Rick stepped closer to Miss Fine. She didn't back away or flinch, which pleased him. He wanted to reach out and brush his fingers down her satiny-looking cheeks, but instead, keeping his gaze fastened on hers and his voice deceptively low to hide his primal feelings and mounting skepticism of her having pure intentions, he asked, "What are you up to, Miss Fine?"

"What am *I* up to?" she repeated, keeping her composure. "I may have been precipitous in coming here without benefit of notice, but now that I am here, we should be discussing what your designs are concerning me."

That comment was more cause to be wary again. "Mine?" She was devoid of fear, but he couldn't let that cloud his judgment. "Perhaps you want to expound on that."

"I find it most disconcerting you seem to be taken aback by my aunt's words regarding your proposal."

His heart thrummed tightly. There was that word again. *Proposal.* That usually only meant one thing when coming from a lady. Her observance of him was as keen as any man he'd ever faced in a shooting match. What did she know that he didn't? Best he find out.

"I am," he said with a hardened jaw.

She glared at him and sucked in a soft breath. "Then why did you send it to me?"

They weren't making much progress on furthering their bizarre conversation, and he wasn't a long-suffering man. Perhaps she'd thought of controlling him through mindless chatter that went nowhere as she had his butler.

"What exactly is it you think I sent you, Miss Fine?"

Her eyes widened in disbelief as she drew herself up proudly once more. "Since your memory is so fleeting, perhaps this will refresh it."

He watched the graceful movements of her hands as she slipped the ribbons of her reticule off her wrist, opened it, and pulled out a folded sheet of exceptional parchment. She extended it toward him with a sense of hesitancy in her actions.

"I received this several days ago."

Guarded, he took the folded sheet from her and looked at it in stunned disbelief. His breath pooled thickly in his throat. There in his bold hand was a somewhat formal offer of marriage: *Miss Edwina Fine, Will you marry me?* With *his* signature.

The muscles in his shoulders and back tightened. More flashes of memory returned as he stared at the paper. He'd been at his mother's feeling like hell and seeming to be burning hot. That's where he'd seen Miss Fine's name. On a list. The dowager had been talking about marriage. But damnation, his mother always talked about marriage. His thoughts had been as blurry as his eyes that night. He'd been tortured with debilitating pain, drenching fevers, and an overindulgence of brandy. After leaving her house, he barely remembered anything for the three or four days while the fever had ravaged his body.

He turned the paper over and looked at the stamp. His gut clenched. There was no doubt it was his mother's. He made a growling noise and took another step closer to her. "How did you get this, Miss Fine?"

She gave him a perplexed blink as her gorgeously long lashes slowly moved up and down. "Mail coach," she said forthrightly. "The way you intended, I assume. Perhaps you would have preferred we answer your letter by correspondence, but it's too late for that now."

Pieces of memory continued to rush back to Rick like a fast-flowing river over flat rocks. Parts of conversation echoed in his mind. He tried to focus through the fog and pull them all together to determine what happened at his mother's house.

Yes, he remembered hastily writing the letter, but he thought he'd thrown it into the fire before he left. Or, maybe, he thought his mother had. But as unbelievable as it was, the dowager had obviously saved it from destruction and mailed the damned thing. Now, he was standing in his vestibule looking at a stunning young lady who was ready to take him at his word that he had offered for her hand and walk with him to the altar.

Miss Fine's lips pursed grudgingly for a moment before she spoke. "I know it's not written on your official stationery and with your seal, but Auntie feels sure it's your mother's. As you can see, it's addressed to me and signed by you. Unless of course, you aren't the one who signed it."

For the first time, she looked at him with apprehension. Her eyes narrowed and tightened as her lips pressed tightly closed. Seemingly without movement, her body went rigid.

Her quick change in demeanor caught him off guard and stirred emotions he hadn't felt in a long time. Compassion surged through him. Perhaps a little sorrow too. She remained still. Quiet. He could see in the depths of her eyes she was suddenly alarmed by the idea she might have come to his home on a fool's errand. Her words had been said with all sincerity. The lady, who only moments before looked fearless enough to withstand any assault or condemnation he might put forth, was unmistakably rattled by the possibility the letter was a ruse. Rick sensed if he said it wasn't his hand that put the quill to the paper, she would accept his word.

He watched as she seemingly reached within herself and pulled from a well of strength she hadn't heretofore tapped. She swallowed hard and lowered her lashes in what he could only perceive as innocence while her hands squeezed the ribbons of her reticule.

"Tell me now if your letter asking me to marry you was a prank or a forgery, Your Grace. I will abide by your word and leave immediately. You'll never hear from me again."

Did she know she was giving him a way out of this unfathomable debacle?

He was certain she assumed he was a man of his word. Instinct told him she wasn't as brave as she appeared or pretended to be. Behind her undoubtable strength, something troubled her. Whether it was his reaction to why she was there or something deeper, he wasn't sure. But he sensed she held a secret. Her heartfelt response, her sudden fragile expression, and her vulnerability tightened his gut.

Compassion for her rippled through him once again. He unfolded the sheet of parchment and looked down to study it. Those few words could alter his life.

Surely, she saw in his face that he knew it was his signature at the bottom of the letter and his mother's seal on the back of it the moment he glanced at them. Yet, she gave him opportunity to admit or deny it. All he had to do was lie and say it wasn't. Or perhaps he could get by with simply hedging on the truth and say it wasn't a prank, but it wasn't exactly an official proposal of marriage either and send her on her way.

Then again, cynical, mistrusting scoundrel that he was, and had been most of his life, he was, above all, a man of honor. She was innocent in the back-and-forth that had happened between him and his mother that night. Her story was legitimate in every way as far as he could tell. In his hand he held her proof of the claim. That's what should make the difference in how he answered her.

A chill worked through him as he studied the paper. Miss Fine had a legitimate marriage proposal from him. He was tempted to take the easy way out of this misfortune and end the discussion here, now, and forever. What was he going to do? Marriage was for better or worse. For life. Could he do the right thing and agree to marry her? Or should he send her on her way?

She would never know the truth.

But he would.

Unable to stop himself, Rick allowed his attention to linger on the delicate line of her nose and delicious fullness of her lips before trailing down to the hollow of her throat, barely visible above the neckline of her clothing. The thought of kissing her caused a whorl of desire to coil tight and spread through him. His attraction to her was real, though he wasn't certain she'd returned it. Thus far.

She remained still, quiet, and continued to watch him as he glanced from her to the letter and back again. Actually, she was being very patient with him.

There was much to appreciate other than her intense comportment and lovely features. Starting with her nerves of iron. She was exceptionally brave, strong-minded, and had a sense of self-reliance about her that impressed him.

And the Duke of Stonerick was not easily impressed by anyone. He'd want his son to have those qualities.

She wasn't very practical, which was evidenced by her showing up at his door, no matter the reason or how good it might be. That could be overlooked in a lady. Many things could be understood or entirely excused when it came to Miss Fine. Including her overzealous attitude that she had the right to confront him.

He was perplexed because she wasn't flirtatious in the least considering she was looking at the prospects of marrying him. She hadn't batted her eyelashes at him once. Nor had she given him a shy smile that so many young ladies liked to present. Someone should have schooled her on the proper way to woo a man. Maybe that was one of the reasons he felt so drawn to her. She wasn't using anything but the weapon he gave her.

However, he couldn't get away from wanting to know more about her. What pushed her to seek out a duke who wrote a proposal on unofficial stationery and had the confidence to hand it back to him. Trust him with it. He could have easily kept it or tossed it into a fire and there would be no proof it ever existed.

She looked sturdy without being robust, healthy, and her lineage had to be solid or she wouldn't have been on his mother's list of those making their entrance into Society. For that reason too, she would have been schooled in all manners of the elite ton, whether she chose to always abide by them, and well-trained to manage an array of extensive households. She'd just tackled the haughtiest butler in London.

The high fevers, sweats, and agonizing weakness he'd experienced the past few days swept through his mind again. It had taken a long time to recover from the ailment both times he'd had it. He was reminded there was the possibility a time would come when the willow bark and other tonics and teas no longer brought the episodes under control.

He didn't know if or when the fever might return. Or, when he married, how long it would take for his wife to get in the family way. It had taken Shubert's wife mere weeks, but Wyatt and Fredericka had been married almost a year and still had no babe on the way.

No matter which way it would go for him, Rick *needed* an heir.

And by gambler's luck—or the more likely scenario, his mother's interfering mischief—he had an acceptable, desirable, and intriguing lady standing in front of him expecting to be his bride. He could handle her bold way, yet there was something delicate about her inner being as well. He felt it and wanted to explore it.

That didn't mean he wasn't going to have a few strong words with his mother for taking this matter into her own hands and not even alerting him to what she had done.

Exhaling deeply, Rick folded the note, tapped it into the palm of his hand a couple of times, and then without further hesitation, extended it to Miss Fine. "It's not a fake. I wrote and signed the letter."

Immediate relief was evident. Her whole body seemed to relax and settle into itself for the first time since he'd seen her. It was obvious from her gaze held firmly on his that she still had questions. She didn't reach for the proposal yet her breaths were short, deep, and choppy.

"Without persuasion or force?"

"What?" She was more formidable than he imagined. This was ridiculous. Why was she questioning his admittance? Didn't she know when she had won? One of his hands sailed through his hair before it landed with a thud on his hip. "You doubt my word or you think someone could have forced me to propose to you?"

"It took you a long time to answer. I don't want to impose myself on you if it was not your intention without unnecessary influence on you."

"Take the letter. I wrote it to you of my own free will."

She did so and carefully stowed the proposal back into her reticule and closed it. Her breathing slowed and her gaze held firmly to his as she returned to the fearless, competent lady he first saw. And why wouldn't she? He'd just acknowledged he'd asked her to be his duchess without manipulation from anyone. He had no doubt she was assuming he was a man of his word.

"I need an heir, Miss Fine. The sooner the better. I stand by the proposal and will now do what I should have done before and ask you in person. Will you marry me?"

She swallowed hard and kept her gaze straight on his. "I accept," she said without hesitation.

Rick blinked as surprise flashed through him. Just that quickly he was betrothed. To a near stranger. He'd never really appreciated how complicated the idea of selecting a bride and marriage would be. Now that it was done, he realized he'd been caught in a parson's mousetrap of his own making. Or perhaps it was his mother's. He supposed fault lay with both. He wrote the letter and his mother mailed it. Yet, Miss Fine wasn't agreeing as happily as he would have expected with a belle who'd landed herself a duke for a husband without doing much more than lifting one of her delicate fingers to do so.

"With some stipulations," she added with quiet resolution.

His heartbeat raced. Damnation, did she know what she was doing? She must. The way she spoke in such a hushed tone, it was as if he felt the weight of her hesitancy on his chest.

She was about to give him another way out of his carelessly written and completely forgotten offer for her hand and his mother's mischief in posting it. One that could quite possibly leave his honor as well as his bachelorhood intact. He was a man of his word, but still, a man. He couldn't let this opportunity pass without further consideration of her intentions.

With a flinch of suspicion piercing him, he answered, "Stipulations can be good, Miss Fine. What are they?"

CHAPTER 4

THE ART OF BEING A FINE GENTLEMAN
SIR DUDLEY SAMSON PEMBERTON FINE

*Patience is a virtue absolutely no gentleman
can be without no matter the circumstances
or the value of them.*

Despite having what Edwina Fine considered steely nerves, she realized she was barely breathing. Her heartbeat skipped with uncertainty. She was literally shaking in her shoes over the enormity of what was before her.

After the butler informed them Aunt Pauline had fallen asleep in the drawing room once she'd had a sip or two of tea, Edwina was ushered into the duke's comfortably appointed book room for further discussions. She declined the offer of a drink from the duke but watched him pour one for himself. It gave her the opportunity to thoroughly study him without his watchful eyes on her.

Standing over six feet tall, the light brown–haired man was formidable and unquestionably handsome. Every ounce of him spoke of strength, privilege, and wealth, along with an abundance of vitality, arrogance, and no short amount of seeming impatience. She was usually astutely intuitive and should have expected this, but to her credit, she'd never met a titled man before. The few she'd read about were older, seemingly reserved, and what she would assume fatherly in appearance. Not so for this one. She hadn't envisioned a duke as someone who might stir a young lady with feminine desires, but this one had drenched her in them.

Broadly built, with a wide chest and shoulders that narrowed to a flat, hard-muscled waist, his frame appeared lithe beneath fawn-colored trousers and a deep purple coat that fit him perfectly. He wore his starched collar high and his neckcloth with the ease of a man well seasoned in the art of tying one. Thick golden-brown eyebrows graced a broad brow and were prominent above his finely chiseled nose and cheekbones. His mouth was outlined with well-defined lips, and he boasted a slightly square chin and jaw.

None of those attractive features could come close to matching the magnetism of his light-blue eyes. She had to force herself not to stare too deeply into their depths for very long. It was difficult to concentrate or consider anything else important when she did. They made her heart thump a little harder and her breath shorten considerably.

She didn't know what it was, but there had been more than mere acquiescence to fact in the duke's expression when he'd glanced at the letter. There was a heart-stopping surprise. That gave her worry. It was as if he were seeing it for the first time. But how could that be? And why had it taken him so long to finally admit writing and signing the letter?

There had been no forthcoming reasons as to why he had chosen to propose to her. Naturally, she was puzzled and wanted answers, but wasn't sure she had the nerve to ask the questions when he picked up his drink and turned toward her.

The power Edwina sensed within him made her

wary. It also made a breathless feeling sweep over her. Walking toward her, he looked more like a dangerous rogue than a distinguished duke in the dark-paneled room lined with overstuffed and highly-polished bookshelves and an inviting glass-wall reading nook at the end of it. To her surprise, she liked his roguish appeal. He seemed so at ease among the predictable smells of lamp oil, dusty leather bindings, and old parchment that hung in the air.

She couldn't feel guilty for taking him up on his offer to marry, but suddenly wondered if she were up to the task now that she knew he was not the older, somewhat fatherly figure she'd imagined him to be.

Expectations she'd had concerning this meeting had not solidified into reality, and suddenly she couldn't take in enough air. A peculiar fluttery sensation stirred restlessly in her chest, and she fingered the ribbon under her chin to loosen it. Heaven forbid the duke think he had two females on his hands that were near to fainting.

"Would you mind if I took off my bonnet?" she asked quietly and with as much dignity as she could possibly muster.

"No." His eyes narrowed in what could have been a flicker of concern. "I should have suggested it. Your coat and gloves as well. Let me help you with—"

"No, not right now. Thank you."

He expelled a breath of frustration at her reluctance for help and asked, "Are you sure you don't want tea?"

"Perhaps a little water," she answered. Forcing herself to remain calm as she unfurled the bow to give instant relief. "If you don't mind."

The duke turned back to the tray that held the brandy. There was no water on it. His gaze then searched every flat surface as if thinking surely there must be a pitcher somewhere in the room. When none was spotted, he cleared his throat and said, "One moment." He placed his glass on the desk and quickly strode out the door.

Lifting the short-brimmed bonnet off, Edwina plopped it onto the seat of the chair in front of the desk along with her reticule and started removing her gloves. It was a great relief seeing him walk out. Thank goodness she now had a few moments alone to gather her wits.

A tranquil and inviting place such as this room with an extensive library was a good place to do it, she thought, looking at the duke's grand collection of reading material. Her father would have considered this space, with its thousands of books and wall of windows giving plenty of light to read by until dusk, Heaven on earth. She'd like to think perhaps he and her mother had spent time in rooms like this one before he'd had to escape from London.

Edwina wasn't too overly tall, but for the past few months she'd had a tall order in front of her. Find a husband. Which wouldn't have been too terribly difficult under ordinary circumstances, even with what some would consider only an adequate dowry.

After all, she was a sensible person, intelligent, strong-minded—a trait that she'd been instructed by her aunt to hide from all men—and fair enough to look upon she reasoned. Since those were the sort of things it took to garner a suitable husband, she'd assumed she'd do reasonably well at the upcoming Season and marriage mart she'd been preparing for, even with red hair. The wrinkle was that Edwina didn't need *a* husband, she needed *three*.

She'd hoped with her reasonableness and instinct to overcome that obstacle as well. All she had to do was convince her older sisters they not only *needed* to marry but *wanted* to marry. A task that had proven more difficult than she'd imagined when broaching the subject with them on many occasions in the past few months.

However, with time and persuasion that could be dealt with as well. Edwina had convinced herself that once she made a match, she could gently impose upon her betrothed to help coax Eileen and Eleonora into finding and accepting husbands as well. But she had a feeling that *gently imposing* may not work on someone like this duke.

As it happened, none of those things were Edwina's biggest obstacle in fulfilling the promise to her father. She faced the prospect someone would know or find out they were the rumored triplets that were born almost twenty years ago. A feat so rare most people still had never heard of the possibility and wouldn't want to believe it if they had.

There were instances recorded of women birthing two babes one right after the other, and both living to adulthood, but three were more than the average mind could comprehend. That it should befall any woman was bad enough, according to her father, but it happening to a lady of quality was a misfortune that couldn't be overcome, so it had to be hidden from Society. Furthermore, there had to be a reason such an unbelievable phenomenon had occurred, and it couldn't have been anything as simple as a blessing.

Their mother had died shortly after their birth. Distraught and overwhelmed at the time, her father had done the only thing he knew to do: He fled to a remote village in York where they had lived somewhat secluded ever since.

Sighing heavily, Edwina pushed aside the stories her

father had told her about how the three tiny babes had managed to defy the odds and live when they were so small and had so many health issues to overcome throughout the first few months. He'd said their infant days were a struggle and Edwina's especially so.

She laid her gloves on the chair beside her bonnet and unfastened her heavy wool pelisse, easing out of it and hanging it over the arm of the chair. On his deathbed, her father decided he must make amends for denying the truth about his daughters' birth. Too ill to take any kind of action, he'd asked Edwina to promise she would do it for him. Go to London and see they were all married or betrothed by the end of the Season.

Now, it was up to her to vindicate her mother and father and set things right for herself and her siblings so they could take their rightful place in Society. Triplets were extraordinary to say the least, but she and her sisters were not monsters. They were not a product of infidelity with three different men, her mother was not cursed, nor was her mother or any of the three sisters witches as some superstitious people believed. Edwina, Eleonora, and Eileen were normal human beings like all other young ladies. Well, except for Eileen's penchant for learning the names of plants, her fascination with numbers, and gazing at the stars every night. But really, could that be considered a bad thing?

She, Aunt Pauline, and her sisters had talked extensively about their births. If Edwina was going to expect others to treat them as ordinary people, she insisted they had to do it first. She wasn't going to offer the information they were triplets to anyone, including the duke, but if he or someone else should ask, she wouldn't deny it. She'd never lie about it but was convinced she didn't have to reveal unnecessary information. As far as she was concerned, she had two older sisters. That was the truth.

With all going against her, prospects had been looking rather dim for a clean sweep during the Season until this miracle of an offer for her hand had come from the divinely attractive Duke of Stonerick. To say she and her aunt were stunned into silence when his letter arrived was too mild a description for such a windfall.

After much ado about the simplistic proposal, the possible reasons for it, and what her answer should be, Edwina and her aunt Pauline decided the best thing to do was pay the duke a visit and accept in person. As luck would have it, they had already arrived in London so Edwina could make final preparations for the first ball of the Season, which wasn't much more than a couple of weeks away.

Having lived with two active sisters, Edwina wasn't one to get rattled. Or so she thought. But an uneasiness skittered up her spine. The Duke of Stonerick had her feeling as if she were standing on a ship that was being tossed up and down by the winds of a fierce storm. She couldn't seem to feel as if she was on steady feet. She swallowed hard and wished her sisters were with her. They didn't see eye-to-eye on everything, but they would be comfort for her.

Her stomach jumped when the duke walked back into the room and stopped just inside the doorway to stare at her. An indecent and entirely inappropriate tingle raced across her breasts and seemed to propel itself right down to her most sensitive spot. He was so handsome and powerful that looking at him caused a catch in her breath. It was difficult to take in the sight of him all at one time. There was an imposing presence about him that was impossible not to notice and be drawn to.

A fluttering developed in her chest when she realized his intense gaze was skimming over her from head to toe. She supposed she did appear a little different without her traveling coat and bonnet. Her long-sleeved, pale-gray muslin dress was adorned with a darker shade of braided, satin ribbon at the high waist and along the scooped neckline. As if being born one of three wouldn't be enough adversity to overcome, the sisters were all blessed with green eyes and thick red hair as well. She was the first to admit their tresses had a beautiful wave and the color wasn't brassy—more of a soft golden-red—but still red enough to have been teased by children and adults alike from time to time.

"Is something wrong?" she asked, feeling a tweak of defiance at his unnecessary and lengthy inspection of her.

"No."

He strode up to her and stopped so close she felt his heat while catching the scent of freshly shaved skin and the smell of his expensive wool coat. He extended the glass to her. That he brought the water himself rather than have a servant do it caused her heart to beat erratically. It seemed a very intimate thing for him to do. The muscles in her stomach coiled and tightened in response to his unanticipated personal attention. Why couldn't he have been like the older, reserved men she'd read about and envisioned in the many hours she'd played this meeting in her mind? It somehow seemed another unfair blow from fate that the man who had proposed to her was so attractive she wanted to lay her cheek on his chest and rest against him.

Stunned and embarrassed by the track of her thoughts,

Edwina avoided his eyes and said, "Thank you," as she took the glass, careful to make sure her fingers didn't brush across his. She didn't immediately take it to her lips.

"Go on," he encouraged brusquely. "Drink."

"You are short and sharp with your words sometimes, Your Grace," she complained, and as soon as the words were out of her mouth, she knew she should have kept her opinion to herself. She didn't need to irritate the duke. She needed to marry him.

"I am a man of few words, and little patience."

She searched his eyes for a reason behind his ungentlemanly tetchiness. "I would venture to say it's more like none."

"You are the most outspoken lady I've ever met. Now, drink before you find yourself feeling faint like your aunt."

She drew in his criticism with an exasperated breath and regarded him with a bit of her own arrogance. "I have never felt faint, sir."

"Then don't let today be the first time." His mouth twitched up as if he intended to smile but thought better of it.

After the first sip of the cool liquid, Edwina found she was too thirsty to be dainty. She quickly downed every drop, and then gently moistened her lips.

"More?" he asked, eyeing the empty glass.

Edwina shook her head as his gaze traced down her face, causing delicious tingles to ripple over her.

He reached over and took the glass from her hand and when he did so, she had the oddest feeling he wanted to tarry and touch her cheek.

"I admit I'm wondering why you chose to ask me to marry you when there are many young ladies who have better lineage, larger dowries, and—" She hesitated.

"And what?" He placed her glass on a side table without taking his attention off her.

"Don't have red hair," she answered honestly.

He grunted a half chuckle. "I picked your name from a list of belles making their debut in Society this year. I had no idea what you or any of the other ladies looked like, Miss Fine, but have no worry." His voice and features softened. The smile stayed on his lips. "Your hair is lovely and so are you."

A flush of appreciation warmed her like a blazing fire on a cold night. She believed he meant his words and was glad he told her. Every wife wanted to please their husband in such a manner as appearance. But she knew from experience that some people still harbored superstitions about women with red hair and green eyes as well as many other things.

"Thank you," she answered, grateful he'd reassured her. But she had to ask, "What kind of way is that to pick a wife?"

The duke shrugged, nodded his head once, and folded his arms across his chest as he took his time answering. "The easy way."

His expression revealed nothing more than his words. Coming from most gentlemen, his answer would be hard to believe, but she didn't doubt the duke at all. She supposed a list was trouble-free for a man who didn't have the patience to bother with the civilities of introducing himself to a lady the proper and usual way—before he asked for her hand.

"Are you saying you didn't know anything about me before you sent your letter?" she asked, assuming that meant he hadn't checked too deeply into her family history. Surely, he would have had a question or two for her if he had.

"You had already been approved by Society by being allowed to attend the Season. Otherwise, your name wouldn't have been on the list, so as shallow as it seems, I didn't. I've been consumed by . . . something else the past few days that has kept me busy since the night I saw your name and wrote the proposal." He paused. "What do you know of me, Miss Fine?" he asked in a lower tone, his attention staying on her face as if he were willing her to say something he expected to hear. "That is, something other than what you've read in the gossip pages."

She blinked rapidly at his question and smiled in genuine amusement. "Gossip pages? My father would never have allowed us to read them. I know what they are, and scandal sheets, but I've never read one."

"Really?" His brows rose as he quirked his head a little and unfolded his arms, clearly showing he didn't believe her. "You never slipped around behind your father's back and read them? Not once?"

Her smile continued. "I wish I had, and perhaps now that I'm in London that will be possible."

She would love to know what was written about this man who held her attention so raptly. No doubt it would be fascinating, but would it be true? From her readings about the much-maligned tittle-tattle not being fit for educated people to indulge in, some believed every word while others claimed none of it was true. Edwina could only assume there was truth *and* fiction in them as her father insisted they were not educational but merely entertainment.

"You truly haven't read one?" he asked, folding his arms over his chest again as he queried her more with his beautiful gaze than his words.

"Where would I get one, Your Grace? You seem to think I lived in a city such as London where such readings could have been delivered to my door, or that perhaps a servant could have gone out to buy one so it could be placed on my breakfast tray and taken to my bed." A breathy laugh escaped past her lips at the thought of something so absurd happening in her home as eating food while in bed. "I am from a small village. My father was lucky if he received back issues of *The Times* once or twice a week. Sometimes not at all in winter. All we had were games, cards, and chessboards to entertain us. We were never any good at chess because Papa wasn't and couldn't teach us much."

"I'm glad to know that and it brings us back to the issue of what did you *know* about me, Miss Fine, before you came to my door?" he said with a lightness in his voice she hadn't detected before now.

The duke seemed to accept her explanation without question and surprisingly that pleased her. A warmth of pleasure washed over her. Emboldened by his undemanding tone and the absence of tension in his features, she answered without any uncertainty. "Absolutely nothing other than you are a duke. And I assure you, all my preconceived ideas of how you would look, sound, and behave vanished the moment you introduced yourself to me." *And how you make me feel delightful things I shouldn't be feeling.*

Edwina took a step back. There was no way she was going to tell him that.

CHAPTER 5

THE ART OF BEING A FINE GENTLEMAN
SIR DUDLEY SAMSON PEMBERTON FINE

*When confronted by a lady who needs help,
a fine gentleman never hesitates to offer
his wise and strong assistance.*

Edwina was pleased her honest account wrung another smile from him, and an easy gleam of amusement glimmered in the duke's blue eyes.

"It's refreshing to meet a lady who knows nothing about me," he admitted. "I don't remember that happening before."

He moved closer and looked intently at her. "What did you think when you first read my proposal?"

She returned his smile and realized how much she liked him smiling at her and enjoying their conversation. "That I needed to find Auntie a bottle of smelling salts because she fainted."

The duke laughed. "And after that and the shock began to abate?"

Edwina couldn't answer as candidly as she would like. She didn't want him to know that her very first thought was that miraculously all her prayers had been answered. Other things came barreling into her mind so close behind that any one of them could have been first. "Was the proposal truth, lie, mistake, or prank?"

He nodded understanding.

Edwina clasped her hands together in front of her. "I've already learned quite a lot about you in our short time of talking," she offered because they were in such an easy conversation for the first time since she arrived.

"That has me curious and requires an answer. What do you think you know about me now?"

Thankfully, caution snaked through her and kept her from immediately saying he was by far the handsomest man she had ever seen. She glanced around the many shelves of books and wondered if she should be completely honest or withhold some of what she'd garnered about him during the past few minutes. Perhaps it would be best if she only mentioned some of his traits.

Her shoulders lifted as if to give credence to her words. "You are argumentative, blunt, impatient, challenging, and more than once you've had me shuddering at your frustrated tone."

One brow rose and his lips twitched a smile. "Is that all?"

"No, but some things I'm still debating and it's best I not reveal them until I am sure."

"A wise decision for you but it leaves me still curious."

His gaze swept down her face in that easy glide that made her breath jump with stirring sensations she shouldn't be feeling and didn't know what to do about. "My father said curiosity is the sign of a healthy mind."

He nodded slowly. "Maybe you would like to add strong, courageous, likable, and persuasive among the attributes you are still considering?"

She swallowed a little harder than she expected, even though his words made her want to smile again. There was no doubt he could be persuasive if he was so inclined.

Edwina studied on that as she looked around the room again and took a moment to enjoy the warmth, the smells, and the beauty of the filled library before her. A touch of sadness flickered through her. Her father would have loved to see so many books in one place and he would have tried to read every one of them.

Focusing her attention back to the duke, she answered, "Reckless would be the only other one I am sure of at the moment."

His eyes narrowed and he leaned back. "How have I been reckless?"

"You picked my name from a list and you are alone with an unmarried lady."

The duke chuckled softly and the sound drifted over her like a soothing breeze on a hot summer day. His eyes connected with hers in a way that had never happened before—as if she delighted him.

"Ah, yes," he nodded. "Guilty on both charges. Would you want to know what I thought about you when I first saw you?"

Edwina's stomach felt as if it were flipping somersaults. No, she wasn't sure she wanted to know, but that didn't matter because she could see the duke was going to tell her anyway.

"From my book room doorway, I had been listening to you and Palmer. I couldn't believe you were taking my formidable butler to task. I thought you were nervy, capable, and the most mysterious young lady I had ever heard."

She flinched at the word *mysterious*. It was true. She had to be. There were things she couldn't tell him.

"You intrigued me and still do. I am of an age and it is a time in my life that I need a wife, and for her to give me an heir. It appears you will be well able to do that."

Edwina was suddenly filled with uncertainty as the very real ramifications of what she was doing flooded her. Having an heir would be the most difficult part of this arrangement between them, should it take place. She understood that having an heir would be of utmost importance to the duke or any man she married. Since first comprehending she was one of triplets, the thought of being with child and possibly having three babes at a time had always filled her with angst. She knew it was a fear she must find the strength to face when the time came.

That the duke hadn't searched deep into her past to know the swirls of rumors about triplets and many of the superstitions that went with them couldn't be considered her transgression. On the other hand, to be fair, perhaps she should tell him some things and let the petals fall where they may.

"I would do my best to have a son, but what you might not know about me is that my mother had three daughters. When I came to London for the Season, I hadn't set my cap for a duke to whom having a son would be so important."

He took his time to digest that bit of news. "Having a son is always important to a man, Miss Fine."

Edwina clasped her hands tightly together in front of her. That was a worry for her. Though a powerful man such as a duke would have a much better chance getting her sisters married, she had to be up front with him about her situation. Some of it anyway.

"I have no doubt that's true, and because of it you may want to consider someone whose lineage has been more fortunate in the prospects of sons."

"I want *you*, Miss Fine."

A breathless surprise like she'd never experienced before washed over her. It felt as if her heart started spinning somersaults in her chest at his profound words that she was the one for him.

The duke leaned in closer to her. "I think it's time for a son to be born in your family, is it not?"

He smiled so pleasingly at her she wanted to throw her arms around his broad shoulders and hold him close to her. Suddenly, she wanted to believe she could unburden all her buried fears about keeping the vow to her father, of being a triplet, and of the possibility of having multiple babes at the same time and opening her husband up to scorn and suspicions. But, of course, she couldn't do that. She had to remain on course and keep focused on her only goal: seeing her sisters married and living normal lives in Society as her father had wished. Only nature could determine if she had one babe or more and that worry should be hers alone to bear.

"I would like to think so," she added. "But I have no way of promising such a feat."

"Nor does any other lady, Miss Fine. You accepted my proposal with stipulations for our marriage taking place. What are they?"

If this agreement with him proceeded, she'd have to get used to his direct manner. She hadn't been around a great number of different men in her near twenty years, but enough to know most of them were more solicitous, and gentle in disposition when speaking to a lady. No doubt, if he and his butler had ever been taught manners, they'd forgotten them. They both could have used a lesson or two from her father.

The duke wasn't the kind, gentle soul she'd envisioned, but he would do. Her gaze swept up and down him once again, taking in the imposing man he was. Oh, yes. He would do.

Clearing her throat, she answered, "I don't just need one husband, Your Grace. I need three."

With the lines around his eyes tightening, the duke's gaze raked slowly over her face. "That wouldn't be possible, Miss Fine. Men don't like to share."

Matching him stare for stare, she retorted, "In case you are unaware of it, women don't either."

He took a moment to deliberate over what she said and agreed it was probably true with a slight nod.

"I didn't mean for me, of course," she added in a softer tone. "I have two older sisters, and I'd like for you to agree to help find them husbands who are not debauched, rakish, or wastrels."

"Consider it done. What else?"

His brusque answer was a little too short for her so she went on. "They should also come from good families and not be given too much to drink or gambling."

He murmured a curse under his breath. "That's not what I was referring to. You've made it clear what kind of man you'd approve of for your sisters." Glancing around, he saw his drink on the desk and went over to pick it up. After having a hefty swallow, he said, "I don't know what the devil is going on here. It shouldn't be your responsibility to see your sisters make a good match. Or that you do

either. Where is Viscount Quintingham? He or his repre-
sentative should be handling this."

"I assume he's at his estate. I've never met him but
have been told he's a recluse. After Papa fell ill, he wrote
to the viscount asking for help. He met with Aunt Pauline and agreed to accept guardianship of us after Papa
passed, add to our dowries, and sponsor me for a Season
since neither of my older sisters would agree to attend. My
aunt was given the task of helping me find a suitable husband."

The duke's brow rose and he looked as if he might
speak, but then thought better of it. She wondered what
he was thinking but because he remained quiet, so did
she.

Finally, he set his drink back on the desk and nodded
as if he understood before asking, "As guardian, why is
the viscount not handling this proposal for you and your
sisters?"

Edwina expected some contention from the duke, but
surely he could see she was handling this situation with
him perfectly well and needed no other help until they had
a promise to each other.

"The viscount made it clear he had no desire to become entangled with three ladies of marriageable age. Financial help and doing what was needed to accomplish
my entrance into Society was all he was willing to do. We
are appreciative, of course. He told my aunt that his solicitor, Mr. Richard Lewis, would handle the details of the
marriage contract for the first sister to marry."

"I'll make sure my solicitor is in touch with him, but
why isn't he here representing you in this matter?"

She hesitated by moistening her lips. "He doesn't know
about your offer yet. After I received your proposal,
Auntie and I decided we'd rather approach you ourselves

and establish whether your intentions were good and honorable before we engaged with Mr. Lewis."

"From what little I've gleaned about you, Miss Fine, I don't find it surprising at all that you wanted to take care of this yourself."

She took his words as a compliment and that made her smile. "I'm quite capable even though Society and the law dictate I must seek Mr. Lewis's help if our arrangement continues."

The duke strode back over to her and stopped in front of her again. "It will, Miss Fine."

There was no reservation in his statement but that was all right. Edwina had enough for both. Handsome as he was, and despite the unanticipated sensations he made her feel at times, she wasn't sure at all that she was going to marry this duke.

"You said your sisters were older than you, so they are content with you doing this for them?"

She hesitated and cleared her throat. She hoped not telling all the truth wasn't the same thing as an outright lie. "They are a little older, and yes, they are content with things as they are. You also need to know that the viscount expects my husband to take complete responsibility for my two sisters. Sadly, now that Papa is gone and he expects we will soon be someone else's responsibility, he's decided to close the house in York where we've lived all our lives."

His Grace shrugged. "I don't see marriage for them as a problem, Miss Fine. I'll find gentlemen your sisters will approve of."

"That might be harder than you think."

"You really don't know how easy this will be for me, do you?" He shook his head in frustration. "I can arrange to have them meet more than a dozen gentlemen tomorrow who would be more than happy to marry them. Surely, they will find one to their liking over the course of the Season."

Edwina pursed her lips for a moment. "One would think, but it's not always the case."

He seemed to study that with deep interest. "Is there anything pertinent about the virtue of either you or your sisters I should know about that would make an acceptable, interested man reconsider?"

The duke could get her back up quicker than anyone she'd ever met. "What are you suggesting, Your Grace?"

His thick brows knitted together in a scowl. "I'm not suggesting anything, Miss Fine. *You* are the one who said it might not be easy to find your sisters husbands. Not me. I've always thought it a woman's nature to want a husband so I was merely inquiring as to reasons why it might be difficult."

Without effort her shoulders stiffened and lifted. "I will stake my life on the fact that we are all untouched."

"Your *life*?"

The duke folded his arms across his chest, took a comfortable stance, and then had the nerve to smile at her in the most charming way. Edwina felt as if heated water was pouring over her with soothing warmth and all she wanted to do was bask in it. She had no idea a smile from a man could make a lady feel that way.

"Well then, Miss Fine, I will not argue with a lady who would do so. Don't let me stop you. Go on."

The warmth she was feeling disappeared quickly. He could have said he believed her. She would have liked to hear that. But for now, she'd let that pass.

"My sisters each have valid reasons for wanting to remain unmarried. Eleonora fell desperately in love with a young man more than a year ago. He never had a strong constitution and, as misfortune goes, he caught a chill and passed away before they could discuss marriage. She's vowed never to consider another."

"Perhaps it's been enough time, and she'll now reflect on the possibility of another."

"That is my hope. Eileen could contemplate making a match if she could get her head out of the clouds long enough to do so. Our father, a learned man himself, educated all three of his daughters quite well, but Eileen's thirst for knowledge has far exceeded mine and Eleonora's. She's especially fond of staying up most of the night and searching the dark heavens for every falling star that streaks across the sky. After only a few hours of sleep, she's combing through the gardens for new plants, bees, bugs, or something new to discover."

"I'll find her a gentleman who desires the same lustful pleasures of looking at the heavens as she does."

Edwina took a step back, staring at him with an air of disapproval. "I don't think that description is an appropriate one to use for a lady and certainly not my sister, Your Grace."

He frowned and rubbed his chin thoughtfully. "What— Which description are you taking exception to?"

Wondering if she wanted to repeat it, she cleared her throat. "*Lustful pleasures* was out of line, sir. Perhaps you meant someone who has the same knowledgeable interests as Eileen."

One of his shoulders tweaked. "Yes, of course, that's what I meant," he agreed with a quick nod, though Edwina could see by his frown that he didn't agree at all.

"She enjoys charting the movements of things in the sky such as how many shooting stars she can see and documents the days and times. She faithfully writes to an astronomer named Mr. Herschel each month, wanting him to invite her for a visit, and hoping she might offer her services as an assistant to his sister, who is also an accomplished astronomer."

"I'll find someone for her who appreciates what the man has accomplished. What else?" he asked impatiently, resting his hands on his hips once again.

Carefully watching him, she worried again about how much she should tell him. "Well, that's it, except . . ."

"What?" He cocked his head back in irritation. "There's no need to dribble out information a little at a time, Miss Fine. Just tell me what you want me to know or do and let's get on with this matter."

With a feeling of dread, she said, "They both look much like me and have red hair and green eyes," she stated as irritably as he had spoken.

He looked at her in disbelief. "That's the second time you mentioned your hair color. Does it bother you?"

"Me?" Why would he say that? "No, of course not."

He looked unconvinced. "Then what makes you think it concerns me?"

"We've read accounts of the past and unfortunately some people still hold to outrageous superstitions about redheads with green or blue eyes, and, well, other things."

"I don't hold to superstitions, Miss Fine."

His blatant answer delivered with such finality lifted her spirits and made her smile. Perhaps things had changed from when her father married her mother over twenty years ago. Maybe most of Society was now more accepting of people who weren't just like everyone else.

"I'm glad. We've heard and read about the things that

have happened to women who look like us in years long past."

He nodded to her with understanding. "There was a time when some civilized people didn't realize that just because something was different about others or someone was an anomaly or rare there was no reason to be afraid or distant. I am not one of those people."

His words touched her deeply and renewed her spirit that perhaps mankind had changed in recent years and no longer held to outdated and unproven superstitions. In any case, the duke held no such fallacies and her heart warmed toward him.

"That is reassuring, Your Grace."

He walked back over to his desk and picked up her glass. He held it up for her to see and asked, "More water?"

She lightly shook her head.

"There's something else you should understand," he offered, replacing her glass and taking hold of his own. "If you are my wife, I will take care of your sisters. Neither of them would ever have to worry about whether they would ever wed. I could bestow a generous allowance on them that no one could take away. They will never want for anything, married or not."

Once again, the duke took her breath away and filled her with excitement over such a possibility. She hurried over to the desk where he stood and looked into his eyes. "That would be wonderful for them. It would give them freedom. Time to figure out what they really wanted. That would—" Edwina's words stopped as the excitement ebbed from her body. She glanced away from the duke as the reality of what she was saying became clear in her mind.

"Go on," he encouraged softly and then sipped from his drink. "Finish."

After a soft cough to cover her feelings, she gave her attention back to the duke. It took every bit of the daring she could muster to say, "That would not change my vow to my father."

The duke placed his glass on the desk again. "I should have known you wouldn't be appeased by a simple answer to your quest."

It was telling that he already knew her so well. Edwina folded her arms across her chest and squeezed her upper arms nervously. "That would be most kind and generous, Your Grace, and like giving me and my sisters the world, but you see, that is not the point to my stipulation." She paused and moistened her lips. "Before Papa died, I gave my word I'd see all of us properly wed or betrothed before the end of the Season. That was his last wish. I must fulfill my promise."

"I appreciate the ramifications of an oath to a dying person, Miss Fine; every lady wants to marry just as every man wants to be master of his house. Together they want to have sons and daughters. I will do my best to find your sisters husbands before the end of the Season. What other stipulations do you have?"

She hesitated. The thought that she wasn't telling him the whole truth, but only part of it, flitted through her head in an aching way again. She felt badly about it but couldn't possibly get a better offer than the duke's. No matter who she accepted an offer from, she would have to keep the secret that they were triplets to herself. Her father had been firm in his beliefs they should be considered as proper as any other lady in Society. His fear was that no man would want to marry a lady who had been born with two sisters at the same time.

Finally, she said, "No others."

"That's all? Good. I'll stop by your house tomorrow and meet them."

"That won't be possible. You see, I couldn't get them to come to London with me."

He gave her that irritated expression she was getting used to but still found annoying. "Where do they live?"

"In the south of York."

"*York?*" he exclaimed with an edge to his voice. "Hell's gate, Miss Fine. What are they doing there?"

Not very good at hiding her true emotions, Edwina raised her eyebrows at his language as well as his tone to her. "What do you mean, sir? They live there."

"But you want me to find them husbands in London!" he exclaimed with what seemed the same passion she was feeling. "They may as well be living in the wilds of Scotland or somewhere in France. I can't be traipsing men up to the moors of York and back again for your sisters to take a gander."

"I know it's a long way to travel," she defended quickly.

"It certainly is, if you want to woo a lady," he shot back, "and by the end of the Season. It's damned well impossible. If they are as eccentric and difficult as you claim, you'll have to get them to London with you so I can see them and understand their reluctance to marry."

Edwina huffed. "Difficult? You are putting words in my mouth. I never said they were difficult. Particular maybe. Peculiar even. At times. However, their reasons to remain unwed are understandable and justifiable. We just need to change their minds."

"In order to do that, I need them *here.*" The duke pointed toward the floor and then ran both hands through his hair and tangled it more. "I need to talk to them, and then find the proper man to woo them out of their unnatural state of not wanting to marry."

"I tried to get them to come with me and be a part of the Season," she stated adamantly. "I swore to them it would be wonderful seeing all the sights of London, which both said they would like to do at some time, but neither of them were interested in the possibilities of parties and dancing every night. The problem is that they are both happy with their lives where they are and have no interest in being a part of a different life."

"Then why bother to upset them? Let them be old maids in peace."

Edwina gasped. His question made it appear he hadn't been listening to a thing she'd said. Edwina advanced on him with purpose and determination. "I told you it was my father's dying wish we all marry. I will not rest until I accomplish that for him. And I do miss not having them here with me." Her chest felt heavy from her rapidly beating heart. "We've never been apart and it's been difficult."

His features softened. "I agree they should have come with you." His tone grew softer too.

She raised her head a little and met his eyes, letting him know she appreciated his softness. Doing so made her want to get closer to him and feel his warmth, catch the scent of his clothing and shaving soap again, but she quickly dismissed those feelings and took a step back for good measure.

"Though they want no part of the Season, I would think they wouldn't want to miss your debut."

Debut? He had mentioned that before. Taking new interest in that, she said, "I'm not actually making a debut, Your Grace. Only attending the Season. I don't pretend to know what all the viscount did for me, but he was the one who arranged for proper clothing and the invitations I've received to various parties, balls, and other events so that I might meet eligible gentlemen."

The way his eyes narrowed was clear he was questioning something she said. But what? She tamped down the slowly rising fear that this match might not be arranged after all.

"Your name was on the list."

"I don't know what list you are referring to," she answered with a troubled frown. "I suppose it's the same one you mentioned before. Perhaps the viscount had my name added to it. In any case, I've tried to get my sisters to come."

"Then try harder, Miss Fine," he countered, his voice on edge again. "Get them to London by any means necessary."

"They would already be here if I could compel them or if I had the power or ability to force them to come," she argued, hoping the words didn't sound as stubborn to him as they did to her. She really wasn't the disagreeable person she was sounding like. His willfulness and her worry were making her seem so. "Can't you just arrange a marriage for them with suitable men and use your power as a duke to make them say 'I do'? Maybe a poet or a painter. Men who have good souls and would appreciate a lady with an adequate dowry to share his life, ambitions, and children."

His eyes widened and his mouth twitched up. "You would want me to do that for you?"

"No." She shook her head adamantly. "Not for me. For my father. This is his wish. I'm trying to fulfill it. I didn't say it would be easy to get them here or married.

I said it was a stipulation to me marrying you or anyone else. Securing my sisters' futures must come first. If it makes a difference as to whether we marry, I understand. I told you I didn't come to London in hopes of marrying a duke. Believe me, if you want to withdraw your offer to me and go to one of the ladies on that list you spoke of earlier, you may do so with no regrets or settlements."

"By the devil, Miss Fine. You try my patience."

"You have none," she came right back, unable to keep her voice as low as his. He was the most infuriating person she'd ever met, and that included her starry-eyed sister, Eileen, who had heretofore held that honor with great distinction.

How many women would ever have the opportunity to become a duchess? Only a handful in any given generation. She was about to throw her chance out the window because she couldn't pretend to be the proper, dutiful, and grateful young lady her aunt insisted she be when talking to a man. Perhaps she was simply being irrational. More than likely, it was her own fears of the wedding night, having a babe, and the duke or anyone in London figuring out she was one of triplets. The same worries that had kept her awake many nights since her father died.

Perhaps in some perverted way she was subconsciously trying to thwart her own goal? She believed if she didn't persuade her sisters to marry before this Season ended, they would be so set in their ways they never would.

The duke slowly moved to stand toe to toe with her as he gazed tightly into her eyes. The tension sparking between them was so lively it felt as if lightning were cracking all around. "You are not getting rid of me that easily, Miss Fine. You fascinate me, and I don't feel that will wane anytime soon. No matter how it came about, I chose you to marry, and I stand by that choice."

His words gave her strength, hope, and urgency. "My sisters are in York. So, tell me, Your Grace, can you arrange marriages for them by the end of the Season or not?"

CHAPTER 6

THE ART OF BEING A FINE GENTLEMAN
SIR DUDLEY SAMSON PEMBERTON FINE

*A gentleman with a fine sense of what is
acceptable would never kiss a lady without
first asking permission.*

It was more a battle of wills than words, Edwina thought. However, she wouldn't give up no matter which, or both.

"Every father wants his daughter to marry the first Season, but for many it just doesn't happen. However, if I can't do it, no one can," the duke stated without a hint of arrogance. Just assurance.

Edwina swallowed hard as her chest heaved with emotion. She wanted to believe him, but once again fear held her back. "So, I have your promise you can do it?"

"Sometimes it seems as if it's impossible for you to see reason, Miss Fine."

"And that seems true of you all the time," she countered. "You are obstinate too."

His brow furrowed deeper than it had since she'd been there, and he gave her a look that said he would do what she asked of him or he would die trying. But he only said, "You can be sassy."

"You can be mulish."

His whole body seemed to twitch and his eyes flickered at her choice of words. Perhaps she had been too hasty in her comeback, but no matter, their standoff seemed to be set on solid ground and his show of determination was welcomed.

"I am rational, Miss Fine," he said more calmly. "The usual kind of man. Simple."

"Simple?" She couldn't help but smile at such an outrageous description of himself, and of all things, she found it immensely charming. And for reasons she couldn't possibly imagine it made her want to hug him and laugh with him. "I have not had many dealings with men other than my father, but you are not simple. You are obviously not used to being thoroughly questioned and don't know how to handle it when you are."

He gave her a slight smile, and she couldn't have enjoyed it more if he'd placed his fingertips under her chin and tickled her.

"True," he admitted without pretense. "Nevertheless, if your sisters are not here, I can't help them. If they stay in York, they will have to choose from the men who are there."

"Unfortunately, only two or three of them are suitable and none they are willing to consider."

She and the duke were at an impasse. Neither of them willing to budge. But what could she do? The truth was she hadn't pushed her sisters to come to London where everyone would see they looked uncommonly alike, even for sisters. There were slight differences they were able to make. Eileen parted her hair down the middle and had a smattering of freckles across the bridge of her nose. They assumed it was because she would sometimes forget to wear her bonnet when she went out into the garden.

Eleonora had tendrils of fringe covering her forehead on both sides, and Edwina swept the crown of her hair back and away from her face. And they were careful to never dress in similar colors.

However, there was always the possibility someone might remember the time when her father said it was rumored a lady had three babes at one birth. Edwina hoped that that wouldn't happen and make them a spectacle in Society before they had a chance to make their way. She intended to follow her father's wishes and see them all married and living normal lives. Her father assured her he'd not read of triplets being born and all three living. Certainly not living to adulthood, and there would be little possibility anyone would believe it anyway. Despite that, the peculiarity and phenomenon of it was a difficult burden for Edwina to bear.

Perhaps no one would ever have to know about the strangeness of their birth if only fate had given one of them blond hair, or maybe brown eyes, or even a mole on the cheek, but no. Not one of them had a distinguishing birthmark to set them apart other than Eileen's freckles, and they were not prominent.

Rick expelled a gusty breath. "Since they are so adamant, I see no way to get them here other than for you to tell your sisters you are ill and need them to come be with you."

There was no command in his voice. There didn't have to be. His intent showed in every word and the way his eyes took in every detail of her face. Edwina straightened her already stiff frame.

"What kind of person do you take me for, Your Grace?" she said in an exasperated voice. "I can't lie to my sisters."

"No." He moved his shoulders and stance uncomfortably, as if he knew he had stepped over the line of propriety with his suggestion. "I didn't mean for you to make it a lie exactly," he added on more of a conciliatory note. "A fib."

"That is the same thing," she argued, thinking maybe she did need more water after all.

"A little one that only shades the truth and pulls on sisterly instincts to rush to your aid. Surely you could use their help with something?"

As impossible as it seemed, he looked at her as if he thought his suggestion was reasonable and had merit. And for a moment, his expression was so endearing and sincere she almost believed it was too. She was furious with herself for even thinking it. Where was her backbone when she needed it?

Thank goodness her sanity returned. "Even though you have given me a headache that has lasted since the day your letter arrived at my door, I won't send for my sisters to come help me when I don't need it."

"Fine," he muttered in a frustrated tone, running his hand through hair he had already tousled twice before. The movement left the thickness of it invitingly attractive.

"It's Miss Fine," she corrected with a slight lift of her chin and twitch of a smile on her lips.

"Yes, it is."

He leaned in closer to her and for some reason she had the feeling he sought to bend his head and nuzzle her neck.

"But it won't be *fine* with you if I can't *find* husbands for your sisters." His voice was grainy as his gaze stayed straight on hers. "That is your demand for accepting my proposal, is it not?"

Her heartbeat raced again. She nodded.

Suddenly, the duke started nodding his head. Irritation disappeared from his brow and from around his mouth and lips. Calmness prevailed in him. Her stomach fluttered. Edwina swallowed back the possibility she had gone too far when his response was to continue to stare silently at her, seeming to weigh his options. He thumbed his bottom lip as if in deep thought once again and completely unperturbed by her.

It was unlike her to be so forceful. He was a duke. She should be dancing with glee at the thought of marrying someone so powerful. And not just that, though it was enough, at times she just wanted to stop talking, look at him, and enjoy the wonderful sensations that flashed through her when he softened and stood close to her.

In a low voice, he all but whispered, "You are strong and clever, Miss Fine. Traits I admire, but I will not be bested by you."

His implication was clear, but what was he aiming to do?

"If you won't agree to manipulate the truth only a little in order to get your sisters to London for their *own* good and yours, then I will have to do it for you."

Excitement shot through her as quickly as lightning flashed on a hot, stormy night. He stood close, overwhelming, and yet she had no fear of his dominating presence. It was more like anticipation.

Edwina's breath caught in her throat, but she managed to whisper, "I don't know what could possibly be stirring around in that masculine mind of yours, Your Grace, but I will not allow you to fib to them any more than I would."

His lips quirked into a slow, easy grin that made her skin chill with expectancy. "Then you will have to tell them the actuality of what is happening to you in London."

She pursed her lips before saying, "That will not get them here. Auntie is not very strong but managing. I haven't been ill, and I'm in no danger here in London."

"I'm not referring to what has happened to you up to this point, Miss Fine. I'm talking about what is going to happen right now."

Without warning, he caught her up to his powerful chest with such impressive strength, astonishing speed, and cavalier ease she rolled to her toes as if she'd expected or wanted his sudden embrace. Her pulse raced. One of his hands pressed firmly into the middle of her upper spine, forcing her breasts against the tautness of his chest. The other cupped the back of her head in his palm.

Edwina's lips parted to object or to gasp, but there was no time before his mouth came down on hers with firm, persuasive warmth. Instantaneously they were sharing breaths, sounds, and tastes in the most intimate ways as his lips brushed back and forth across hers. Her body stiffened and then trembled. His fingers sliced through the curls of her chignon and massaged her nape with such excruciatingly slow and sensual movements they radiated stimulating sensations throughout her body, causing her to melt against him.

Her pulse throbbed in her chest, her ears, and all the way down in her most womanly part.

By all the holy saints, she and the duke were kissing! Worse, it wasn't horrible or offensive. Just brash and overpowering. The way his lips roved over hers with demanding pressure gave her the stunning, surprising feeling he was eager and hungry for *her*. It was an extraordinary experience and she didn't know what to make of it. Having never been kissed, she didn't understand what to do or how to react to how he was making her feel.

She'd never even *seen* a kiss except from her father to his daughters' foreheads or cheeks, and that was mostly when they were younger. What was she to do other than shudder in astonishment.

Seeming almost as quickly as he'd pulled her up to him, he let her go and stepped back. His breath was deep, heavy, and quick. So was hers. His expression intense but not worrying. A hot, willful silence stretched between them. They watched each other as if they were hunter and prey, facing off to see who the victor would be.

It had to be her. He'd wronged her by his sudden and aggressive ungentlemanly behavior, which led her to feel things she'd never felt before.

Edwina slowly backed away from him without taking her gaze off his face. "I can't believe you did that," she whispered, wondering how he'd taken her by such alarming surprise and why she wasn't feeling more offense. She barely managed to add, "You, sir, are an uncivilized animal."

"Only when I must be, Miss Fine. You wanted to tell your sisters the truth," he said in an undertone so husky and sensual she was nearly ready to forgive him for the grave offense. "Now you can. Send a message to them today. Say the worst rakehell in London is pursuing you, and you fear if they don't rush to your aid, you will marry him."

CHAPTER 7

It is perfectly fine for a gentleman to pat himself on the back, but only when no one is watching.

The solicitor, account managers, and anyone else who was expecting to meet with the duke today would have to wait until he returned. With all he had to do he would be up half the night to get it finished, but that didn't matter. Rick wanted to see his mother and find out why the letter had been mailed to Miss Fine, and he didn't intend to waste any time doing it.

The relatively small house in the oldest section of Mayfair looked much like all the others as he walked up the crushed stone walkway. It was well tended with a tall, neatly trimmed yew hedge lining each side and short boxwood shrubs acting as a fence along the front. There were bigger, more elaborate homes in which his mother could reside but this was the one she preferred. It was an easy walk to Hyde Park where she loved to stroll, and she'd known most of her neighbors since first coming to London as a bride.

He would have never expected such manipulation from her no matter how desperate she was feeling now that Shubert had a son. Was it possible she could have known or even sensed how ill he was that night and decided to take matters into her own hands after all? Had the apothecary told her of his recent bouts of high fever, or could it be possible one of his servants had tattled to one of hers?

After the kiss, Miss Fine awakened her aunt and they made a hasty exit from his house. It was just as well. Rick had a lot to do. He left instructions with Palmer and Mr. Wrightmyer concerning things he wanted accomplished by the end of the day, and since there was nothing more to be done regarding Miss Fine—except keep the intoxicating kiss he gave her off his mind for the rest of the afternoon—he hurried over to his mother's house.

"Maman," Rick called, letting himself in the front door. He threw his gloves and hat onto a chair and called to her again. The butler came rushing into the vestibule and Rick tossed his cloak off to him. "Where is she, Webster?"

"In the garden. I'll send someone for her immediately."

"There's no need," he declared. "Does she have guests?"

"No, Your Grace."

"Good." Hardly slowing down, Rick headed toward the rear door.

When he stepped outside, he saw his mother walking from the end of the garden toward him with a book in her hand. The parcel of land behind her house wasn't much bigger than the house, but kept in glorious fashion spring, summer, and autumn. At a glance, he caught sight of multiple colors of flowers embedded among intense shades of green.

"What's wrong?" Alberta asked in her usual elegant voice. "I heard you calling to me from inside the house."

He skipped down the steps and stopped before her, folding his arms across his chest, hoping to leave no doubt he was annoyed about something. A breeze fluttered the blue-and-white-striped ribbon that banded the straw hat and was loosely tied under her chin.

"You mailed the letter," he stated with no question to the correctness of his comment as she stopped in front of him.

Tilting her head back, she smiled, and replied, "What's this? I don't get an affectionate hello kiss on the cheek or even a '*How are you today, Maman?*' from my son?"

Keeping his determined gaze tightly on hers, he said, "I can see you look quite well as usual. Why did you post the letter?"

Her eyes narrowed curiously from under the wide brim as she took in his serious expression. "Which letter are you referring to? I sometimes write three to four a day to various people."

Rick unfolded his arms and shielded his eyes from the bright sunlight to watch every muscle movement in her face. Best he could tell, she wasn't being coy or evasive. She truly looked as if she didn't know what he was talking about, but he was convinced she had been the one at work to send Miss Fine to his door.

"Indeed, Maman. I am talking about you mailing the proposal I wrote to Miss Fine a week or so ago asking her to marry me."

"What madcap nonsense is this?" She gave him a breathy laugh and moved her hands behind her back like an innocent young maiden being falsely accused of a ridiculous offense. "A proposal from you? I did no such thing. I don't even know a Miss Fine. Why do you ask about it?"

Rick's mouth twisted into a frown as he tried to ascertain if she was avoiding telling him the truth. They were both silent for a moment. He heard the soft noises of spring buzzing around them. A light wind rustled the new leaves on the trees and shrubs, and a bird twittered as it flew overhead. Neighbors' muffled conversations could be heard in the houses next door as they mixed with distant sounds of street traffic.

"She has the letter," he said, the breeze fluttering the ends of his hair across his forehead.

"What letter are you referring to, Stonerick?"

Rick's curiosity grew. His mother wasn't faking ignorance. She really didn't know what he was talking about. "Miss Fine has the letter I wrote at your house several nights ago asking her to marry me."

The dowager lowered her lids over her eyes as if she were trying to get a better look at him to decipher exactly what his words meant. "Impossible."

"I saw it, Maman. It was written in my hand and closed with your wax seal."

"Mine?" Her mollifying tone changed abruptly with indignation. She retreated a few steps back. "It can't be. There is no way she could have that letter and certainly not under my seal. I never even looked down at it when you handed it to me. I gave it right back to you and watched you throw it into the fire and then I walked away with my brandy."

Strange as it was, that was the foggy memory he had as well, but Rick wanted the mystery solved. "It was mailed to her."

"It would have to be a forgery, of course." Alberta brought her hands around in front of her to cup the book to her chest as if to give validity to her words. "Who knew you wrote it?"

"You."

"Pshaw," she muttered in an agitated tone he seldom heard. "I would never have mailed that letter. I told you so that night. No one knows better than I that you are reckless beyond reason at times as you were to even think of writing such a proposal. You were basically throwing a dart against the wall and hoping for a good match."

"It worked for Wyatt when he married Fredericka."

"His solicitor had met her. I may not care who you marry but there is no way I want you to marry a lady neither of us have met. She might be missing a tooth, be walleyed, or have red hair and green eyes."

That stopped Rick cold. He relaxed his arms to his side. "What's wrong with red hair and green eyes?"

"Everyone knows women with those two features can read your mind and accurately tell one's future."

He blew out a gruffly murmured curse. "Please, Maman. That's rubbish. This new group you have joined is taking you too far with superstitions."

"No, no, it's true," she said with conviction, turning the front of the book over for him to see the title.

Rick looked down. *Ten Superstitions That Have Been Proven True.*

"Our Insightful Ladies of London Society read about it in this book. And, of course, I've heard stories from time to time throughout my life about such oddities."

"What are you reading that rubbish for?" He scrunched up his face. "Queen Elizabeth had red hair and so did probably a host of other monarchs. I don't believe they would have made some of the decisions that were rendered if they could read minds."

"Of course they couldn't do such things, Stonerick," his mother agreed, walking over to place the book in a nearby chair. "They all had brown eyes according to paintings and writings. Which is the common color for redheads. It's not just red hair or green eyes, but the two together."

Rick looked at her in puzzled amusement, and then shook his head in dismissal of such a preposterous claim. If Miss Fine could read his mind, he would have never caught her unawares when he kissed her so suddenly and shocked her down to her unmentionables.

"Why is this irrational superstition of yours just coming to light now that you've joined this new group of ladies?"

"We're studying a series of books on superstitions." She nodded toward the book in the chair.

"Stop reading the blasted thing," he mumbled. "And it would probably be best if you stayed away from that group too." He didn't care what color Miss Fine's hair was. Or her eyes, which were beautiful. She was the first lady that had been able to attract him and hold his attention in a very long time. Considering his reaction to her, it no longer bothered him the letter had been sent. He only wanted to know how it happened. "For now, let's get back to how Miss Fine got the letter."

The duchess pressed her hand to her forehead as if that might help her think as she looked from one side of the garden to the other and back to him, clearly distressed. It was unlike her not to know exactly what she wanted to say.

"I know I saw you—" Her voice halted. She compressed her lips in concern and looked up at him. "Wait, no, I remember now." Lowering her hand, she continued. "I didn't give the letter to you. I laid it on the desk in front of you without looking at it and walked away. You stayed there, and I didn't return to the desk for the rest of the evening. The list of names my assistant made for your consideration was lying beside it." Horror filled her eyes. "Is it possible you threw the list into the fire instead of the letter?"

Anything was possible that night with the way he'd felt. He barely remembered going to his mother's house and had no memory of getting back home. Her explanation was probably true. The letter wasn't a forgery. He was certain of that.

Rick bit back an oath and with a grumbling pitch to his voice, asked, "If you didn't mail it, who did?"

"I have no ide— Oh, dear saints in heaven!" Her eyes widened as she covered her mouth with her hand for a moment. "My new assistant. I'll turn him off immediately. No, I'll strangle him first and then let him go."

"Maman, what has he to do with the letter?"

Shaking her head, his mother started pacing in front of the steps. "Probably everything." She stopped and looked at Rick. "He failed to post an important letter for me his first day of work. I was quite put out about it and told him if a letter with a signature was left on my secretary he was to seal and mail it promptly that day. I might have been a bit harsh with him, but he has been overly attentive since."

Rick's mother was never harsh with anyone.

"This one had my name on it," Rick reminded her. "It wasn't even on your stationery."

She looked aghast. "Perhaps he thought I was mailing it for you. I don't know what he was thinking, but I do know he wouldn't read my private correspondence."

Did she really believe that? "It was one sentence. Anyone could have read it with a passing glance."

"I didn't," she swore almost defiantly. "As I said, I didn't even know who you wrote the proposal to. I'll discuss this with him tomorrow, of course, but I'm sure he'll confirm that he simply saw her name and *a* signature and did what he was supposed to do. There isn't that much difference between the *Duke* of Stonerick and the *Duchess* of Stonerick if one is only glancing at something. The poor man is so afraid of being dismissed he jumps at his own shadow."

"How in Lucifer's name would he have known where she lives, Maman?"

"And how would I know that, Stonerick?" she asked just as quickly. "It's his job to find out such things, not mine. I can't be hunting down addresses for him. What would I need him for if I had to address my own letters?"

The sound of carriage wheels rolling over the street in front of the house caught Rick's attention and he looked away from his mother. What she said was true. At least he felt better knowing she hadn't intentionally set him up to marry, even though that night he'd given her permission to do so. Besides, for all her tart retorts, Miss Fine fascinated him. She was loyal to her father and passionate about her sisters.

"So." His mother's voice returned to its normal softness. "Miss Fine received the letter of proposal and came to see you about it?"

"Yes."

Alberta folded her arms across her chest, drummed her fingers of both hands lightly on her arms, and asked, "To say or do what?"

"Query if it was a legitimate offer from me." There was no reason to reel off the particulars of their conversations or Miss Fine's stipulations.

"Oh." His maman seemed to hum low in her throat, letting him know she was warming up to the idea of him marrying, even if it was brought on by such extraordinary circumstances and to someone she had never been introduced to. "I don't recognize the name Fine. What do you know about her family?"

"She's related to Viscount Quintingham. Distant cousins."

"Oh," she said again, softer, clasping her hands behind her back again and shrugging. "I don't know much about him or his extended relatives. No one in the family seems to be social. Do you know him?"

He couldn't say he did, but that wouldn't make his mother rest easy so he said the next best thing, "Enough."

Alberta brushed at a strand of hair that had escaped from beneath her hat. "Is she pleasant? I'd be pleasant if a duke proposed to me."

"One did, Maman. Father."

She smiled and so did Rick.

"Besides, days are pleasant," he added.

"Well, yes, of course they are, Your Grace. Females are either comely or homely. There seems to be no in-between these days. Being with her for a time, did you find out sufficient things to know whether she might be an acceptable bride?"

Rick thought back to his invigorating and contentious conversations with Miss Fine, and then to the way she felt so pleasing in his arms, and the softness of her lips beneath his. He wished their first kiss could have been different. He hadn't wanted it to be so shocking and hard, but she'd left him with few choices. He would make it up to her with the next kiss. And the next. And the one after that. The breeze fluttered his hair, and suddenly he envisioned Miss Fine brushing it away from his forehead. The nice thought made him feel good and eager to see her again.

"She is lovely."

His mother's lips twitched in a near celebratory smile. "I'm glad to hear that."

"And outspoken," he added.

Her smile faded and she brought her hands around front and held them together at her waist. "That doesn't exactly reassure me of her suitability for you, Stonerick. You need a wife who always knows her place in all situations."

The muscles around his eyes tightened. "I thought you had great respect for women who are outspoken."

"Oh, I do. For mothers. Not wives," she answered with sincerity. "However, if her deportment doesn't change, I'm sure one of your solicitors can easily get you out of this offer for her hand any time you wish. They'll know how to explain to her this was an unfortunate mistake. If her family insists on restitution, you can arrange an appropriate settlement, which I'm sure they will be happy to accept."

Her words made Rick's back twitch as thoughts of the fevers returned. No, he was not letting Miss Fine get away. He needed a wife, and she was the one he wanted.

"I'm going to marry her."

Confusion settled in his mother's features. He knew she wanted to feel relief that he was finally going to marry but wasn't certain he'd picked the right bride—the right way. He understood all her worries. He had wrestled with them too.

"All right," she said, braving a smile. "After you've gone through the Season with her, you'll know if her outspokenness continues or if there are other unflattering traits."

"It's done, Maman. We will wed within the next few days."

Alberta's eyes went wide again as a gust of wind blew the ribbons of her hat across her cheek. "That soon, Stonerick?"

"I'd rather she attend the Season as my wife."

"Why? There's no reason when the Season is so close and you still have so many young ladies to meet."

That's what the ravaging fevers had him thinking too until he met Miss Fine, but all he said to his mother was, "Did you forget Shubert and his newborn son?"

Her lips pressed together again in a distraught line for a few seconds. "I suppose I did. It's disconcerting that all this time I've longed for the day I'd hear you were to wed, and now that you are, the feeling isn't the joyful one I'd always expected."

Rick understood her meaning. There was always a bit of sadness when a long-sought goal was reached. Especially the unusual way this one had come about.

"I may be an ill-tempered brute most of the time, Maman, but I'm a man of honor as well. I wrote the letter. I will honor it."

"You are a duke," she said with pride beaming in her voice and countenance. "You don't have to marry anyone you don't want to."

"I asked. She accepted. Be happy knowing I will marry soon. You've been waiting to hear this news since the day my father died."

"Of course I have," she said without pretense. "I've never denied that. But the truth is, I don't think I meant it when I said it didn't matter who you married. It does."

Rick gave her an understanding smile but remained silent. He wasn't going to change his mind.

"I never dreamed your betrothal would be conducted in such a haphazard manner, and though I agree with the necessary haste because of Shubert's good fortune, it makes me worried for you. I do want you to be happy. Your father and I had a short marriage but we were happy when we were together."

Now that he knew what had happened concerning the letter, Rick resolved that he may never have another bout of high fevers but was no longer willing to take the chance. He needed an heir and was *fine* with Miss Fine. With all the qualities he liked about her, there lingered an air of mystery surrounding her and it was intoxicating. He could wait to find out everything about her. A little mystery about a lady was good.

Fate had directed him to stop on her name that night. Fate had caused him to throw the wrong piece of paper into the fire, and for his mother's inept secretary to have mailed it was all the proof he needed that she was the one for him.

"I appreciate her candor. She'll do nicely, Maman."

"Very well, I will do my best to trust your decision on that. When will I meet her?"

Rick's mind swirled with possibilities. Dinner at his house or his mother's would probably work. But then his gaze landed on the chair with the book about superstitions. He didn't want his bride to see that kind of book or be subjected to prattle about his mother's recent leanings into what he considered hocus-pocus nonsense. If she had to hear it, better it be after Miss Fine said "I do."

"At the wedding, Maman."

"What?" She let out a soft laugh. "You can't mean that, Stonerick."

"I do," he answered quietly. "It will be easier for all of us to keep everything simple. We'll have the wedding at my house as soon as all the plans can be made. I'll keep you apprised of how quickly the negotiations for the contracts can be settled and properly signed."

Alberta gasped, sniffed, and then looked away before turning back to say, "That's not fair, Your Grace."

Rick gave her an affectionate smile. "No, but it will

be best. You can invite a few friends if you like. That should make you feel better."

"No, it doesn't," she admitted. "But, of course, I'll invite a friend or two. What about Miss Fine and her family? Is this what they want? A rushed wedding with not even one small dinner party to announce the engagement before the Season even starts?"

"It starts the next day, Maman. Besides, I plan to see her tomorrow and will make sure she's accepting with the short notice." His gaze strayed to the book again and he debated what he should do. "There's one more thing I need to tell you before I go."

The dowager braved a smile and lifted her chin. "What's that?"

"She has red hair and green eyes."

"Oh, dear, Your Grace. Get my sachet quickly. I think I might faint."

CHAPTER 8

THE ART OF BEING A FINE GENTLEMAN
SIR DUDLEY SAMSON PEMBERTON FINE

*A gentleman should never overburden a lady
with too much information.*

Familiar sounds of harnesses rattling, wheels rolling on hard-packed ground, and horses clopping along echoed around as Rick drove his curricle down the quiet streets of St. James the next morning. Most of the two- and three-story houses he passed had been built years ago and were close together. Some people called the nestled residences a cozy way to live, while others insisted it was nosey. Either way, there were no secrets among the people in this neighborhood.

The homes in this section of town were separated by fences made from wood, iron, or sometimes a simple hedgerow, but Rick knew such enclosures did little to add to one's privacy. Aside from some variations in styles and colors, the things that made every home different were the distinctions of flowers, trees, and shrubs gracing front lawns, and the occasional fancy awning of iron or lattice-work around the front doors.

Bright midday sun had the skies blue and took a bite out of the cool spring air. Rick tapped the ribbons on the horses' rumps to keep them moving when they slowed.

In his eagerness to get to Miss Fine's leased house, he ignored the friendly greetings of waves, nods, and hat-tipping from pedestrians and other drivers as the horse clipped down the road at a brisk pace.

Rick had already missed Wyatt's early morning fencing match and would probably miss seeing Hurst run his newest thoroughbred as well, but what the hell. He'd see them in time for his shooting match later in the day. His friends would forgive him for his absence, after they picked themselves up off the ground. News of his upcoming nuptials was sure to have them rolling in laughter.

Hurst was the only one of the three friends who'd been eager to marry, and it looked as if he was going to be the last to tie the knot of matrimony. For reasons Rick didn't understand, Hurst always talked of wanting to fall in love before saying "I do."

In order to secure a sizable inheritance he was about to lose, Wyatt had agreed to an arranged marriage last year with a young lady he hadn't known until a day or two before the wedding. Now he was devotedly in love with Fredericka and happy as a lark perched on the highest branch of a tree on an early summer morning.

News of an impending marriage would be the last thing they'd expect to hear from Rick. He hadn't seen it coming either. Now that his decision to wed had been made, he was feeling impatient and wanted to get on with it and do right by his father and the title and have an heir as soon as possible. He no longer wanted to leave to chance the possibility of another fierce fever and not living through it. Twice was enough to get his attention.

Besides, Miss Fine captivated him more than any lady he could remember. Yet, his strong, physical reaction to her was interesting, to say the least. He'd never been attracted to redheads, but her hair was beautiful, lush, and made her green eyes twinkle and sparkle seductively. Especially when she was irritated with him. Which was most of the time they'd spent together yesterday.

When he'd first walked back into his book room with the water for her, he'd been stunned at the sight of her. Not from the color of her hair, but because he immediately envisioned seeing it unpinned and draping across her pale, bare shoulders, delicately covering the tips of her breasts. The image had seared into his mind and he enjoyed remembering it.

Thinking about Miss Fine made him smile as he maneuvered the curricle around and ahead of a slow-moving landau packed full of a family of three or four children who were talking and laughing, and at least one was squealing to the high heavens! He quickly gave the horses leeway to go.

He supposed he most admired Miss Fine's determination to fight for what she believed was fair when asked repeatedly to leave his house. In the end, she was right to be so insistent. The letter that had been sent to her was not something he'd want her discussing with Mr. Wrightmyer or Palmer.

Perhaps some of her strength came from the fact she wasn't just fighting for herself but also had a duty to see her older sisters married. The problem was she thought he could create a miracle and do that for her. And he would. Eventually. But by the end of the Season might prove a challenge.

Rick chuckled under his breath. Miss Fine had tried to hide it, but he'd seen how she'd hedged when saying her sisters were a *little* older. No doubt that meant they were *much* older and perhaps not as gorgeous as their younger sister and had already become settled in their lives as spinsters. Which was probably the true reason they didn't want to come to London and marry. All they needed was the right man to tickle their fancy and they'd be ready for the altar.

There was one possible hitch but he could overcome it. Because he'd never made a lot of friends in the ton, Rick didn't know any of the older bachelors. He'd have to call on Wyatt, Hurst, and others to help him find suitable men to call on the sisters—once they made it to London. He would have them married or betrothed by the end of the Season if he had to wrap the men in pastry dough and sprinkle them with sugared apricots. Perhaps her sisters didn't know it yet but would learn—dukes could accomplish most anything.

The warmth of the sun on the back of his neck reminded him of Miss Fine's warm, inviting lips. Their kiss was intensely vivid in his mind. He had no doubt it had been her first. That pleased him and substantiated her claim to innocence. Kisses should be anticipated and wanted but never forced. Unfortunately, Miss Fine was being unreasonable, so on impulse he had been unreasonable in return. The kiss was only meant to give her a truthful purpose to summon her sisters to Town, but it managed to give him a little foresight into his newly betrothed as well.

When he'd held her in his arms, he liked the way she'd felt next to him. Natural, warm, and womanly. It was as if he knew she was the one who belonged in his arms. No other. He'd never had that feeling about a lady before. She smelled of freshly washed skin and hair, not even a hint of rose, lavender, or any other perfumed water on her. Her bosom wasn't billowy or puffed above the neckline of her dress in a showy manner but seemed to fit nicely with her slender frame.

In the short time he'd held her, he learned she had a

narrow waist and gentle, feminine flare to her hips. She'd been so caught off guard by the kiss that she trembled. He wasn't happy his quick action frightened her, but it was necessary, and her reaction had told him a lot about her. The fact that she was appropriately abashed with shock and outrage at his tactics, and wasn't willing to lie to her sisters, let him know her standards were high.

By all he could tell, it appeared that fate had been good to him when his finger stopped on Miss Fine's name. Now he hoped fate would be equally generous and make their first babe a son.

Rick continued to ponder as he guided the horses onto the street where Miss Fine was residing. Though he was committed, he wasn't without concerns. He didn't know how successful he would be at having a wife. All his life he'd enjoyed being alone. Something that had never been allowed him as a child or young man. His mother saw to it there were always servants, governesses, or tutors hovering around waiting and wanting to do everything for him. Even as he grew older and managed to slip away to explore the woods or take his horse out for an early morning ride by himself, it wouldn't be long before he realized someone had followed to keep watch.

Eton and Oxford were worse. Who could ever be alone in schools that had over two hundred boys and headmasters who appeared to have eyes in the back of their heads? Somehow, he'd managed those years.

The Dowager Duchess of Stonerick wanted to make sure nothing happened to the heir to the title. Rick vowed he would never be that overly protective of his son. Whenever he had an heir, he was going to give him all the freedom he wanted to just be a boy and not worry about the title.

Rick smiled as he slowed the horses to a walk on his approach to Miss Fine's house. She was sitting in the shade on the top rung of the front steps, her attention on the book in her hands. When she realized the horse and carriage had stopped, she looked up. His stomach clutched as their eyes met across the distance. It felt good to see her, and that she was doing something so normal was a lovely sight.

Without wasting time, he secured the reins, and jumped from the curricle. The mares were well schooled to a carriage so he had no fear of them wandering off as he strode toward Miss Fine.

"Your Grace," she said softly while rising and giving a curtsey as he approached.

Rick stopped at the bottom step and took in her natural beauty. She was fetching in a light honey-colored dress with a dark-brown spencer. Her hair looked as if it had been hastily penned and the cool breeze fluttered wisps of strands about her face. There was a freshness about her that looked pure, sweet, and untouched. It made him want to catch her up in his arms and show her the proper way a man should kiss a lady.

Her eyes were steady but wary, almost distrustful as he watched her swallow hard. Was she thinking he might accost her again? He didn't want her to be apprehensive with him about anything, but he wasn't good at knowing what to say so she would feel comfortable around him. Especially after yesterday. He never had a reason to worry about such things. Ladies were usually watching what they said around him for fear they wouldn't please the duke.

"You look lovely, Miss Fine." It was true, but he was hoping to put her at ease as well.

She twitched her shoulders a little. "Thank you," she offered softly, continuing to hold her wary gaze on his.

"You left so quickly yesterday we didn't make arrangements for a time to see each other again." He looked at the book.

"It was necessary. I needed to get Aunt Pauline home to rest."

"I know," he answered truthfully, wondering if he should mention the kiss, apologize, or leave it unspoken between them. "Am I interrupting anything?"

"No." She held the book to her chest in much the same way his mother had held hers yesterday afternoon. "Just reading. Would you like to come in for refreshment?"

He shook his head and propped his booted foot on the first step. "I can't stay long. I wanted to make sure you and Mrs. Castleton were feeling better."

"I'm quite all right, Your Grace." Her countenance strengthened. "Auntie hasn't come belowstairs yet today but she was feeling more rested when I checked on her before I came out to read."

"Good to hear." Rick wasn't any good at stepping around questions so he simply asked, "Did you get a letter mailed to your sisters yesterday as I suggested?"

She lifted her chin and scoffed with defiance. "Is that what it was? A suggestion?"

His features softened. "Perhaps a strong one."

Edwina seemed to prickle at his words. "Definitely a strong one, sir, but I sent the message immediately upon my return home."

Rick consciously settled his breathing and the desire to catch her up to his chest and kiss her long, soft, and often. There would be time for that after they married, and he suddenly realized he was looking forward to that.

"What did you say to them?" he asked quietly, not

wanting to start an argument with her but needing to know she was holding up her end of their bargain.

"The truth, of course," she murmured under her breath and then said more plainly, "That a scoundrel of the highest order had offered for my hand and was pursuing me in a most ungentlemanly manner."

"Good." His gaze caressed her face in a leisurely way. "I like that. They will come. I asked my solicitor to be in touch with your solicitor, Mr. Lewis, today so they can start preparing the marriage contracts."

"So soon? There is no hurry is there?"

He leaned back and regarded her. She was tense. That was to be expected for a bride. If not for the possibility of the fever returning, he wouldn't mind giving her more time. "There may be no hurry for you, Miss Fine, but there is for me. I need to marry as soon as possible."

She hugged the book tighter and seemed to consider his words carefully before saying, "All right. Thank you for letting me know. I shall be in touch with Mr. Lewis too."

Rick nodded once. Her tone indicated that she thought their conversation was now finished and he would be leaving. But he wasn't. There was something about her that made him want to indulge in all she had to offer.

"The other reason I came by is because I have something for you."

Miss Fine looked at his hands and smiled at finding them empty.

"I'll be right back." He turned and strode to the carriage and picked up the large wicker basket from the floor of the curricle. It was stuffed full of newsprint pages that had been rolled and tied with colorful ribbons. Just the sort of thing a lady would like. He walked up and placed the basket near her feet.

Peering down at it, she seemed baffled at first, but then faced him with a gracious smile. "Newsprint? I do believe you need to read my father's book, Your Grace. I'm sure he suggested flowers or confections were appropriate for a lady you'd expect to marry."

"No doubt, he is right." Rick chuckled softly, realizing how just looking at her pleased him and teased his senses. "I should have added flowers on top."

"The ribbons are a lovely touch," she added, unmistakably trying to keep from widening her smile as a gleam of humor danced in her eyes.

Rick gave her a slight shrug, not minding at all she found amusement as well as pleasure in his unexpected gift. "This isn't ordinary newsprint, Miss Fine. They are scandal sheets and gossip columns."

Her lips parted with a silent *O* and her arched brows lifted. "Really? Are this many printed every day?"

Rick let his gaze scan over her face. She really had no clue about the gossipmongers' mischief. It was intensely refreshing. "No, only a handful. Most of these are from the past year. Since you had never read a scandal sheet, I thought it was time for you to see what you've been missing. Most of these have something written about me. I assumed you might want to read about the man you're going to marry."

"Yes, yes, I do. This is superb! I should like to read these very much."

Her words were soft and breathy, but he could see the excitement in her beautiful face. There was no doubt, he had delighted her with the old *newsprint*. Rick found her enthusiasm for the gossip sheets enchanting.

She knelt before the basket and laid her book aside.

Rick could see the title. *Literary Anecdotes of the Eighteenth Century* by John Nichols. A far different kettle of fish from what his mother was reading. A tinge of concern shuddered through him as he remembered his mother's most recent book. A sudden feeling of needing to protect Miss Fine buried in his chest. The Dowager Duchess of Stonerick was going to have to bring her reading standards up to match her future daughter-in-law's. And she was going to have to do it fast.

Miss Fine glanced up at him. All the earlier wariness was gone from her features. Glee seemed to radiate from her as she dug both hands into the rolled papers and then let them drop back on top of each other as she laughed. "How did you get so many? Do you keep them?"

"Me? No. I seldom look at them." Bending on one knee near the opposite side of the basket, he added, "I think my mother has a copy of everything that has ever been written about me. She keeps them, good or bad, and enjoys reading them from time to time. I had her butler gather some of them for me."

"I'm so glad you did. I'll get started on them right away, but . . ." With eyes sparkling, she paused and offered him a teasing smile that only lifted one side of her mouth in a sensual way. "How will I know what is true and what isn't?"

Rick enjoyed her eagerness to read the gossip pages and learn more about him too. "If you want to believe it you will."

"Thank you for bringing these."

She looked at him with such fondness and appreciation that he had the feeling she wanted to reach over, pull him close, and hold him in a tight hug of thanks. His body responded to the tug of attraction that passed hot and thrilling between them.

By the saints, he'd been with women through the years

who had excited him, made him come back to them time and time again, but he'd never felt the strength of the pull Miss Fine had. It was different. Before, he always wanted what the women in his life could give him. This time, he wanted to give, and that filled him with excitement.

Filled with impatience to kiss her, Rick quickly glanced around. The portico was small with stalwart, wide posts that shielded most of the front from the street and gave the feeling of warmth and intimacy. He owed her a proper kiss, he reasoned, and it would be easy to reach over and buss her softly on the cheek and then move on to her lips. He knew he needed to start slow and keep his advance tender and intimate.

Feeling anticipation inside him, he leaned forward and watched her shoulders relax as she looked at his lips. An invitation. A slow roll of enticement worked its way from his chest to low in his stomach. He moved closer, and her lips parted. Suddenly, a door slammed from somewhere down the street.

Miss Fine jumped at the sound and stood up so hurriedly Rick didn't have time to help her rise or convince her they could recapture the desire to kiss that was filling them.

CHAPTER 9

THE ART OF BEING A FINE GENTLEMAN
SIR DUDLEY SAMSON PEMBERTON FINE

*One of the first things you must do in order
to become a fine gentleman is learn how
to win and lose with honor.*

Rick pulled the reins to slow his racing gelding as he reached the large grassy field on the outskirts of London. Some of the fifty or so men gathered there clapped and whistled at his approach, signaling they were happy he'd finally arrived. So was he. It looked as if he'd made it in time to honor his commitment to his opponents and friends who'd laid down their wagers. He'd hate like hell to lose by default because he was late.

But he would have been if Miss Fine's neighbor hadn't picked the most inopportune time imaginable to shut the door. Rick had wanted to stay and once more evoke the closeness that was building between him and the lovely miss and he would have if she hadn't told him she needed to check on her aunt. How could he argue against that?

He might not be sure he wanted marriage but he was damn sure he wanted Miss Fine.

Shouts from the small crowd regained Rick's attention. Men often challenged him to contests, pitting their skills against his, so he regularly obliged and participated in games such as this one. It helped keep his eyes sharp and hands steady. He'd always considered them practice for the bigger sporting events he participated in.

The flat, open land called The Field was a favorite spot for shooting matches. It wasn't so far from the streets of London that it made the ride out weary, yet not so close the noise of the continuous shots being fired would bother the townspeople.

As Rick hoped, Wyatt and Hurst were waiting for him and rushed to help when he stopped.

"Where the devil have you been all day?" Wyatt asked, not trying to hide his annoyance at the late arrival.

"Is it the fever again?" Hurst questioned as he started removing the leather straps that held Rick's wooden pistol case onto the back of the saddle.

"Later," Rick answered, swinging down from his horse, and handing the reins off to Wyatt. There was no time to tell them about Miss Fine. "I have to ready my pistol, sign up, and place my wagers."

"We'll do that for you and hear your excuses later," Wyatt grumbled. "Get yourself in line for your first shot."

Rick complied with Wyatt's command and took his place. The early rounds of the competition dragged on longer than Rick expected, giving him plenty of time to remember the breeze ruffling Miss Fine's hair and the attractive lilt to her soft laugh as she looked at the abundance of scandal sheets. He also had to bear in mind there were things he needed to get done now that he'd decided he was going to wed in a matter of days.

After many sips from brandy flasks between turns, an assortment of cheers, heckles, and groans from the crowd along the way, and more than a dozen rounds of competition, the small group of seven competitors had dwindled to only Rick and a young, sandy-haired buck, who talked a line as well as he aimed. Mr. Matthew Malcolm was a damned good marksman.

The man didn't look to be much past his twenty-first birthday, but he was dripping in confidence and arrogance. Together with his boyish good looks and affable personality, his eyesight was sharp as an eagle's and his aim was solid as a tree trunk. He'd tried to engage Rick in conversation each time their pistols were reloaded, but Rick wasn't one to pass time with idle chatter. Especially with people he didn't know and had no plans to ever know. And he had yet to meet the man who could intimidate or impress him by bragging about his shooting skills.

Along with the usual crowd of gentlemen who'd followed Rick's exploits in marksmanship through the years, the fresh-faced blade had brought a fair number of onlookers to place bets in his favor. Rick was always happy to have a new opponent to go up against, except for the fact the man was having a damn good run of luck. He'd hoped to put him away after a couple of rounds but the upstart was shooting like an experienced challenger.

Unfortunately, Rick was having a difficult time maintaining concentration on his aim. He was usually good at keeping other things off his mind while in a match but thoughts of Miss Fine, his agreement with her, and the things he needed to do kept vying for his attention.

Hastily scheduled matches like this one were usually a simple contest for Rick to win and fatten his followers' coffers as well as that of the charitable hospital he and Hurst helped Wyatt support. A tin cup was placed on a stand about the height of an average man's chest. All the contestants had to do to advance to the next round was shoot the target off in one shot. After the end of each rotation the stand was moved a couple of feet farther down the field. The match went on until only one man was left with a clean shot.

The sun beamed hot on the back of Rick's neck and glinted off the barrel of his expensively crafted pistol. He'd long ago shed his coat and gloves but kept his hat pulled low on his brow to minimize shadows, movements, or any other distractions. His nape was damp from where moisture had caught against his collar and neckcloth.

The tin cup was getting smaller and harder to see with each completed round, and Mr. Malcolm continued to try and engage Rick in the jovial conversation he'd carried on with the man who'd reloaded his gun after each shot. Rick had learned long ago not to allow opponents, comments from the crowds, or other gunshots that might be going off at the same time to distract him. He couldn't let his own thoughts do it either.

Mr. Malcolm's constant banter throughout the afternoon wasn't taunting Rick but he sure as hell was irritating him. The man had a lot to learn about the correct way to participate in a shooting match. Starting with how to be quiet.

But his dialogue continued.

"Do you ever get tired of gentlemen telling you what a good marksman you are?"

"I've heard you never practice. Is it true?"

"How did you learn to shoot so damn well if you don't practice?"

"You may not have heard about me, but I haven't lost a match in over a year."

And on and on it went. When Rick's time came around again, he settled the pearl grips comfortably in the palm of his hand, tightened and pulled back the hammer. He seldom changed his routine and always took his time. After another steadying breath, he aimed and settled his focus. At the instant he squeezed the trigger, it was as if the sun had moved from behind a cloud and glinted off the cup at just the right angle to spark in his eyes. The shot rang out, but the ping of the ball hitting the metal never sounded.

Rick missed. A flicker of shock jolted through him. "Bloody hell," he whispered. It had been years since he'd missed such a simple shot. He pushed his hat up farther on his forehead with one hand while he lowered the pistol in his other.

Jubilant clapping and shouts of congratulations sounded from the gallery of younger men who were there for Mr. Malcolm. Moans, gasps, and curses echoed from Rick's supporters. They were stunned. So was Rick, but he wasn't a sore loser to anyone who played fair. And, except for his chatty attitude and occasional bragging remarks, common in such games, the young man had.

Rick walked over and shook hands with the happy, blond blade who, up close, looked even younger than his years. "A win on your first match with me. I'm impressed."

"Not nearly as much as I am," he answered with a laugh as he received more claps on the back and the usual jostling about winners received from their friends after a great feat. Mr. Malcolm handed off his pistol to one of the men beside him and said, "I've been hearing about how good you are since I was sixteen. I'm glad I won. It's been an honor to go against you and a pleasure to win. My friends here had their doubts, but not anymore. I showed you all!"

His friends roared again and two of them lifted him off his feet as he raised his arms up over his head in victory.

Rick tipped one corner of his hat in a tweak of salute and a nod before he turned away. There wasn't anything left to say. He'd done his duty as a gentleman by congratulating the man. If he was a true sporting gentleman, he would stay quiet and move on without further discussion about the matter until he celebrated in a club, a tavern, or a brothel.

"I'm in Town for the Season, Your Grace, and available any day of the week you're up to a rematch," Mr. Malcolm called out. His friends backed him up with more jeers and laughter.

Seeing no reason to answer, Rick headed toward Wyatt and Hurst. He received several *better luck next time* claps on the back of his shoulders and an encouraging comment or two from some of the fellows as they moseyed over to their horses and carriages to start the trek back to London.

"Damned good shooting," Hurst said as he came up beside Rick, took the pistol, and started placing it back into the box.

"Damned bad fortune," Wyatt added.

Rick swore under his breath. "I don't need you two trying to make me feel better about a loss to a cocky kid."

"What happened out there?" Wyatt asked. "I could tell you were distracted by something."

No, he wasn't. True, he had a lot on his mind, but Rick knew it was a kind of fluke, a vagrant sparkle of sun on the tin that made him miss the shot. He was never impatient and never allowed anything or anyone to disturb him when he was shooting.

Rick stared at the two men who had been his friends since their days at school. Wyatt, the Duke of Wyatthaven, and Hurst, the Duke of Hurstbourne. Wyatt had married last spring, and he and Fredericka seemed happy as turtledoves. Having a wife he adored had changed Wyatt's lifestyle. He didn't compete with their sporting team, the Brass Deck Club, or spend as much time with Rick and Hurst at the clubs or hunting ventures, but their friendships were as solid as ever.

Hurst, with his uncommonly light-blond hair and green eyes, had the charming good looks and easygoing attitude women couldn't seem to resist and most men respected. He had been the thinker of the trio in the wild days of their youth. His clear, level head had saved them from making many mistakes, and at times kept them from participating in outright foolish endeavors that would have surely gotten them killed.

"Where have you been all day?" Wyatt asked as he handed over Rick's coat and gloves. "You didn't show up for my fencing match, or to see Hurst's new racehorse."

Rick blew out a short laugh as his booted feet crunched on the dry rocky ground. He wasn't sure he was going to answer that question right now. They wouldn't believe him anyway. Hell, he still couldn't believe it himself . . . until thoughts of how Miss Fine made him feel filtered through his mind.

He was still mulling over whether he should wait until they made it back into Town and have them over to his house to quietly tell them about her after a brandy. Or was it best to give them the news at White's? Oh, hell. He might as well tell them here and now and get on with it.

When he reached his horse, he took a deep breath and looked at his surroundings. A brassy sun was sinking toward the horizon and a medley of puffy, disjointed clouds were gathering overhead. The patchwork of grasses in the flat field were bearing fresh new growth and the first of the wildflowers and weeds had started unfurling their blooms. Sounds of men talking, and horses and carriages riding away echoed in the distance. Everything around him looked peaceful. Rick felt at peace too. In his gut, he felt that marrying Miss Fine was the right thing to do.

He took in a gulp of the late afternoon air and stated without preamble, "I'm getting married."

"Hell no, you aren't." Wyatt cursed and helped Hurst secure the pistol case onto the back of the saddle. "So, what's wrong?"

"It's true." Rick's tone was even, but as he spoke an unexpected flicker of anticipation tightened low in his stomach. Yes, she was the one he wanted. He couldn't say he was interested in marriage and all the trappings that went with it, but he was interested in her. Of all the proper young ladies he'd met over the years, and all the mistresses he'd enjoyed, she was the first one who had captivated him enough that he wanted to know more about *her*. And it had been that way since he heard her voice down the corridor.

Hurst whistled low under his breath and brushed his hair away from his forehead. "So, miracles do happen. Hmm. I had always doubted their existence."

Rick arched a brow and looked at Hurst. "You once studied to be a clergyman. How could you not believe in them? I thought all clergy believed in miracles."

"What are you two talking about? Never mind about that," Wyatt said testily. "Who did you compromise?"

"No one," Rick defended with ire in his voice. "You know better than to suspect me of ruining a young lady's reputation."

"Apparently not," Hurst injected with a mumbled curse.

Wyatt didn't pay attention to either of them but continued with, "Who is she? Where were you? And who found you with her? If we put our heads together, maybe there's something that can be done to settle this another way and leave her reputation intact. And keep you away from the altar."

"Damnation, Wyatt, I haven't compromised anyone and I'm not being forced to marry. It just so happens I like her and it was my idea."

"It must be the fever." Hurst gave a shake of his head and a *tsk*ing sound in his throat.

Wyatt took his hat off, brushed a hand through his hair, and then settled it back on his head. "You're right, and it's come back worse than the other two times he had it. If he's thinking about marriage, I'm worried."

Hurst nodded. "Nothing else would explain why he missed your fencing match, my new horse, his easy shot, and be talking nonsense too. Let's get him home and a tonic in him before it gets worse."

"I'm not sick," Rick insisted, as several whoops and laughing came from the group of young bucks who weren't far away and obviously too joyous to start heading back to Town. "The fevers have precipitated my need to marry and have an heir, and you both know it's best I get on with it and take a wife."

"Who the hell is she?" Wyatt asked, his frown and voice deepening. "You've never looked twice at a lady that we know of."

"It is a long story and best told over a strong drink."

"Stonerick," Mr. Malcolm called in a cheerful tone while the others continued to whoop and laugh behind him. "Another word with you, if I may?"

Rick's jaw clenched and he bristled at the young man's

familiar tone. They weren't friends. Nor was it likely they ever would be. He looked in Malcolm's direction but didn't respond to his question. The blade won fair and Rick had no desire to rehash the event with another afternoon of the man's company. Nor did he want to listen to any more of his prattle. As far as Rick was concerned, they were finished. What little patience he had was fading fast. He had more important things to do.

But obviously Malcolm didn't. He refused to let his question rest. "My friends and I decided that all of us should meet here tomorrow at the same time for another match. But it would be just you and me competing. No others. You and your companions deserve a chance to win back your blunt."

For his answer, Rick made a short, gruff sound deep in his throat that was almost a laugh before turning back to Wyatt and Hurst.

But the young man called to him again. "To show you I'm not a poor winner, I want to buy you a drink. We're going over to Little Sorrell Tavern. Come with us. I'll introduce you to Mademoiselle Rivoire. She's favored among all the wenches and has never disappointed me. I'll make sure she takes good care of you, and I'll find someone else to take care of your friends. I'll see they leave happy too."

More whoops, hoots, and hollers erupted from Malcolm's cohorts.

"That does it," Rick remarked and swore under his breath. He wasn't interested in any woman but Miss Fine. "I'm going over to teach the young tosspot the respectable way to win a match. Since he doesn't know how to pick up his winnings and move on, I'll teach him. I've had all the braggart I can take."

"Let it go." Wyatt put his hand to Rick's chest to stop

him from leaving. "He's not worth the bother," Wyatt assured him. "I believe he's from Lord Derrybrooke's family. The third or fourth son. They are all soft in the head when it comes to knowing how to behave like a gentleman. He's not important."

Hurst handed the reins to Rick and climbed onto his own horse. "Wyatt's right. Leave him be and let him show off in front of his friends if he wants to. It seems you have more important things to worry about than he does." Hurst looked at Wyatt. "We need to get him back to London. I'm not convinced he doesn't have a fever coming on again."

CHAPTER 10

THE ART OF BEING A FINE GENTLEMAN
SIR DUDLEY SAMSON PEMBERTON FINE

*A fine gentleman should be discreet about all things,
at all times when a lady is present.*

Edwina touched her lips for what had to be the thousandth time in the past few days. Looking out the drawing room window of the modest, leased house in St. James, she could see her reflection in the windowpane. Behind her, Aunt Pauline was busy looking through boxes of fabrics and occasionally humming to herself.

No matter what Edwina was doing, she couldn't get the feeling, the taste, or the heat of the duke's kiss off her mind. The freshness of his mouth and scent of newly shaved skin added to the clutter of recollections. She didn't remember exactly what she'd imagined her first kiss would be like, but it hadn't been what happened between her and the duke a few days ago.

She'd read enough romantic poetry to know there would be urgent passion from the man she married. Apparently, it was man's nature to be filled with such emotions. Yet, she hadn't known the kiss would be so sudden, primal, and shocking in how it made her feel.

One of the confusing aspects was she couldn't make sense of the little swirls of pleasure that twisted inside her and how it wasn't as horrific as it should have been given the brashness and lack of tenderness in the kiss. But even all that paled when she thought of how she was so caught up by how wonderful the duke had made her feel when he brought her the unexpected gift of gossip sheets, she was going to allow him to kiss her again. On the front steps of the house! Why? She had no idea. The thought of him kissing her again should send shivers of revulsion through her but instead, it sent shocks of inappropriate desire spiking inside her.

So, every time her contemplations drifted in that direction, she tried to think of other things. Like her sisters. She wondered how they were doing without her. They obviously were not missing her as much as she missed them. Edwina hadn't received one letter from them. She had written several times since she arrived, including the message the duke insisted she send. And they still hadn't found their way to London yet.

And, of course, thinking of that made her think of the duke and ponder his admirable qualities once more. That wasn't as easy to do as one might think.

After she made it past his obviously handsome face and magnificently fit body, there didn't seem to be much recommendation. He wasn't even-tempered, in no way malleable or patient. There were times during their discussions when he was only modestly polite. Then again, he had managed to get water for her to drink when she desperately needed it and promised to see her sisters married or betrothed to proper gentlemen.

Some of the scandal sheets she'd read heaped praise on him for his looks, his title, and his marksmanship abilities while others considered him aloof, blunt, and much too querulous to adequately give attention to any one lady. Edwina agreed with all of them. After reading everything that was written about him, more than once, she wasn't surprised that when he got ready to marry, he'd picked her name off a list.

Sooner or later, however, when thinking about him, she always came back to her fear of the wedding night. And when she did, she was flooded with a mixture of anxiety and interest, wondering what it would be like. Her father was a brilliant man. He'd taught her history, literature, religion, philosophy, art, science, and so much more. But he never once mentioned the most important night of a young lady's life. Her wedding night. Would the duke embrace and kiss her with such hunger every night as he had that first time? And if he did, would she feel—

"You're looking pensive, Edwina," her aunt said from behind her.

"I am," she answered honestly.

"You should stop pining for the duke and come look at the fabrics that were just delivered to you."

Pining? For the duke!

"What a dreadful thought," Edwina mumbled. She was merely thinking about him. Again. And not because she wanted to. Because he was an impossible man to keep off her mind. That wasn't pining. Was it?

Edwina turned to her aunt and suddenly smiled. Mrs. Pauline Castleton was bending over a box and digging through its contents with relish, her face almost buried in it. The room was a mess. Swatches of cloth, folds of lace, and sheets of clothing designs were scattered over both settees, a tea table that stood between them, a chair, and most of the floor. It didn't appear her aunt was trying to maintain any kind of order to the boxes that had been so meticulously packed when they'd been delivered earlier that day.

Picking up lengths of fabric along the way, Edwina stuffed her arms full and walked to where Pauline stood and added her bounty to the collection on the settee.

"The duke's such an insightful man as to your needs," Auntie said in a voice that was as soft as the brush of angel's wings. "Such a gentleman," she added dreamily.

His kiss came vividly to her mind again. His lips pressing hard on hers, his hand rubbing up the back of her neck and into her hair with such zeal. Were they talking about the same person?

"When we were in his home, he realized I was about to faint and needed to sit down, have refreshment, and rest. Imagine a duke being that attentive of a stranger's care."

Edwina had forgotten about that when she was listing his finer attributes. That was indeed perceptive of him. And Edwina appreciated it. Since her aunt's lung fever illness last winter, she would, at times, have trouble catching her breath and would suddenly become weak and shaky.

"You were right, my dear, to insist we confront the duke face-to-face. Everything has turned out splendidly. You'll soon be married and can properly chaperone your sisters. I can go back to my quiet cottage in Dover."

Edwina's heart pinched. Her mother's sister had come to live with them when her father became ill. She had been a great help to the three sisters during their mourning. Edwina didn't want to think about losing her. She walked over and placed her hand on top of her aunt's hands. "I wouldn't want you to leave us, Auntie. Besides, I will need you to continue to help me. What would I do if Eileen wanted to go to the park to look for butterflies and Eleonora wanted to go to a bookshop?"

"You would manage to go to both places."

Edwina laughed. "Auntie, I know you get tired easily, but don't think of leaving us. We need you."

"All right, dearie. And thanks to His Grace, we now have a carriage and driver at our disposal—not that we've made use of it yet." Pauline sniffed. "But we will certainly make use of it to go to the balls when they begin. And he sent over the footman he hired to aid Mrs. Needlesmith and the other maids. It will be so nice to have him on hand for whatever we might need. There's all the places the duke opened accounts for you—none of which we've visited. But soon, I hope."

Perhaps she should add those things to the duke's "nice" qualities too. Edwina pursed her lips harder as her aunt talked. All in all, the duke had been more accommodating than she was willing to admit. In truth, she would be having feelings of uncertainty about the wedding night, having a babe, and all the rest of it no matter who she was marrying.

"We'll go out in the carriage tomorrow, Auntie, and ride through St. James' Park and Hyde Park. I promise."

"Lovely, dearest. Let's do." Her hands stilled and she gave Edwina a smile. "Now, come closer and let me see how these beautiful fabrics look with your coloring. They are the finest materials I've ever seen. It's simply luxurious to feel them in my hands, and so considerate of the duke to have the best modistes in London send samples of their work to you. Look at this marvelous shade of pink. It looks as if someone crushed rose petals and added milk to them."

"We just prepared for the Season, Auntie. My wardrobe is filled with everything new."

"I know and isn't it wonderful? We'll pass those gowns, dresses, and other things along to your sisters when they get here, and have new ones made for you.

It's best anyway. Those gowns were made for a young belle out to capture the heart of a beau. There's very little color or trim to any of them so that you might look as pure as you are. Now you are going to be a duchess, Edwina, and must adorn yourself as one. The duke expects you to take advantage of his generosity and pamper yourself with all the finest things available. Don't disappoint him."

A shiver washed over Edwina. "Disappoint him?" Yes, of course. But not because she hadn't taken advantage of his luxuries. Perhaps because she hadn't told him the whole truth about her birth. She had made an attempt to dissuade him by reminding him there were only girls in her family. But was that enough? And the truth was that she supposed she didn't really want anyone to know of their unusual birth, which would set them apart.

"Take your chignon down, dearie. I want to see this color against your hair and your skin."

Wanting to make her aunt happy, and to get her mind off worrisome things, Edwina obeyed and removed the combs, letting her hair cascade to her shoulders. Fabrics and laces were not of interest to her when she had so many gowns she hadn't worn yet. Her sisters' reluctance to marry, the wedding night, and a host of other delicacies concerning marriage were swirling around in her head.

"While we are doing this, Auntie, I want to ask you something of a personal nature."

"Yes, do, my dear," she encouraged, giving Edwina a glancing look before immediately pulling a pin from a sewing cushion and fastening the piece of milky pink silk to Edwina's bodice at the neckline.

Clearing her throat, Edwina asked, "What happens on the wedding night?"

"You get married," she answered, adding a garish orange-and-purple brocade onto Edwina's simple pale lavender shift.

Edwina took in a deep breath. "I'm talking about when I'm alone with the duke in our chambers and it's time to retire?"

Pauline's hands stilled on the fabric, and her head started shaking. "No, no, dearie. Never mind about that. You'll find out soon enough." She began humming and digging through the box before her.

That didn't go well. Edwina decided to try again. "I would like to know a few details."

"And you will when the time comes." Avoiding Edwina's eyes, she pulled a busy swatch of a multicolored flower print from the clutter and commenced pinning it between the other two colors. "But that time is not today. You must wait."

"Why is it such a secret?" Edwina asked, exasperated, but she held still as her aunt pinned on the third piece of cloth. "Am I to talk or be quiet? Am I to lie down, stand up, or bend over?"

"Edwina, please don't be crude," her aunt implored, covering her ears with her hands. "Your father would be shocked to hear such talk come from you."

She supposed he would. He'd brought his daughters up as ladies even though they were far from London Society. "I'm sorry, Auntie."

Pauline lowered her hands and gave Edwina an understanding expression but remained silent as she turned her attention to a new box of samples.

But Edwina wasn't ready to put the subject to bed. "It's so frustrating, Auntie. I was taught to read and comprehend difficult books. I studied the history of countries I'll never visit but can find on a map. I know the constellations and can point them out in the dark sky, but I'll never see any of them up close. I've been taught to add and subtract large sums of numbers but I will never hold that amount of money in my hands. However, the wedding night, something I *will* experience, has been kept a mystery."

Her aunt seemed to study on her answer before saying, "The rosy pink is not the color for you. Let's try a different one."

Edwina took another deep breath. After her father concluded she would have to be the first sister to wed, she looked in their extensive collection of books. Not one of them mentioned what a wedding night would be like when a man and woman joined together and became one. She scoured all the poetry books that would have been the likeliest ones to share information, and the volumes on the study of the body. None of them helped her to understand.

Why was her aunt so bashful about this? She was married close to thirty years before her husband passed. Edwina wasn't trying to be high-handed. She needed help understanding what would be forthcoming. Softening her voice, she said, "This conversation is important to me, Auntie."

Sighing, her aunt didn't take her attention off the bolt of lace in her hand. "That is the way of it, my dear, and it's not going to change. The only thing you need to know about the wedding night is that it's a most private affair and not something a lady would ever discuss with another. It is the husband's duty to reveal to his bride everything he wants her to know and not for any other person to meddle in." Pauline laid down the lace and, picking up one of Edwina's hands, she clasped it in both of hers. They were soft and warm as she gently squeezed with confidence, sighed deeply, and smiled as if she'd answered every one of Edwina's questions to her satisfaction. "The duke will know what to do and that is enough. He'll take excellent care of you."

"How?" Edwina contended, hoping to persuade her aunt to reconsider. "He is the most impatient person I've ever met."

She wanted to know more about how babies were made and, more importantly, how many she might have. Her father had always said Edwina was more like her mother in temperament, actions, and thoughts than either of her sisters. What if she was so much like her mother, she had multiple births too? That was probably her biggest fear of all. What would she do if she had triplets? What would the duke do? Would he be as resourceful as her father had been?

Would such a phenomenon leave the duke open to suspicions and doubts about her purity or faithfulness to him? What would she do if he rejected her and the babes? Edwina had no answer for that. She only knew she and her sisters *were* normal. This was her chance to prove it. Edwina just had to have the courage to do it.

Her aunt wasn't going to relent and supply additional details. Vexing as it was, she had to give up. "All right, I'll take your advice and be completely surprised by what is expected of me on my wedding night."

"Excellent." Pauline smiled contentedly. "That's what I wanted to hear. Now, let's see how this red-and-white stripe looks on you."

"We have looked at enough fabrics for one day, Auntie. Do you feel up to a short walk to clear our lungs?" And thoughts.

"I think so, but maybe I should have a bit of a rest first. It would be good for you to have one too. You seem disquieted. We can't have you overwrought for the up-coming marriage, can we?" She dropped the fabric she was holding. "I'll meet you down here in a little while, dearie."

Instead of heeding her aunt's suggestion and following her up the stairs, Edwina went back to the window that overlooked a narrow strip of garden. The start of spring was transforming wintery gray days into warm sunshine and empty trees into unfurling buds of green leaves. In a couple of weeks everything in the garden would be green. An assortment of flowers was beginning to bud but most blooms hadn't opened yet to reveal their vivid colors. It seemed as if life would be so much easier if she only had flowers and walks in the park to contend with.

"I'm sorry to interrupt you, Miss Fine," the house-keeper said from behind her.

Edwina turned and greeted the housekeeper. "It's not a problem, Mrs. Needlesmith. If more boxes have ar-rived, place them on the settee with the others. Auntie will look through them later."

"I'm afraid I wouldn't fit into a box, Miss Fine."

At the sound of the duke's voice, Edwina's pulse quick-ened. The duke bypassed the housekeeper to enter the drawing room. Looking at him made Edwina's heart feel as if it were lifting. Fluttering warmth filled her chest. It didn't matter if he was as impatient as the first day they met or caring and thoughtful as he was the last time they were together. She was happy to see him. Her breath grew uncomfortably shallow. Heat flared inside her and settled low in her abdomen.

"Your Grace." She curtsied as the housekeeper quietly left the room.

Stonerick nodded as he regarded her closely. "I'm sorry if I stopped by at an inopportune time."

"No," she answered softly, enjoying how handsome he was. He wore a perfectly fitted dark-brown coat and waistcoat, and buff-colored trousers stylishly stuffed into shiny, below-the-knee boots. She wondered if he would always look so commanding and powerful that her insides quivered with exciting little squeezes every time she saw him.

"These are for you." He handed her a small nosegay.

Her gaze caught his again and held for a moment before she glanced down at the delicate cluster of early, pale-yellow primrose blooms that looked as if they had been hastily and unevenly cropped and bundled with small fragrant twigs of rosemary and sage. She doubted the gardener or the duke's very dignified butler had composed the bouquet. There wasn't even a ribbon to hold the stems tightly together. Obviously, flowers for her were a last-minute thought, but a nice one. She couldn't help but smile when she imagined the duke bending down to grab a handful of whatever was nearby as he passed.

"Thank you. They are lovely—but." Hooding her eyes with her lashes, she asked, in a silky voice, "Does this mean I won't receive any more gossip columns?"

The duke shifted his stance and grinned. "So, you read them?"

"Every word. My favorite story was when you shocked the entire ton by having two dances with four different young ladies on the same night and had all of them believing you would ask for their hand. It seems everyone in Society was aghast when you didn't ask for anyone's hand but snubbed them all."

He did his best to not look guilty by clearing his throat and coughing a little before he responded, "There might have been an overindulgence of brandy and a wager involved in that unfortunate evening."

Edwina nodded and gave him an amused smile. "Would you like to sit down and tell me about it?" She turned toward the settee and saw the strewn pieces of fabrics and strips of lace and suddenly remembered the unbecoming squares of cloth pinned to her dress. No wonder he assumed he'd arrived at an inconvenient time. He had!

Mortified, she felt a blush searing up her neck. In a panicky moment of racing thoughts, she first wanted to start yanking at the pins, but then she saw a glint of amusement sparkle in the duke's beautiful blue eyes. He had found delight in catching her in such a state. And no doubt even more pleased that it appeared she was indulging so feverishly in the samples he'd sent over for her.

It took all her inner strength, but she wouldn't give him the satisfaction of seeing her flapping around like a fish out of water while trying to remove the swatches from her bodice.

Searching for the right words to say, her chin lifted and her shoulders eased back. "I'll just take a moment to move these so you can make yourself comfortable." She placed the flowers on a nearby table and headed for the settee.

"Don't bother for me, Miss Fine. I can't stay long."

All the better. Wonderful, in fact. Maybe she could find a way to recover from her embarrassment after he left.

"All right," she calmly said. "What can I do for you?"

The duke took a more relaxed stance. "I just left my solicitor. He informed me you are insisting on reading every page of the contracts for our marriage settlement before they are sent to the viscount for his acceptance and signature."

Taking interest in what he said, she answered, "Yes, of course."

With silence and a firm set to his jaw, he joined her near the settee. It didn't appear that was what he wanted to hear. From beneath thick lashes his eyes questioned her, but she remained quiet too.

"Assurance the contracts are satisfactory is what your guardian's solicitor, Mr. Lewis, and your trustee are for. They are looking after your best interests for the viscount. But more than that, as your betrothed, it's my responsibility to take care of your future and see you are protected."

Edwina believed the duke was a man of honor and would see to fairness in the settlement, but that didn't keep her from wanting to read and understand them. She was learning to read by the time she was learning to walk. "I understand," she answered. "Is there a problem with me looking at the documents as well?"

"It is unusual. Most ladies don't want to worry about matters having to do with money, properties, and such."

She inhaled a deep, confident breath as she watched him study her intently—as if he couldn't figure her out. "Perhaps some haven't been as well-schooled as I. I'm quite capable of understanding difficult-worded documents. Thankfully, my father taught me to be diligent in all my studies."

"So you've mentioned before."

Perhaps she had commented on her father's forward-thinking attitude in wanting his daughters well-read a time or two. "You sound as if it upsets you that I want to read what is being settled about my future."

A slow, devilishly attractive smile eased across his face. "It doesn't bother me at all."

His words made the fluttering return to her chest and her heart beat faster again. He was good at making her feel wonderfully delicious sensations that were new and exciting. She wanted to always be proper and in control, but with the duke that was impossible. Like now, she wanted to enjoy every improper feeling and thought he was causing her to experience.

"I find it unnecessary, Miss Fine," he continued in a reasonable tone. "You have three men doing it for you." He took a step closer to her. "The problem is that at this rate, with you holding up the contracts for your own satisfaction, we won't be married for a month."

She didn't see that as a problem. "Most engagements are far longer."

With resolute determination, he crossed his arms. "I'm not willing to wait that long, Miss Fine. I need an heir and that takes time. You may look at all the documents you want and take as long as you want to read them. Some of them can even be changed if you wish, but we will marry Friday morning at my house."

Her throat tightened as she tried to swallow. She knew the duke had said he needed to marry soon but she'd hoped to put off the wedding longer than that. At least to the end of the Season. Autumn or Christmastide would be better. When she'd first come to London, she'd also thought it would take her the entire Season to find a husband and get him to agree to help her sisters. The duke's letter had catapulted her into something she'd always known she wasn't ready for. Marriage.

But she had to do this for her father. It shouldn't surprise her the impatient duke was moving everything so fast. Her father could teach the duke a thing or two about slowing down and being a proper gentleman. Besides, she needed her sisters here to remind her how important this marriage to the duke was to all of them.

"What if my sisters haven't arrived by then? I would really like to wait until they do and then set a date. They would be disappointed to miss my wedding."

His eyes flashed with displeasure as his brows and forehead creased into a tight frown at her news. "They should already be here."

"You have lofty expectations, sir, which are, no doubt, common to your title. There's been hardly time for them to get here."

He didn't move an inch from his uncompromising stance and his gaze didn't leave her face. "It's been several days since I was here and you assured me the letter was mailed the day before I arrived."

"It was," she insisted, bristling. "But as you said, York is a long way from London. Besides, they would have needed time to prepare for an extended stay . . ."

"Then let's hope they arrive on time. I've been quietly making inquiries about possible husbands. Gentlemen I think they will consider as quite suitable and attentive. I want to make introductions at the first ball of the Season."

His tone, words, and softened expression swept the breath from her lungs and compelled her to soften toward him too. "It's good to hear you've made progress, but I don't think you should count on them being there. If they come to London at all, it will be difficult to get them to attend balls."

"We'll find a way, Miss Fine."

Without warning, he reached out and brushed his fingertips through the length of her hair. His arm brushed ever so lightly across her breasts. She quietly inhaled a startled breath. Tingles rushed over her body. She couldn't have been more stimulated by him if he'd been caressing her cheeks or neck.

He bent closer, his face mere inches from hers. "When I kissed you the other day," he said huskily, lightly trailing his finger pads down her cheek, "was it your first?"

His nearness and touch caused a feeling of expectancy to tremor inside her. Edwina was barely breathing but found enough air to whisper a raspy, "Yes."

A twitch of a grin lifted his mouth. "I admit it was rash of me to kiss you the way I did."

"Rash indeed, sir," she managed to say, as a shudder of delight shook through her at the remembrance. It couldn't be natural for her to be so beguiled by him. She took a step back.

He straightened but kept his gaze tightly on her face. "I had to so you could experience rakish behavior. Otherwise, you would have never written to your sisters how dire your situation was." He moved closer to her again. "I regret it had to be that way." His expression softened as he picked up her hand and kissed her fingers.

His movement startled her at first but the warmth of his touch sizzled through her and seemed to settle in her soul as his lips pressed firmly against her skin. His apology, his kindness was so unexpected her breathing became even fainter. Not sure what to do, she pulled her hand away from his and clasped it in her other.

"You do understand there are different ways to kiss, don't you?" he asked.

A tremble started in her limbs. His voice was husky, low, and seducing. His gaze swept up and down her face until it lingered on her lips, causing her insides to tighten with anticipation of what he was going to say or do next.

"My knowledge of kissing is quite limited but from the poetry I've read, I would assume there is a softer way."

He gave her a brief smile. "There is. I think I should show you what a tender kiss is and how it feels."

Well, maybe.

"No, no, really," she whispered on another raspy breath, trying not to let the direction of the conversation, his seduction, and her reaction spiral out of control. "We should follow the rules of Society and wait until we are wed for such things."

"Would your father say that is the right thing to do? Wait for the wedding night to kiss my bride?"

"Yes. I'm sure that is exactly what he would say." She forced herself to relax and not be further seduced by the gleam of amusement she saw sparking in his eyes. "And probably add that you are being a rake, a scoundrel, and anything but a gentleman."

"Did he write in his book how a gentleman should behave toward a lady?"

"Concerning kissing?" Her heartbeat labored to stay constant. "Oh, no. I'm certain he made no mention of that in any of his many writings. But there is also the possibility Auntie might come in at any moment."

"What would she do?" A teasing light shone in his eyes. "Might she insist you have been compromised and we must rush to get married in order to avoid scandal?"

Edwina found his relaxed manner so attractive her body responded with an ache to be held and cuddled against his strong-looking chest. "You are teasing me again," she offered softly.

"I am speaking the truth again. We are already getting married in a matter of days. What more could be done to a man other than he be forced to marry a young lady he had ruined by kissing her?"

Edwina had no answer to his question because she wanted him to kiss her. Despite all her efforts to the contrary, she wanted to experience the thrill of it again.

"Still not convinced?" he asked when she didn't respond. "You know it's acceptable for a kiss after an engagement has been set. Ours has been duly offered and accepted."

"A soft kiss?" she asked, almost yearning for his lips to touch hers.

"Yes. The way a man kisses a lady he is wooing, a lady he desires with all his being."

Wonderful sensations spun through her. Could he possibly be feeling the same way, or was it just her? He gently slipped his arms around her waist, pulled her up to him, and leaned his hard, muscular body into hers. The strength and heat she felt was thrilling and enticing. He hadn't startled her as he had with his first kiss. He was taking his time, seducing her so she would be prepared to accept his advances.

The duke smiled gently. "I'm going to kiss you the way I wanted to the first day we met."

His voice was low and persuasive. A hot dizziness whirled in her head as a tempest of emotions surged inside her while his face descended closer and his arms tightened.

Fluttering, her lashes started to close but Edwina caught a glimpse of movement behind the duke. Something came sailing through the air.

Whack!

It came down hard with a flap on the back of the duke's head and shoulders.

In the blink of an eye, a different object came flying at him from the other direction.

Whack!

"Unhand her this second, you vile creature!"

"Damnation!" The duke swung around to confront

his attackers and was struck for a third time with a blow that landed across his neck and jaw.

Edwina jerked in shock.

Her sisters had arrived.

CHAPTER 11

*A true gentleman knows when to accept defeat
with dignity, especially when it comes
from the hand of a lady.*

The duke held up his hands and took a slow step away from Edwina. "Put your reticules down, ladies. I am unarmed."

Flushed and astounded for a second, Edwina struggled to pull herself together after almost being caught kissing the duke, and then realizing it was her sisters who were flailing him. It was as if every thought in her brain scattered with panic. She couldn't move or speak. Eileen's arm was poised, ready to strike again. Her beaded, fringe-tipped purse dangled menacingly from her hand.

Edwina glanced from her sisters to the duke. His expression was intense, but thankfully not angry. Definitely surprised. A red scratch showed on the side of his face near the edge of his jawline where one of the beads must have struck hard. He kept looking from one sister to the other and then to Edwina. She knew why but couldn't dwell on that right now.

"Eileen! Eleonora!" she demanded, feeling her breath still trapped in her chest when she tried to speak. "Papa would be scandalized by your behavior. What were you thinking?"

"That you were being attacked by a beast. We're here to save you from this scoundrel!" Eileen exclaimed, her green eyes wide with fortitude.

"And looks as if we arrived just in time," Eleonora added and raised her reticule too. "Step back, sir. If you make another advance toward our sister, we will be forced to defend her again."

Gaining some measure of composure, Edwina sputtered, "No, no. You both have it all wrong. He wasn't attacking me, we were going to . . . he was . . . only . . ."

"I don't need you taking up for me, Miss Fine." The duke interrupted her pitiful attempt at an explanation in an impatient tone as he lowered his hands.

Good. She didn't know how. His brow furrowed deeper and his gaze skimmed with uncertainty over each sister before giving Edwina a look that indicated she should accept whatever he said as truth and not argue with him about specifics. By all means she would do it this time and stay quiet about whatever he said.

Not that he didn't deserve some of their admonishment. If Edwina didn't believe there was no such thing, she'd think he'd bewitched her. However, her sisters didn't need to know that.

"What you witnessed when you arrived was all very innocent," the duke said tightly. "I was helping your sister remove a pin from her dress that was sticking her and causing pain." His eyes pointedly looked at the fabrics pinned to her bodice.

Eileen huffed and lowered her arm, zeroing her attention on the pieces of cloth fastened to Edwina's dress.

"Your selections are dreadful. None of those shades go with your coloring."

Edwina's hands flew to the swatches, fingers spread wide as she tried to hide the offending things. Her whole body stiffened. Why hadn't she taken the ridiculous pieces of cloth off the moment her aunt left the room? Or when the duke mentioned them? Why had she even allowed Auntie to put them on? It was too late to do anything now. As the duke had indicated, they were a good cover for what was transpiring when her sisters arrived. She hoped they would let the subject drop.

"Yes," she whispered, looking down at the horrible colors on her chest. "I've decided that too."

"And what happened in here?" Eleonora asked, scanning the disorderly drawing room with a frown of disbelief. "It looks as if the two of you have been throwing fabrics at each other and they only stuck to you. How else could you make such shambles of a room?"

"Don't be ridiculous, Elle," Edwina argued. "Aunt Pauline was in here helping me with the samples earlier. You know how she can get carried away, but then the duke stopped by—but never mind all that right now. It's not important."

"Duke?" both sisters said at the same time.

"Blessed Galileo, Edwina," Eileen whispered as the sprinkling of freckles across her face reddened.

A deep wariness flickered in Eleonora's eyes and she moved closer to Eileen. "Did we strike a duke?"

"I'm afraid so, ladies," His Grace said dryly.

Despite his arrogance, he sounded amiable enough and her sisters were bound to know he wasn't too terribly upset by their wild blunder. Though the strain in his features told Edwina he was working to hold his agitation in check.

"May Jupiter save us," Eileen whispered as the two sisters huddled closer together, clasped hands, and watched the duke.

With a brief squeeze of her eyes and summoning the inner strength her father had sworn long ago was inside her, Edwina turned to the duke. "Your Grace, may I present my sisters, Miss Eileen Fine and Miss Eleonora Fine. Ladies, the Duke of Stonerick."

Eleonora sucked in a hasty breath. Eileen cleared her throat uncomfortably, and both immediately turned loose of each other and curtsied while contritely mumbling apologies. The duke continued to look from one to the other and then to Edwina. A chill shook her as she wondered if he was assessing their unmistakable likeness.

"We assumed you were the rogue who is after our sister to woo her into his clutches for nefarious purposes and ruin her reputation," Eileen explained in an appropriately repentant tone. "I'm sorry we mistook you for someone of a lower character."

Bracing, Edwina's gaze aimed straight as an arrow at the duke's. She had no idea how he was going to respond. Forgiving or revengeful? Would he even possibly confess to being the scoundrel they thought he was? The only thing she knew for sure was that he wasn't amused. There was no sparkle in his eyes.

"I do hope you'll excuse us for being so aggressive, Your Grace," Elle offered sweetly before giving him her prettiest smile. "We assumed we had good reason after receiving Edwina's letter of concern. It just makes one feel wretched when mistakes like this happen. It's an embarrassment of the highest order, and we always wish to never make another. But somehow the tide of fate turns viciously against us and we manage to do something dreadful again."

He looked at Elle as if he wasn't certain he'd understood what she'd just said. Edwina wasn't sure she'd comprehended it all either. Eleonora had been effusive with her words as long as Edwina could remember. Her sister would start talking sometimes and simply not know when she'd said enough.

"No apologies are necessary, ladies. I've made a few mistakes myself," he said a little too calmly for a man who had just been attacked and bore the ever-reddening wound near his chin to prove it. "No harm done," he added with a twisted smile, continuing to glance from one sister to the other with more curiosity than Edwina would have liked until his glance landed on her. "I didn't expect the three of you to look so much alike."

Fear shot through Edwina and her spine stiffened again. Would he ask if the sisters were twins or the three of them triplets? Surely not, she dismissed quickly. It was too rare for anyone to suspect. Her father had assured them of that, but admitted, living away from Society as they always had, he missed a lot of research and news.

Eleonora smiled pleasantly at the duke, and calmly answered, "I know. No one ever does."

"I really find it quite dumbfounding when people mention it," Eileen added. "To think one would be surprised sisters coming from the same two parents would favor, and a strange phenomenon when they don't."

The duke rolled his shoulders and shifted his stance as if he was trying to figure out if Eileen was indicating he wasn't a rational thinker. But all he did was turn to Edwina and say, "Now that they are here, I'll excuse myself and take my leave so you can have a proper reunion." He turned to her sisters. "Good day, ladies," he said tersely as he looked at each sister, nodded once to Edwina, and turned to leave.

"Wait for me please, Your Grace," Edwina called. There was no way she was going to let him walk away without knowing what he was thinking right now or what he was going to do. He could decide the idea of marriage to her was too much trouble and he was dismissing the idea. "I'll see the duke out while you two take off your bonnets and capes," she told them as she hurried past.

Edwina and Stonerick walked in silence to the vestibule, where the duke opened the front door for her and closed it after they stepped out onto the stoop. A comfortable chill to the spring air felt good and Edwina embraced it heartily. It was calming to inhale a deep, refreshing breath. Overhead, a light-blue sky was streaked with white, windswept clouds. A couple of houses down and on the other side of the street, two women spoke to each other over a waist-high hedge. The light breeze carried the lilting sound of their voices across the way.

"Why didn't you tell me your sisters are dangerous?" the duke accused the moment he shut the door behind them.

Edwina's shoulders tightened and her spine stiffened. He needed to do a better job of watching what he said about her family. "What?" She drew herself up taller. "How dare you speak so ill of my sisters. They are not dangerous."

"Really?" he asked, looking at her as if she'd said something in a foreign language.

"Well, you do have a red mark on your jaw," she added with a fair amount of dismay and concern.

He touched the scratch and grimaced.

"They were worried about me and only trying to help," she offered, feeling terrible they had left a mark on him. She reached out her hand, wanting to touch the scratch, but quickly drew it back. "I hope it doesn't hurt."

"I am fine, Miss Fine," he retorted. "Which is more than I can say for your sisters. I am wondering how in the world I am going to get the two of them wed. They have serious aggression problems."

Edwina huffed indignantly. "Don't be ridiculous."

He leaned his face close to hers so quickly it startled her. "I am a lot of things, Miss Fine, but that is not one of them. I have a tendency not to trust people who hit me before they speak to me."

Yes, she could understand that but wasn't about to admit it when he was being so sensitive about their behavior. They had sound reasons that he seemed to be forgetting.

Not giving him the satisfaction of seeing her lean away from him, she simply said, "They explained their actions quite well. And remember, *you* are the one who wanted them to think I was being pursued and seduced by a scoundrel."

"We weren't even kissing." He glared, then added, "Yet."

Her breath fluttered at the thought of his kiss. They'd been so close she'd felt his heat and strength. She couldn't help but feel slightly bereft the touching of their lips hadn't happened. If only her sisters could have waited another moment or— Mercy! What was she thinking?

Clearing her throat and her thoughts, she grimaced and insisted strongly, "They couldn't see that. It wasn't their intention to harm you. Only to stop you. Don't deny your arms were around me and you were being extremely forward."

"That's what men do when they are in pursuit." He let out an exasperated sigh. "At least now I know why they aren't married. They obviously jump to conclusions and act before asking."

Flustered, Edwina declared, "That, sir, describes you, not them."

The blue of his eyes darkened. "There are better ways to announce yourself when you interrupt people no matter what they are doing."

"You, sir, are trying to besmirch my sisters when you are the one who needs some discipline in your life," she answered hotly.

The duke mumbled an oath under his breath. "And who's going to teach it to me? You?"

Suddenly aware of the two ladies down the street who could see and hear them without hindrance if they were of a mind to pry, Edwina calmly drew herself up proudly once again and kept her voice level. "If I must. How dare you rush to judge them on a first meeting."

He casually folded his arms over his chest and snared her with a penetrating stare that seemed to be daring her to stop him.

"I admit it was quite astonishing what happened just as you were about to . . . to be a rake again."

Apparently, her fierce denial of her sisters' dispositions hadn't appeased him. Edwina didn't know what madness had come over them, but the blame belonged on the duke's strong, wide shoulders.

She lifted her chin and squinted against the glare of the afternoon sun that hung above the roofline of her neighbor's house. By crossing her arms at her waist, she mirrored his defiant stance. "The incident was *your* fault, Your Grace."

He scowled, obviously not ready to forgive and forget.

"Mine?" His eyes narrowed perceptibly. "You are unbelievable."

"And you are being grumpy for no good reason," she answered, feeling her tension ebbing. She then harrumphed cheekily.

"Perhaps I have reason."

He touched the back of his neck and his fingers came back with a trace of blood.

Edwina flinched. "Oh, my," she whispered, suddenly feeling wretched again. She reached up to touch him and offer comfort, but a loud laugh from across the street stopped her just in time. "You really are hurt. Should we go back inside where I can tend it for you?"

"I'm fine. It's only a scratch."

But that meant he had at least two marks and maybe more from the fringe of beads.

He pulled a handkerchief from his pocket and placed it onto his nape. "I've never been attacked by two ladies at the same time."

Really?

She tilted her head a little to the side and gave him a quizzical expression. "So, does that mean you've been attacked by one woman before?"

Her responsive question must have tickled his fancy. His frown eased. She could see he was trying to keep it from happening, but as if against his will, the corner of his mouth lifted attractively.

She smiled with a bit of a teasing smirk and suddenly they were both chuckling.

"That was for an entirely different reason, Miss Fine."

Edwina relaxed and relished the good feeling of communicating with him on such a lighthearted level. "I'm sure it was. I'd enjoy hearing about when it happened and the reason."

His stance loosened from his rigid pose. The crease between his brows faded completely away. "I have no doubt you are eager to hear it all. Rest assured you never will."

"Such a disappointment."

"But best that you don't." His eyes sparkled with amusement as he stuffed his handkerchief back into his coat pocket. "You know I am not tolerant of most people, Miss Fine, but I find you an exception."

His words sounded solid, genuine, and made Edwina feel as if butterfly wings were fluttering in her chest. With all the wonderful things the duke made her feel, could the wedding night be so dreadful no one wanted to talk about it?

Drawn to his mellow manner, she smiled too and watched sunbeams make the golden streaks in his light-brown hair shine and sparkle. For a moment, she had the wild thought to reach up and brush her hand across its silkiness and let her fingertips trail softly down his cheek. She wanted to kiss the red scratch near his chin to thank him for not being angry with Elle and Eileen for their impetuous behavior.

Instead, the sound of a door slamming across the street and the screech of a young child brought back her sanity. She clutched her hands together behind her back for fear she might forget the neighbors were so close and touch him anyway. "I'm glad you aren't hurt too badly. Aside from that inappropriate mishap, I know you must be pleased your plan worked and my sisters are now in London. I didn't think your plan would, which is why I didn't mind reporting your ungentlemanly manner to them. You must feel like crowing from the rooftops."

He gave her an appreciative shrug. "I'm very glad our

ruse worked." He moved in close to her. "However, *you* still have some explaining to do."

"What about?" she asked curiously.

"You misled me when it comes to your sisters."

Fear she'd been caught withholding the truth gripped her and she stilled. Had he seen at once they were triplets even though they were all dressed completely differently? Tension held her rigid, but she tried to keep all emotion out of her face. "I don't believe I know exactly what it is you are referring to."

His eyes focused harder on hers. "You said they were older than you."

Edwina's hands tightened into fists. She had to force herself not to turn away from his probing stare and dissolve into a puddle of despair. She didn't want to reveal to him all the story of their birth but if he asked, she would be truthful.

Softly, she admitted, "I didn't mislead you. It's true. Both are older than me."

His voice softened. "I assumed much older because they didn't want to marry. I imagined spinsters of an older age who had long ago given up on the prospects of marriage and families of their own. Probably gray hair, plain, or shy. Maybe all three."

Her back stiffened again but the duke held up his hand before she could respond to his assessment of her sisters.

"They are as lovely as you, and don't appear to be a day older. Quite frankly, it's remarkable how much they look just like you. If not for their bonnets, I'm not sure I would have known who was who. They are just as bold and spirited as you are. When I think of older sisters who haven't married, I don't envision someone so young, beautiful, and sure to catch the attention of any man."

His words settled her and she started breathing easier again. "Why does it even matter how they look?" she asked, more composed now that she knew what he'd been thinking. "A true gentleman would be more interested in their intellect and disposition."

His brows rose on her last words.

"Don't say it," she whispered, condemning herself for unintentionally setting up whatever remark he had in mind to say. She'd rather not hear any more of what he thought about their disposition.

A knowing grin widened into a full-blown smile. "I don't have to say it."

No. He didn't. Edwina wanted to smile too but refrained, and instead took to defending them again. "Their behavior in the drawing room has nothing to do with their true natures. They are ladies, Your Grace."

He barely concealed his grin again, before answering almost under his breath, "That is my hope."

She inhaled a deep breath of warning to him. "I'll have you know Elle is quite tenderhearted, impressionable, and writes beautiful poetry, as did our father. Eileen is so knowledgeable and, like my father, could talk with any man on any subject and hold her own."

"And what about you? How are you like your father?"

"I'm the sensible one, of course."

A whisper of a chuckle passed his lips. "You really think that?"

"My father told me many times."

He quirked his head. "Would a sensible, well-brought-up young lady stand in a duke's vestibule and demand to see him?"

By the light in his eyes, she knew he was teasing her and she was determined not to be any more affected by his infinite charm than she already was. She could tell herself she wasn't attracted to him but knew it wasn't true. It helped to distract her that the child across the street started squealing gleefully as a carriage stopped in front of the house. The neighbors' bids of happy welcomes helped give her time to collect herself.

"I did what I felt was right."

"And you were right. Did any of you take after your mother? You never mention her."

"Oh," she whispered, softly, quickly. A pang of sorrow slowly cut through her and she grew still as she looked at the handsome man in front of her. There was much regret that she never knew her mother. The beautiful, strong lady who had given her life for her three daughters. Somehow, Edwina felt her mother would have liked the duke. "I never met her."

His lids lowered over his eyes a little. A sincere expression settled on his face. "I'm sorry, I didn't mean to bring up sad memories."

"I never mind being reminded of my mother or father. They were both extraordinary people. It gives me the opportunity to tell you that we all three took after our mother." She smiled pridefully. "She had red hair and green eyes."

"That doesn't surprise me." After giving her a mischievous, yet somewhat sympathetic, expression, he nodded. "The gentlemen I was considering introducing to your sisters will not be good matches. The men are much too old and stodgy for them. I'll have to rethink my selection to include younger gentlemen with—" He paused.

Edwina's eyes narrowed and tightened. "Perhaps you should be on guard with what you are about to say."

His answer was to hide more amusement dancing in

his eyes by clearing his throat and looking away for a few seconds before his gaze swept sensually up and down her face with something akin to longing. It pleased her. This time he didn't try to hide his amusement. "I am always on guard with you, Miss Fine."

She didn't believe that for a moment. The duke was never on guard about what he wanted to say.

"You are right that it might be harder than I thought to find your sisters husbands, but I got them to London," he said softly. "Half the battle has been won, has it not?"

The duke's expression was warm and infectious. It filled Edwina with a sudden intimacy with him. It was as if the neighbors, the carriage noise, and the squealing child were no longer across the street. She and the duke were the only two people in the world, and she wanted to enjoy that feeling.

"Will you at least give me that concession?" he asked when she didn't immediately respond.

"Yes, you deserve to feel quite good about that." A small laugh escaped past her lips. "I am happy they are here. We've never been away from each other before. I've worried about them as well as missed them. I have always been sensitive about what people say about them."

"Why would anyone say anything unkind about two beautiful young ladies?"

"The usual superstitious things I don't want to mention," she said, realizing her error in what she'd stated. She didn't want to go into the things she'd read about women who didn't measure up to someone else's standard—be it having a black cat, more than one babe at a time, or a wart on the nose. If Edwina was careful and fate kind maybe she'd never have to tell him about the strange phenomenon of her birth.

He nodded his understanding and she felt a closeness to

him, as if he really understood how she felt about being different from most young ladies. "You said there were few eligible bachelors to choose from where you lived. There are many here in London, and I will introduce them to every gentleman in Town if I must. The sooner we can get them used to Society, the better chances we have of getting them married. That would settle my commitment to you, and yours to your papa so that he may rest easy in his grave."

Stonerick's mention of her debt to her father warmed her heart. "Yes, thank you."

He reached and opened the door for her. "Now, Miss Fine, stop dawdling over every word in the contracts and get them back to your solicitor tomorrow. We have a wedding date set."

Realizing she didn't want him to leave, she asked, "Will I see you again before then?"

"Probably not. I have many things to do, and so do you."

He looked down at the fabric pinned to her dress. "You'll be busy with your sisters too. They may want new gowns for the wedding and Season. I'll give you the time you need to be with them."

His consideration warmed her even more. "Thank you for that, but shouldn't I at least meet your mother before we marry?" she asked, even though she felt apprehensive at the prospect. She may not be as forward thinking as her son about old superstitions and falsehoods.

The duke remained calm but suddenly seemed in deep contemplation before stating, "That can wait until the wedding."

Edwina tensed. There was only one rational reason he would want that. "You are afraid she won't like me."

"No." He quirked his head again and gave her a dismissive smile. "My mother has been waiting a long time for me to marry. She's very happy about you. And don't worry about Palmer either. I've already spoken to him and told him to be expecting a copy of your father's book."

Lightly shaking her head, she unfolded her arms and clasped her hands together at her waist. "I'm not sure I agree, Your Grace. He seemed very adamant he needed no instruction or suggestions from anyone."

The duke shrugged. "I thought about it and decided one of us should read it and determined it would him."

"Oh!" Edwina laughed. "You are terrible."

"And you are beautiful."

Edwina could hardly contain her happiness. The way he looked at her so sweetly let her know he meant what he said.

He nodded and made a move as if to go, but then stopped and looked at her with what seemed to be quiet respect.

"I agree with your sister, Miss Fine. None of the fabrics pinned to your dress work with your coloring, your countenance, or your spirit, but I would love to see you wearing a dark lilac to enhance your hair and eyes."

She had never worn such an exceptional color.

The duke moved closer to her again and bent his head toward hers. "Maman suspects you can read minds." He gave her playful grin. "I know better."

Even though he had told her he wasn't superstitious, and she'd believed him, he was so confident and cocky with his statement, Edwina had to challenge him. The color of her eyes and hair might be easy to dismiss, but how would he feel if he knew she was one of three at birth?

With the same cool assurance he presented to her, she asked, "And how can you be so sure, Your Grace?"

Without batting an eye, he reached up and ran the pads of his fingers slowly down her face. Every nerve ending in her body came alive with his touch and she swallowed hard against the soaring inviting sensations.

"If you could read my mind, Miss Fine, you'd be blushing right now," he whispered in a suggestive voice. "I can't wait to make you mine."

CHAPTER 12

THE ART OF BEING A FINE GENTLEMAN
SIR DUDLEY SAMSON PEMBERTON FINE

*A gentleman of good breeding should always
speak well of his intended's family.*

Edwina pulled the pins and offending swatches of fabric off her bodice as she walked back to the drawing room. Her sisters' bonnets, gloves, and capes were off but determination to get to the bottom of what was going on with her and the duke was evident in their posture. Eileen stood with hands pressed lightly on her hips and one leg cocked out to the side while she gently tapped her foot on the floor. Eleonora seemed a little more relaxed with her arms folded casually across her bosom, humming to herself.

A broad smile stretched across Edwina's face. "It's about time you two got here. I've missed you terribly." She rushed over and hugged and kissed the cheeks of first one sister and then the other as they laughed, hugged, and kissed some more.

"I hope I am never away from both of you at the same time again. I had no one to talk to but Aunt Pauline. I'm so glad you came."

"We've been dreary without you too," Elle said, and planted another kiss on Edwina's cheek. "We felt as if a part of us was missing. We missed Auntie too. Where is she?"

"Resting. She'll be down shortly. Come sit down," Edwina said, scooping up a big pile of fabrics to make room on the settee.

"After being in that carriage for days, I don't want to sit down for a week." Eileen rubbed her backside and smiled. "It feels good to stand up straight, walk around, and put some weight on my legs."

Edwina agreed and dumped the armful back into one of the empty boxes. "It's such a beautiful day. We'll go for a walk with Auntie when she gets down. I'll go ask Mrs. Needlesmith to bring tea and apricot tarts."

"In a moment," Eileen said, stepping in front of Edwina so she couldn't leave the room. "First things first, little sister. Why didn't you tell us in your letter the scoundrel who was after you is a duke?"

Eileen's question caused Edwina to hesitate for a moment before she started gathering more of the scattered swatches. Her oldest sister had always been very perceptive and observant. She seldom missed a twitch or blink.

"How did you know he was the man I was talking about in my letter?"

"Several things," Eileen answered with a slight roll of her eyes.

"To begin with, we were not fooled by the excuse of you needing his help because the pins were sticking you," Eleonora replied with a glowering expression that said no amount of argument would convince either of them otherwise so best not to try that again. "You are quite capable of such a small task."

"What was the attractive duke really doing here, standing so close to you it seemed as if you could have been in one another's arms?"

He *did* have his arms around her. And it felt heavenly. He was about to catch her up to his chest so she could feel his warmth and strength. But surely, she didn't need to admit to that.

"Yes," Eleonora agreed, with a curious smile. "I noticed the lovely spring nosegay lying on the table over there." She cut her eyes over to the flowers. "He must have been with you for a while since the primrose have wilted."

"He wasn't here that long, and they were already— never mind," she finished with a silent sigh of vexation.

"Was he calling on you?" Elle asked, with a hint of disbelief in her tone. "In a matter of a couple of weeks have you managed to catch the eye of a young and handsome duke who looked as if he could be a prince?"

Yes, he was quite something to look at, Edwina agreed silently, remembering his broad, muscular chest, beautiful golden-brown hair and blue eyes, and chiseled features. No question about it. He was an amazingly fit man, and more stimulating than any gentleman she could have hoped would give her notice.

"Would you have come to my aid if you had known it was a duke pursuing me?"

"Of course." Eileen assured her, snapping her hands to her hips and sounding slightly offended.

Elle gasped in outrage. "How can you ask us that?"

"Easily. You might have presumed I was safe and in no danger with a duke." Edwina's tone was a little sharp too. "You've both been so adamant you wouldn't come to London and help me find us husbands. How was I to know?"

"Jumping Jupiter, Edwina. We don't want to attend the marriage mart as you so desperately wanted us to. Of course we'd come if you needed us no matter where you were because we love you."

Edwina's irritation settled down and she smiled affectionately from one sister to the other. "I'm so glad. At times, I've felt lost without you."

"We missed you too," Elle said, hugging Edwina again.

Eileen slid her hands up to her waist and started tapping her foot in that no-nonsense way of hers again. "It's time for you to confess. Is he courting you?"

Hope, excitement, and worry all seemed to converge inside Edwina's chest. She was thrilled the duke was helping to fulfill her father's last request. And she wanted more of the wonderous feelings he created inside her. But there was worry too. What he'd expect of her on their wedding night; what he would do if he discovered the sisters were triplets.

"I suppose you could say he's already done that. He came to tell me we are getting married on Friday."

"Married?" Elle blurted on a broken gasp.

"Already?" Eileen sounded astonished too. "You haven't been here a month. You led us to believe it might take the entire Season to find someone to your liking."

"That's what I thought." Edwina inhaled a deep breath. "I had expected to have more time to think about marriage. But a miracle of sorts happened. He asked and I accepted."

Elle's long lashes fluttered and her bright green eyes turned dreamy. "Oh, it sounds as if it was love at first sight for the two of you. Just as it was for me and Mr. Climperwell."

"Not exactly like that," Edwina admitted. "After meeting, we came to an understanding rather quickly."

Eleonora hugged Edwina tightly. "I believe it can happen instantly."

"I'm sure it can," Eileen agreed, "but it doesn't."

Eileen had always been pragmatic about everything and not poignant about anything.

"Hush, Eileen," Elle admonished. "Love is such a beautiful emotion. If you are desperately in love you shouldn't wait to marry. You never know how much time you have. Things can happen very quickly and you must share all the happiness that you can while you can."

"Yes, of course it's wonderful for you." Eileen kissed Edwina's cheek and then gave Elle a quirky smile. "She also needs to be sensible. There is nothing wrong with waiting until the end of the Season, is there? The viscount gave us until then to vacate the house so you have several weeks."

Challenging as it was to think about, she must satisfy her end of their arrangement. Edwina started picking up some of the design sheets from the table between the settees and stacking them together.

"No, nothing wrong with waiting." Edwina placed the drawings on top of a stack of cloth. "But we're not going to. You know I never could have imagined a duke would seek my hand. A distant relative of a titled man with an adequate allowance was the best I had hoped for, and you know I was prepared to accept an offer from a merchant's son if I had to. The viscount has left us no choice. We must believe him when he said he'd be turning off the servants and closing the house in York by the end of the Season."

"We do understand that." Eileen's eyes searched Edwina's. "But, you aren't forcing yourself to marry him just because one of us needed to say 'I do,' are you?"

"No, of course not," she denied with conviction. "I mean, just look at him. He's the handsomest man I've ever seen and he's quite persuasive. I'm sure we'll be happy together once we know each other better."

"How did you meet the duke?" Elle asked. "The Season hasn't started."

Edwina supposed there was no harm in telling her sisters the whole story. Most of it anyway. She'd always shared everything with them throughout their lives. She started with, "I received an offer of marriage from the duke by post," and finished with when she and Aunt Pauline left the duke's house. Her sisters hung on every word she spoke and had many questions about the kiss that prompted her letter to them. Edwina conveniently left out the part about how passionate the duke's kiss was and how the sensations had stayed with her even until now.

They didn't need to know every little detail.

"What kind of man picks a bride from a list?" Eleonora blustered after talking of the kiss died down.

"A beast," Eileen said, as she picked up a handful of the fabrics and tossed them into one of the boxes. "And that man is no beast." She quirked a smile at Edwina. "There must have been a reason other than it was simple. I'm not believing that. Why didn't you question him further about it?"

"Eileen is right. A list of possible brides is the least romantic thing I've ever heard. Usually, men at least ask for a painting of the ladies before they choose one, if they don't plan to get to know them first."

"Elle, I wasn't searching for romance and neither was the duke. We were looking for an arrangement that worked for both of us." But as the words left her mouth the duke came to mind as easily as slipping a shift over her head and down her body. His heat, scent, and power were suddenly as present with her as if he were standing beside her. She could have done far, far worse but wasn't sure she could have done better in her hunt for a husband to take responsibility for her and her sisters.

"I suppose that is true, but it would have been nice." Elle sighed. "I've read that dukes think they have the right to do as they please and ignore all rules that don't suit them."

"So have I," Eileen echoed. "They are not ordinary people. They go around with their heads in the air."

Edwina huffed a short laugh. "What do you think you do all day and all night with your looking and studying the skies?"

"Their heads are in the clouds because their noses are in the air. I am trying to learn something when I look at the skies. However, I admit it was highly clever of him to give you a little kiss without permission to get us here." The edges of Eileen's lips twitched with a smile. "You've probably never been so shocked in your life."

"I don't think I have. Until . . ."

"By Jupiter, you can't leave us hanging. Until what?"

"You two started attacking the duke with your reticules."

Suddenly, the three started laughing. It was delightful to feel something other than anguish or desire over the incident. "I must stop thinking about all of it. For my own peace of mind so I can enjoy being with you again."

Eileen shook her head and plopped down on the settee. "Not yet. We want to know more. What did he say when you followed him outside?" She cut her eyes to Edwina. "You were gone a long time."

Her sisters seemed reluctant to give up the conversation and continued to pepper her with questions about the duke. Edwina remained firm that she had nothing more to say other than she had to be ready to marry him come Friday and needed their help. It was more how he looked at her and how he made her feel than what he said, but Edwina didn't want to share everything with her sisters. She'd told them enough.

Eleonora picked up a strip of white border lace from the settee and looked at it as she asked, "Did you tell him we are triplets?"

"No," Edwina said without hesitation but with a full measure of guilt at what she was doing. She was constantly asking herself if it was fair not to warn him and be completely honest about their births. But it was best she just go forward and not look back.

"We all agreed we wouldn't tell anyone," Eileen reminded. "That hasn't changed."

"He's promised he's going to find husbands for you," Edwina said cheerfully.

Eileen leaned forward, stretched her back and shoulders, and pinned Edwina with a bold stare. "*You* are the one who wanted a husband. Not us."

"Papa wanted all of us to wed," Edwina answered without equivocating.

"Only to prove we are normal and accepted," Eileen insisted. "We already know that."

"There are people who still have superstitions."

"There always will be, Edwina," Eileen countered.

"What anyone thinks about us doesn't matter to me," Elle said softly as she joined Eileen on the settee. "If they consider us an oddity it is their failings. Not ours."

"You know she's right, Edwina," Eileen added. "We know we are normal and don't need validation from a man or Society to prove that to us."

"But we do need sustenance," Edwina reminded her sisters, thinking she was so happy to have them with her even if they didn't agree on everything. It was comforting just to have them near. "We can't expect Aunt Pauline to care for the three of us the rest of her life with the small allowance she receives."

"I don't want much," Elle said with a carefree air to her voice. "Only to read poetry, write down my thoughts, and take long walks on beautiful days like today."

"And I have my astronomy books and Papa's old telescopes to keep me happy. I am looking forward to seeing the night sky here since I've never been far from York. Perhaps I can even find a way to get to the roof of St. Paul's Cathedral since it is the tallest building in London. Tomorrow I will write another letter to Mr. Herschel and his sister, Caroline. I know one day he'll allow me to visit so I can prove to him how knowledgeable I am."

Edwina shook her head and pursed her lips for a moment. She knew it was Eileen's deep desire to work with the astronomers but not their father's. "You have been trying for over a year, sister. You haven't received one answer. Besides, it isn't what Papa wanted for you," Edwina said earnestly and turned to Eleonora. "It's the natural order of life. You know that. Surely you want to have those wonderful feelings of love for a man again."

She gave Edwina a contented smile. "I have my memories of Mr. Climperwell and they make me happy."

"Papa did what any father would do for his children," Eileen said in a matter-of-fact tone, rising off the settee. "He fed us and saw to it we were clothed. He educated us far beyond what some, if not most, fathers do for their daughters. We do appreciate him for that, but now we must live our lives. It helped that our mother was strong and

healthy and took care of us until after we were born,"
Eileen responded.

"Papa was real," Edwina argued pointedly. "Mama
has always been just a vision of an angel in my mind."

"I think all angels have red hair and green eyes, don't
you, Edwina?" Elle asked as she continued to look at the
strip of lace.

The gentle words about angels instantly calmed Edwina. She guessed she'd always been a little miffed they
didn't want to help her fulfill Papa's dying wish. That was
all right. She had enough fortitude for all three of them.

"I've never seen a real angel and I don't think I've ever
thought about it much. Most painters prefer golden hair.
It doesn't really matter. An angel is what each person sees
in their own mind."

"Yes, it is what each person sees, wants, or believes
that matters," Eileen said, looking directly at Edwina.

No, it was what a person promised that mattered. Edwina wouldn't give up on that vow. And now she had the
duke's help.

"I see something behind your eyes," Eileen said, walking closer to Edwina with her hands on her hips.

"What? Don't start with that *I know what you are
thinking* because you know you don't."

Eileen lifted her chin and gave her a sisterly smirk.
"I may not know what you were thinking but I know it
wasn't about angels. I could sense that whatever it is worries you. Tell us and we will help you. We rode that
bumpy carriage all day and night so we could get to you
as soon as possible."

"Nothing." Edwina dismissed their intuition and then
realized that wasn't the truth and added, "Nothing that is
important anyway so don't worry."

"I sense your worry too," Elle said, dropping the lace and moving closer to Edwina. "Something's bothering you—or at the very least, something more than our being triplets or getting married."

Edwina blew out a sigh of frustration. "I am worried about the wedding night. Before now, getting married was just an idea that would happen in the future. Suddenly, it's not just a possibility. It's real and I must prepare myself for the intimacy of it without knowing what I'm supposed to do."

Her sisters looked at each other and then back to Edwina again.

"Blessed starry night, Edwina," Eileen said irritably. "We can't help you with that. We don't know any more than you do. Why haven't you asked Aunt Pauline to explain it to you? She has been married."

"Yes, of course," Elle encouraged her with a smile. "She is the one you must ask."

"I did ask. She refuses to tell me anything other than my husband will let me know what to do. I'd have better luck trying to pull a coach loaded with baggage down the street than getting one peep about the wedding night from Auntie."

Her sisters seemed to study over what she'd said, looking as confused as Edwina.

"You need to ask Henrietta," Eileen finally said with a measure of confidence that gave Edwina hope someone might know about such a secret night. "She can tell you."

"My maid?" Edwina gave her sister a skeptical look. "I'm not sure about that. She's never been married."

"I know," Eileen agreed confidently, rubbing her lower back as she continued to circle the settee. "But I feel sure she knows about such things. It's part of her duties to

know about the ways of a man so she can properly prepare you for bed that night."

"Do you really think she does?" Elle asked, as riveted
as Edwina by the prospect the maid might know details
about such a private encounter as the marriage bed.

"If she doesn't, she can find out for you. That is part
of her duties too."

"All right," Edwina answered, feeling comforted by
the possibility someone might help her. "If you are sure,
I'll ask her tonight."

CHAPTER 13

THE ART OF BEING A FINE GENTLEMAN
SIR DUDLEY SAMSON PEMBERTON FINE

*There is no better way to show the art
of being a fine gentleman than to allow
a lady to win an argument.*

Staying in his chambers at the behest of his mother posed no problem at first. Watching all the preparations for his wedding was the last thing Rick wanted to do. He had three morning newsprints to read and two account books to look over. Now that those were finished, there wasn't much to occupy his time but stare out over the kitchen garden or pace in front of the fireplace. Neither he wanted to do.

With all the constant talking, laughter, and moving around coming from belowstairs, he wondered if the staff would manage to get everything finished in time. They all seemed to be having one jolly of a time.

Nervousness wasn't something Rick had dealt with before. Not that he could remember anyway. As one of the best marksmen in England, he had participated in more shooting contests than he could count. In all of them he'd never had the tightness in his chest or jittery feeling in his stomach that he had now. But the stakes had never been this high. Getting married was an entirely different experience from any he'd ever had, and though he'd never admit it to anyone, he wasn't sure he was handling it well.

The fidgety feelings started when Palmer told him Miss Fine's belongings had been delivered. The sound of luggage hitting the floor in the rooms connected to Rick's chambers brought home the reality of marriage. The permanently vacant adjoining rooms would now be occupied. By his wife. Only a few steps from him. That would take a bit of getting used to.

It could be that he hadn't really thought through the idea of marriage and all the ramifications of it the past few days. He knew how to conduct himself and manage a proper young lady, a mistress, and his mother. But a wife? He wasn't sure. Miss Fine intrigued him immensely, but still, the thought of a wife was obtrusive. No doubt it was going to take some getting used to.

With all thanks to his overprotective mother and hovering servants, except for Hurst and Wyatt, he'd never enjoyed having people around him for any length of time. Miss Fine would be with him for life. A responsibility that would never cease. There was so much more to a relationship called marriage—love and cherish, protect and honor, in sickness and health, until death. The last was a worry he kept pushed to the back of his mind. He couldn't dwell on the possibility of the fever returning.

Rick hadn't mentioned the recurring fever to Miss Fine for good reasons. Most important was that his physician and apothecary assured him there was the possibility he'd never have another. Why worry her about something that might never happen? But they'd also reluctantly admitted there was no guarantee he wouldn't have another. And if the fever came again, they had no way of knowing how bad it would be.

Perhaps it wasn't a wife, marriage, or a fever at all, but just his mother's machinations about the wedding that had him feeling as if he were sitting on the edge of a cliff and about to fall off. She had arrived well over an hour ago now and had every servant in the house bustling about, changing out flowers, moving furniture, and obviously making a nuisance of herself to Palmer and the rest of the staff. She'd insisted Rick must go abovestairs and wait until Palmer came for him. That would be the signal his bride was ready to enter the drawing room and take her place beside him.

Rick considered all the prewedding planning unnecessary and couldn't wait for the ceremony to be over.

The wedding was to start at eleven. Ten minutes before the hour, Rick decided he'd had enough of his mother's instructions. He started down the stairs. Before he managed to get halfway, he saw it wasn't servants making all the noise but a crowd of handsomely dressed people gathered in the vestibule and corridor, spilling over into the drawing room.

No wonder he'd heard such chatter and stirring about. What the hell were all these members of Society doing at his house?

He made it to the bottom and had to thread his way through the buzzing throng, brushing past the bows, curtsies, and congratulations from all he passed with little to no acknowledgment in return. The trail of well-wishers funneled into the drawing room, which, to his irritation, was packed as tightly as the vestibule and corridor. Thankfully, at his appearance, the chatter of the crowd reduced to a low respectful hum that seemed to roll like distant thunder all around him.

"Damnation," he muttered to himself. Where did these people get the idea they were invited to his wedding? He caught a glimpse of his mother near the fireplace, looking regal in her summer sky frock, talking to the vicar with a delighted expression on her face. Knowing he'd found the guilty party, he headed toward her.

After nodding a greeting to the robed clergyman, Rick turned his attention to his mother and the minister stepped away. In a low voice, Rick whispered to her, "Who are all these people?"

She looked at him with genteel surprise in her blue eyes. "What do you mean, Stonerick? They are friends who are here to help celebrate your wedding."

"No, Maman. I have three friends: Hurst, Wyatt, and Fredericka."

"Yes. They arrived moments ago and are just over there waiting to speak to you after the ceremony." She pointed to the far side of the room but they were nowhere in sight. "Well, perhaps it was down the corridor where I saw them, but I know they are here."

He should have known the duchess was up to mischief when she arrived early. It wasn't like her to insist he'd be in the way and should excuse himself so the servants could get everything ready.

"These people are *your* friends, Maman. Not mine."

"Oh, botheration, Stonerick." She lifted her chin and smiled defiantly and then looked around the room as she proclaimed, "You know everyone here. Maybe not well because you never put forth the effort, but you know who they are. You've played cards with all the men here and you've danced with most of the ladies. It's so near the Season, everyone is in Town. Why are you being ungenerous on such an important day in your life?"

"You know I don't like crowds," he said with rough impatience as a throbbing started in his temples. For a fleeting instant, he worried the fever might be returning.

It always started with a headache. He quickly pushed that possibility from his mind. "There must be more than a hundred people here."

His mother smiled as sweetly as she ever had. "Maybe a little over," she said innocently. "You told me I could invite some friends."

An undercurrent of frustration crept into his voice again. In a hushed tone, he replied, "I said a few, Maman. A few is a handful. Five, not half the ton. You've invited everyone you've ever met."

"Don't be ridiculous." Her eyes remained steadfast, but her lips formed a tiny smile. "I did no such thing. I had to leave many off my list because I didn't want to outshine the ball tomorrow evening. But, I don't mind if we come close. Don't worry. In the end, you will be happy I did this for you."

He expelled an exasperated breath. "I never have parties here. Palmer is not prepared to serve this many people."

"Of course he is," she answered with confidence and a look that told him she had everything under control. "Do you think I would have left him to manage your wedding alone? What kind of mother would I be? I sent over some of my staff earlier with food, champagne, flowers, and other things to help with the wedding buffet. Unlike you, Palmer has been a gemstone about the unexpected number. The day is beautiful. Tables have been set up outside in the garden. I didn't ask you about this because I knew you'd never agree."

That was for sure.

"Besides, it would be bad luck to have only a few people to show up at the wedding of a duke."

Rick's head pounded harder and his neckcloth

suddenly seemed too tight. He forced the thoughts of the fever from his mind again and concentrated on what his mother was saying. "What are you talking about? Did you get that ridiculous idea from the books you've been reading?"

"No, one of my friends in the Insightful Ladies of London Society told me. She's wise about such things as good and bad luck."

That comment was so outrageous, Rick almost smiled. "You must stop with this superstitious poppycock."

Wanting to avoid mischief like this was the reason Rick hadn't wanted to set a time in advance for his mother to meet Miss Fine. He should have known she'd find an opportunity of some kind, seize upon it in any way she could, and put her stamp on it.

"But your wedding is important so why take the chance? Now look on the bright side for a change." She breathed in deeply and surveyed the crowd. "Everyone will see your duchess and be properly introduced to her today, so you won't have to worry about it at future gatherings."

Rick sighed and whispered a curse low in his throat. He pushed the tail of his coat aside and settled one hand on his hip. With the other he rubbed the back of his neck, trying to tamp down the pounding in his head. Getting married was bad enough, but now he had to contend with the ever-increasing crowd watching every move he made.

"The only thing we needed was a vicar and to say *I do*."

"I always enjoy swapping banter with you, Stonerick, but don't be combative today." His mother shifted her gaze to scan the room again without moving her head.

"I've waited almost thirty years for you to marry. And

you decided to do it in little more than a week. You gave me no time for announcements or parties to celebrate your engagement."

The duchess knew no amount of feeling sorry for herself was going to pull on Rick's heartstrings. She'd been trying to do it for years with no success.

"This will be my only time to show off my son, the duke, and his bride. I don't intend to let it go unnoticed by anyone in London. If you are upset with anyone about what is happening today, Stonerick, be upset with yourself for not having a proper betrothal period with dinner parties, teas, and other social gatherings befitting your title."

Rick reluctantly accepted the inevitability of the teeming crowd bearing witness to his vows. His mother's somewhat contrite expression remained and so did his frustration at what she'd done.

He blew out a short laugh of surrender. "I'll give you today, Maman, as it seems I must, but no more meddling. This ends it."

"Yes," she answered as innocently as a young child. "I'm happy you are marrying, but . . ."

"But what?" he asked, suspiciously. Had she done something else he didn't know about?

"I was wondering if you did as I suggested in my note to you yesterday and asked the apothecary to give you a potion Miss Fine could wash into her hair to tone down the red? I would hate for anyone to—"

"Maman," he warned with a scowl and mentally shook himself to keep from saying more than he should. It might help his attitude if the damned pounding in his head would cease. "I don't care if she was born on a full moon, All Hallows' Eve, or any other day that might bother you and your group. She's beautiful, she's mine, and I don't want to hear another word about your tales."

"Yes, of course," she agreed without a hint of petulance. "It was only a suggestion, Stonerick. I guess you would know by now if she could indeed read your mind. We'll just be happy she's not one of three."

"Throw away those cursed books and stop attending those meetings. They are warping your mind."

"They are enlightening me."

"Excuse me, Your Grace," Palmer said, amazingly composed despite the chaos that must be going on with the servants and kitchen staff. "I've just been alerted the bride is ready to enter the house."

Rick's stomach tightened.

"Right on time." His mother smiled at him triumphantly. "That's a good way to start a marriage. See, having a large crowd has already brought good luck." She turned to the butler. "Clear a path for her entrance, Palmer." And to Rick, she said, "You and the vicar stand here and ease the frown off your face and smile. You are about to be married. With some of Shubert's good luck you'll have a son by this time next year."

That's exactly what he wanted. And in the meantime, Rick intended to enjoy his beautiful wife. He bent his head and quietly said to the elderly vicar, "Do you remember what we have discussed in the past about your lengthy services?"

"Yes, of course, Your Grace. You always ask that I keep them short."

"Keep this short too."

"But this isn't a Christmastide blessing," he answered firmly but respectfully, the chin of his beard bobbing as he talked. "I have some leeway there."

"You have it here too. I just gave it to you."

The vicar cleared his throat and puffed out his chest. "May I remind you it is highly irregular not to have a complete sacred marriage ceremony."

"I appreciate your concern, but I'll take my chances with missing all the blessings."

"As you wish, Your Grace," he said, closing the book he held in his hands with a disgruntled clap.

Along with the guests, Rick settled his gaze on the entrance to the drawing room and his attention fell on the cocksure marksman, Mr. Matthew Malcolm. Rick went rigid with anger. What was that braggart doing at his wedding? If Alberta Fellows Cosworth weren't his mother, he'd have more than a word or two with her for inviting that man. Rick was of a mind to stalk up to him and throw him out. But as that notion took root in his thoughts, he noticed Miss Fine's sisters and aunt slipping into the back of the room. They melded unobtrusively into the crowd of guests near the doorway. From the corner of his eye, he saw Hurst, Wyatt, and Fredericka move closer to the front near him.

Everyone was in place.

A moment later, a violin and pianoforte started playing and his bride walked from around the doorway and into the room. Rick's breath caught in his chest. Everyone but her was forgotten.

Edwina was stunning, but more than that was the realization that she would be his to have and to hold forever. Suddenly, Rick felt as if hundreds of horses were galloping in his chest. She looked almost angelic, dressed in light ivory-colored silk that shimmered and flowed elegantly against her legs with every step she took. The crown of her hair was covered by a wide band of beaded silk the same sparkling shade as her dress. In her hands she held a single pink rose with colorful ribbons streaming from the stem to flutter down her gown.

Somehow, he'd known she was the right lady for him the first day he met her. And now he was surer than ever.

Though none of the guests had seen her before, they had no doubt who she was when she entered. In a rustle of shuffling feet and swishing taffeta and silk, they backed up and widened the short path to where Rick stood. Miss Fine held her chin modestly high and her shoulders confidently straight.

An odd sentiment came over him, and for a fleeting moment he felt as if he had been waiting for this lady all his life. Odd as it seemed to him, it just felt right and exciting that she should be in his house and joining her life with his.

She had an aura of sensuality that seemed to envelop her every time he looked at her. It wasn't something he could define, but it was soft and vital. He saw, felt, and was drawn to it in a way he'd never been with any other woman. It was as if she radiated a seductive heat. He sensed it the first time he'd seen her standing in his vestibule, even though her back was to him. That same quality now had him eager for their wedding night.

As she came closer, the throbbing pain in his head receded to a dull ache, and then, thankfully, along with the quiet whispers from the crowd, it faded completely away. His thoughts were consumed by the sight of his bride; it was as if everyone in the room had disappeared by the time she stopped beside him.

With painstaking concentration, his gaze moved over her features when she turned to look at him. Her rosy lips were closed and softly tilted upward. Sensing she was nervous and hiding it well, he gave an encouraging smile. She acknowledged it by lowering her chin and lashes and giving him a brief nod. He may not have wanted to marry at this time but thanks to fate, his mother's constant harangue for a grandson, and the worrisome possibility of another fever, he had no doubt he had chosen well. Now he would make sure she knew she had chosen well too.

They faced the vicar, who at present was desperately trying to find his place in the book he'd snapped shut earlier. While the musicians finished playing the last chords of their score, Rick took the moment to whisper to his bride, "You look exceptionally beautiful today."

"Thank you," she answered softly, and immediately added, "You are most handsome too, but you could have warned me you were inviting half of London to our wedding."

"I would have, had I known."

"There are more people here than in the entire village where I grew up. I'm not comfortable around so many people and was expecting something a little more intimate."

His brows rose and he harrumphed softly. Keeping his voice a whisper, he said, "I'm glad we have that in common. In time, you'll get used to the way my mother does things. She thought it best you meet everyone she knows today and get all introductions over with."

"Then I must give her my gratitude for that. I believe I should like getting it all over with today."

The vicar started speaking and their attention shifted to the clergyman. He kept to his word and led them through the consecrated vows and only two short prayers at an even pace without adding a sermon, an opinion, or a lecture concerning the state or sanctity of marriage.

When the minister asked for the ring, Rick took hold of her hand. It was cold but not shaky. She was handling the ceremony well. Her eyes were steady but tentative as he slid the gold band bearing the Stonerick crest on her finger.

A few words later the vicar said, "I pronounce you husband and wife. You may kiss your bride."

CHAPTER 14

THE ART OF BEING A FINE GENTLEMAN
SIR DUDLEY SAMSON PEMBERTON FINE

*It is incumbent upon a fine gentleman to consider
the day he weds as the luckiest day of his life,
and to make sure everyone knows it.*

Edwina had no idea how or why it had become a proper tradition, necessary even, for a husband of only a few seconds to kiss his bride with everyone in the crowded room watching.

The divinely dashing duke stood beside her in his crisply pressed white shirt, tastefully tied neckcloth, white quilted waistcoat, and black formal coat looking as calm as if marrying was something he did every day of the week. No different from putting on his hat. Knowing she had to marry for her sisters' benefit as well as her own, knowing this was the first step in fulfilling her promise to her father, Edwina had been quite composed throughout the ceremony. Until this moment.

After the vicar announced they could kiss, all she could hear was the pounding of her heartbeat thundering in her ears. She looked into the duke's eyes and for an instant wondered if he would kiss her as he had the first time.

Seconds passed, and the room remained quiet. He

made no move to touch her but waited and let his gaze slowly caress down her face as he gave her a small, tender smile. It was as if he was telling her not to worry. She inhaled unevenly and caught the faint scent of the rose she clutched tightly in her hand, the new wool of his coat, and the heady, masculine scent of his woodsy shaving soap. Smells that pleased her. Calmed her.

A cloak of warmth spread over her at his patience and pulsated inside as she pushed away all thoughts of the crowd. She was transfixed by his face as his came closer to hers until his lips brushed lightly, invitingly upon hers with feather softness. Her stomach tumbled and twirled at the amazingly soft contact. Her chest seemed to expand. The kiss was exactly how she imagined a first kiss would be: sweet, tender, making her insides tighten, and making her want more.

All too quickly he eased away from her a mere fraction, moistened his lips, and, surprisingly, kissed her in the same manner again, with slightly more pressure and urgency than before. Tingles of delicious pleasure rippled across her breasts and down into her lower stomach. She wanted to hold onto the ecstatic feeling so it would last, but he lifted his lips from hers, straightened, and took a step back.

A smattering of applause and several hearty comments of congratulations and good wishes rumbled throughout the packed room. Distantly, she heard the violins and a pianoforte start playing again and chatter from the crowd. The wedding was over, and the celebration was about to begin, and later there would be the wedding night. That filled her with trepidation.

A soft breath of laughter passed the duke's lips as he looked into her eyes. "Was that kiss more to your liking than our first one, Duchess?"

His tone was sweet and inviting. "Much better," she answered softly, hoping that would be the way he kissed her tonight, when the guests had gone and they were alone.

"I am a lucky man you received the letter I wrote."

"Both of us were," she answered, feeling nervous jitters in her stomach again. "I hope you will continue to believe that."

He eyed her keenly. "Is there any reason I shouldn't, Duchess?"

"None that I know of." Right now. "I only meant that ours is a curious arrangement. If you don't mind, now that we are married, I think I should be more comfortable if you'd call me Edwina."

He nodded once. "And I am Rick. After today. For now, we must address each other properly or forever have the ire of the ton." He bent closer to her ear and in a low voice said, "We'll begin with my mother. She's been in a dither to meet you for almost thirty years, and she's standing behind you. Don't let her intimidate you. She respects strong women."

That was good to know, but Edwina wasn't feeling very strong right now. There were too many people in the room and too many unsettled feelings about the wedding night. She was overwhelmed. Tamping down those feelings, she turned to see a distinguished, confident-looking lady with tawny-brown hair, trying hard not to reveal she was giving her new daughter-in-law more than a curious once-over. His mother stood the same height as Edwina but with a slightly fuller figure. She had an elegant countenance, and beautiful blue eyes like her son. Wearing a stylish frothy gown the shade of a summer sky, she appeared regal and almost celestial.

"Your Grace," the duke said to his mother. "May I present my wife, the Duchess of Stonerick."

The two greeted each other with the required formality and Edwina was thankful to have the introduction over. She noticed the duchess couldn't seem to keep her gaze from straying to Edwina's hair, then to her eyes and back again. She cleared her throat and tried not to let the obvious appraisal bother her. In time, she would realize Edwina had no power to read minds. Or any other superstitious control or powers. Watching the dowager's face, Edwina didn't detect any snobbery or malice but there was a heaping amount of interest in her expression.

"Well, my dear," his mother said with conviction, "you are every bit as . . . lovely as the duke said."

The unexpected compliment eased a little of Edwina's tension. "That was kind of him." She glanced at the duke and received an encouraging smile. "Thank you for letting me know."

The dowager gave a confident nod toward her son. "What he indicated is true. Since his father died, my only goal has been to see him married and with a son of his own to protect the title."

His mother's voice had a soft, cultured tone, making it seem as if every word she said was important. They were, of course. That truth was Edwina's new role in life: to produce an heir. She was healthy, strong, and had no doubt she could do it. The terrifying worry was, would it be one or three?

"We have the same aspirations," Edwina answered, thankfully not feeling as nervous as she expected to be in front of his mother.

"Ah, here's champagne." Rick lifted two glasses from the server's tray, handing one to his mother and the other to Edwina before taking one for himself. He raised the glass in a salute as he looked at Edwina with a smile and a nod. "To our future."

As Edwina lifted her glass to the duke's, his mother added in an undertone, "And to the enduring continuation of our family forevermore."

The dowager's comment made Edwina's burden heavier. Before having a babe, she had to get through the wedding night. Perhaps the champagne would help ease her fears concerning it. According to Henrietta it wouldn't be an enjoyable experience. Her maid had offered to make her a tonic to sip while she dressed for bed, insisting it would help with wedding night apprehensions. Perhaps the champagne would be enough.

Never having tasted the drink, Edwina took the smallest of sips and found it to be pleasant enough, reminding her of apple cider without the sweet richness of the fruit.

The dowager turned to Edwina with an affable smile and said, "I understand that your sisters made it to London in time for the wedding. You must be so pleased."

"Yes. I missed them."

"I'm sure," she offered with a genuine sweetness to her voice. "I should like to meet your aunt too. I look forward to talking with her and hearing more about your family. I'm sure she can—"

"But not today, Maman. There will be plenty of time to discuss families later."

The duke moved closer to Edwina, brushing his arm against hers. His protective gesture warmed her.

"Yes, of course you're right, Stonerick. I must remember . . ."

Suddenly Edwina was pounced upon by her sisters, nearly knocking her over as they squealed with delight and hugged her tightly. Her champagne spilled down the front of her dress and her headpiece almost slipped off her hair. Eileen, Eleonora, and her aunt were oblivious to interrupting a dowager duchess in the middle of a sentence and showered Edwina with kisses and laughter as if they were seven-year-old girls again.

Among the giggles, Edwina heard a sudden and sharp intake of breath. She cut her eyes to the dowager, whose brows had risen high on her forehead in an arch of shock. Her champagne glass was shaking so much Edwina felt it was about to hit the floor. Edwina quickly calmed her sisters' jubilant greeting.

"I can't believe all of you have red hair and green eyes," the dowager said, keeping her tone soft, even though her eyes were wide while looking from one triplet to the other.

Edwina knew she needed to get the introductions over with in a hurry. Thankfully, the duke stepped in and handled them while she continued to take in the fact that she was now truly married. The duke's mother continued her assessment of Edwina's family.

"I'm startled by how much the three of you look alike when you stand so close together."

"Do you think so?" Edwina asked innocently, purposefully not looking at the duke while she sipped from her glass to cover her concern of the dowager's question.

The dowager cleared her throat, seeming a little taken aback by Edwina's question. "Yes." She lifted her chin as if to give strength to her answer. "Quite certain. Three in a family with such colorings isn't even referenced in the book I'm reading about strange marvels."

"Perhaps that's because this isn't one, Maman."

Edwina glanced at the duke. She gave him an appreciative smile, and then turned to the dowager in the manner he'd suggested. "We've often had people mention that we're remarkable," Edwina answered lightheartedly.

Besides, as they had done all their lives, they did their

best to look differently. While Edwina wore pale ivory and a wide headpiece covering most of her hair, Eileen had on a pale, pink-colored gown with a small gold crown in her hair, and Eleonora dressed in a dark copper color with a trio of pheasant feathers delicately woven into a band at the top of her head. The difference helped disguise their similarities, but there was nothing to be done about their vibrant green eyes.

"I believe it's true, Your Grace," Eileen said, joining the conversation with ease, tenaciously looking from the duke to his mother, no doubt hoping one of them would challenge her. "Some sisters don't favor at all. Not even the same color of hair and nowhere near the same height or size. You would think they were from entirely different families with no relation whatsoever. With others, like us, you can hardly tell one from the other." Eileen finished with a satisfied smile.

"I suppose you are right," the dowager answered with a fair amount of conviction in her voice and expression. "Tell me, are you enjoying your stay in London?"

"Yes," Aunt Pauline added to the conversation. "She spent all night charting the few stars she could see and then slept all day."

Eileen twisted her face into a frown.

"Oh." Her Grace's eyes widened again. "That sounds strange." She glanced at her son with an expression that seemed to say *Did you hear that?* She then cleared her throat and added, "Strangely lovely."

"She uses our father's old telescope to look at the heavens," Edwina explained, fearful the conversation might get out of hand. "I told her we are due a clear night soon."

"Much like gentlemen who spend all night playing cards and then sleep long after the sun comes up, Maman," the duke added with a smile, before seeming to search the room for someone.

"Actually, I study the heavens," Eileen clarified with a pert lift of her shoulders.

"Oh, you study them." The dowager looked at her son and gave him a knowing smile. "Yes, I understand now. I'm so glad you told me. Many people believe in reading the moon, stars, and planets to tell their future and all manner of other things. I've read about when they are aligned on specific days of the year or the date of your birth you can expect certain things to happen."

"That is not what or why I study the heavens, Your Grace," Eileen said with an arrogant tilt to her chin but thankfully her tone remained polite.

"Excuse me, Maman," the duke said. "I believe Palmer is looking this way. Perhaps he needs a word with you."

"Of course." The duke's mother turned to Edwina and gave her an elegant smile. "I'll return shortly and help introduce you and your family to everyone. That way you'll have plenty of people to talk to at the ball tomorrow night."

"Ball?" Eileen questioned as the duchess left with the butler. "Certainly not me. I won't be attending," she assured Edwina with an expression that could leave no doubt she meant what she said. "We've hardly had time to take a deep breath since we received Edwina's letter. I'm much too weary from the hectic schedule of getting Edwina ready for the wedding to attend a ball anytime soon."

"I'm afraid I won't be joining the festivities either." A wistful light shone in Eleonora's eyes as she looked around the crowded, teeming room. "I'm still in mourning and couldn't possibly join another joyous occasion like this one. It wouldn't be right."

"What's this?" A troubled frown appeared on Rick's forehead.

"Mr. Climperwell passed away over a year ago," Edwina said to help cover the silence that was stretching.

She could tell the duke couldn't see at all why such a young and lovely lady would be in mourning past a year. Quite frankly, Edwina couldn't either. She had told the duke it would be difficult to get them to agree to participate in Society balls. Perhaps now he would believe her.

"It's not only that, Your Grace," Edwina felt compelled to add. "Viscount Quintingham didn't secure invitations or tickets for them to attend any of the parties or balls, so it would really be impossible."

"I am responsible for them now," he said with quiet assurance, keeping his gaze only on Edwina. "I'll get the invitations. You get them ready." He looked at her sisters with his frown still in place. "I do understand neither of you are ready for dancing or enjoying the celebrations of a grand ball, but you do have to attend to assist your sister at her entrance into Society. She'll be more comfortable with a large crowd if you are there."

"She will have you and Auntie with her," Eileen reminded him.

"Oh, I wouldn't miss it," Aunt Pauline said. "I remember the days when I was young and would dance until my feet would ache. I can't wait to go again but fear my dancing days are over."

"Mrs. Castleton will spend most of her time on one of the velvet chairs with all the other widows, spinsters, and chaperones," Rick said, not letting the sisters' defiance deter him. "You two will be wherever Edwina is."

Eileen moved her lips from side to side before saying, "I suppose I can go for a little while. Until she feels comfortable."

He nodded to her and then pointed his gaze at Elle.

"Well, yes, of course, we want to help Edwina. That's why we left York. Of course, I'll go for a little while."

He gave Eleonora a nod and turned to Edwina with a smile.

Edwina felt as if she'd taken her first easy breath of the day. Her sisters were beautiful and had done excellently. They handled the duke's mother well, and Edwina was thrilled they were in London and in Society. Their possibilities of making a match were far greater than they had been in York.

"Good," Rick said. He stopped a passing server and grabbed two glasses of champagne and gave them to the sisters and then handed one to her aunt.

"I've never tasted champagne," Elle said and quickly took a sip. She smiled. "I think I should like this."

"You might as well start getting used to what a grand ball is like. If you don't care for it there is always punch."

"I'm feeling a little tired, Edwina," Aunt Pauline said. "Would you mind if I found a chair and took a rest while I enjoy this glass of champagne?"

"Of course not, Auntie."

"I'll escort you, Mrs. Castleton," the duke said.

"You will do no such thing," Eileen said, slipping her hand around her aunt's upper arm. Eleonora immediately took the other arm. "You two need to be together. We'll take care of Auntie."

Edwina's family left and she placed her glass and rose on a small table.

She turned to Rick. He was once again scanning the crowd. She looked out over the room too. The hum of talking, laughing, and generally moving around was a little intimidating. Being an active participant in Society was going to take some adjusting for her and her sisters.

"Are you looking for someone?" she asked.

He turned his attention back to her. "I was hoping out of all the people here my mother would have invited a few bachelors, so I could introduce them to your sisters. The only one I've seen I would not want either of them to consider."

"I had noticed most of the people here are a few years older than we are," she answered with a smile. "And thank you for being so firm with Elle and Eileen about attending the balls. It makes me hopeful you can succeed where I have failed."

His gaze easily moved to hers. "You have nothing to worry about, Edwina. Now, I should do what everyone is waiting for and introduce you to all the guests. I feel none of them will go home until they've met you." He smiled. "Once this is done, you can relax and enjoy yourself. The hard part will be over."

Edwina wasn't sure about that, but she returned the duke's smile.

The whirlwind of formalities and introductions seemed endless as they moved about the room meeting the guests. Rick was right about how formal the occasion was. Every gentleman bowed and every lady curtsied and referred to them as Your Grace. Though some wanted to tarry over conversation, the duke didn't stay long to chat with any of them. He kept moving until they came upon two exceptionally tall and powerfully built men who were just as handsome as Rick. A beautiful young lady with dark-blond hair was with them. She had a healthy blush on her cheeks and immediately gave Edwina a friendly smile.

"Your Grace," Stonerick said to Edwina, "may I present the Duke and Duchess of Wyatthaven and the Duke of Hurstbourne."

Edwina smiled to the threesome as appropriate greetings were exchanged. She was delighted to learn the friends didn't stand on formal ceremony with each other when she was asked to call them Hurst, Wyatt, and Fredericka. That made her feel more at ease in the bustling room.

"Rick told us your sisters and aunt are with you and perhaps more of your family are here," Fredericka said to Edwina.

"No one else," Edwina replied affably, seeing only friendliness in Fredericka's face. "My mother died shortly after I was born, and my father passed early last winter."

"I'm sorry to hear it's so recently."

Edwina appreciated the sincere light of sympathy in Fredericka's golden-brown eyes. "Thank you. He was scholarly and loved to impart his knowledge to others."

"I think I would have enjoyed meeting him."

"Yes, you would have," Edwina agreed. "He often put his thoughts in journals and wrote many papers on topics that interested him. We have his writings and take pleasure in reading them from time to time."

"How wonderful to have something of such a private nature as his daily thoughts," Fredericka said. "I was recently given some poetry I had written as a young girl. My cousin had kept the collection and returned them to me not long ago. I was very happy to have those memories from my past."

"I would like to read them one day if you wouldn't mind," Edwina said.

Fredericka laughed softly. "I will consider it, but I'm sure you wouldn't find them as thoughtful and interesting as your father's writing."

Edwina smiled sweetly. "Not all Papa's writings were private musings. He had a book published a few years ago."

"What is the nature of the book? I wonder if I might have read it."

"Probably not," Edwina said with a friendly lift of her eyebrows. "It's a reference guide for gentlemen. You wouldn't have had much need for such a book, but perhaps Wyatt or Hurst might have read it or heard talk of it among gentlemen in one of their clubs. *The Art of Being A Fine Gentleman*." Edwina looked from one duke to the other, eager to know if they had by chance indeed heard of it.

"I haven't read much other than newsprint since I left Oxford," Wyatt said with a grin. "There are other things I'd rather do."

"I might have come across your father's work when I was younger," Hurst replied, brushing his light-blond hair away from his forehead. "Forgive me for admitting I don't remember all the books I've read."

He gave Edwina an easygoing smile and she knew he was the type to make friends quickly and without much effort.

"Forgiveness isn't necessary, Your Grace. I don't remember all I've read either," Edwina assured him shyly, wondering if she was talking too much about her father again. She knew she tended to do so, and to boast of his accomplishments without shame. Trying to temper her bragging, she added, "Besides, my father's book wasn't widely acclaimed."

"Have you read it?" Hurst asked Rick.

He shook his head, cleared his throat, and looked at Edwina. "No, but perhaps one day."

"It has a very intriguing title, Edwina," Fredericka said, further continuing the thread of conversation. "I'm sure these three gentlemen could find some wisdom in your father's book." She looked at her husband and gave him a bright smile. "Right?"

Fredericka's tone was sincere but her lips twitched and her eyes sparkled with mischievous humor.

Wyatt quirked a brow at his wife. "A gentleman is *always* interested in wisdom, my darling."

Edwina could see the love he held for Fredericka and was tweaked with a sudden rise of hope that she might look at Rick like that one day. "I'm sure he only wanted to inspire gentlemen in a subtler way, almost like poetry," Edwina answered, brushing aside the stray, unexpected thought from her mind.

A sudden hush fell among her companions, and they all shared an odd glance. She had no idea what caused the instant, uncomfortable silence. She focused on Rick, hoping for a sign or insight as to what she might have said that seemed to stun them all.

"Poetry, you say?" Fredericka was the first to speak. She turned to her husband and gave him an even bigger smile before turning back to Edwina. "I think we should have tea soon and talk about poetry and other things."

Edwina felt herself beam at the invitation. She'd had her sisters all her life, of course, but because they lived so far from the village she'd never really had a friend she could visit and share things with. "I would like that very much." She then looked at the duke and gave him a sweet smile, hoping it carried into her eyes so he would know how appreciative she was that he'd introduced her to his friends. He nodded and smiled too.

Over the course of the next few minutes, lighthearted

conversation flowed through the group. Edwina recognized a strong bond of friendship between the three men and that Fredericka had found a comfortable niche for herself among them. It gave her hope that, in time, with work, she could do the same.

Soon, she and the duke moved on to meet other guests. Edwina was certain she had been introduced to most everyone attending when Eleonora came up beside her with an unusual exuberance, giving her another hug and kiss on the cheek.

"Auntie sent me to check on how you are doing."

Edwina stepped aside from the couple they were talking to. "Quite well considering the occasion and number of people here," she said, wondering at the liveliness of her usually subdued sister.

Eleonora's attention was caught by something or someone over Edwina's shoulder. It was the most intriguing expression Edwina had seen from her sister in over a year. Her entire countenance seemed to soften as a pretty blush stained her cheeks.

Curiosity made her turn to find the subject of her sister's interest and she caught a glimpse of a tall, handsome gentleman with golden-blond hair. He was staring at her sister as if he were looking at the woman of his dreams before he turned away.

This was wonderful! It proved the duke had given Edwina a good chance in helping her sisters find husbands by the end of the Season and keeping her promise to her father. The duke had introduced her to most everyone at the wedding but she was certain she hadn't met this man.

She turned to Rick with a sudden and overwhelming urge to reach around his broad chest and strong neck and hug him tightly. She was so happy she wanted to feel his strong arms around her and place kisses all over his face. Rick saw her and returned her appreciative expression with a smile.

Suddenly, the heady delight was dampened by other thoughts of good news that came to mind. Even as it seemed the duke was keeping his promise to her, Edwina wondered if she could give him what he wanted: a son. A shiver flashed over her as she continued to watch her handsome husband give his attention back to the man talking to him.

First, she had to get through the wedding night. It was no wonder her aunt had been evasive and hadn't wanted to tell Edwina anything about it. Henrietta had no problem telling Edwina about the joining of a man and a woman—in great detail. And none of it sounded like the romantic affair Edwina had always envisioned. In fact, it sounded dreadful.

CHAPTER 15

THE ART OF BEING A FINE GENTLEMAN
SIR DUDLEY SAMSON PEMBERTON FINE

*The finest married gentleman denies his
own desires and pleasures and seeks
to please his wife first.*

The afternoon had stretched on longer than Rick had thought possible. He made sure everyone in attendance had been introduced to the new duchess, except Mr. Matthew Malcolm. It didn't appear the man had stayed a lengthy amount of time after the wedding, which was good, and everyone was gone shortly after dark.

Edwina had looked as exhausted and wrung out as Rick felt when all the wedding guests had left. She'd nodded with appreciation when he suggested she retire to her rooms to rest for a while; he would be up later in the evening.

Rick's head had pounded off and on all afternoon but thankfully now that his house was quiet again, he was feeling fine as he went into his book room, thinking he would look over correspondence, documents, the wedding contracts again, or something to distract him while he gave Edwina extra time. He found the only thing he'd been able to focus on was his beautiful wife and wanting to join her in her room.

He'd been surprised to learn Edwina's sisters and aunt had been some of the first to leave, until he discovered Miss Eleonora had enjoyed the taste of champagne but was unaware of the effects of drinking too much of it.

Rick would have thought the eldest sister would have stayed with Edwina and let the aunt go back home with Miss Eleonora. Though, he supposed, her family might have considered it was now his place to be with her. Which it was. But it might take him a while to get used to the responsibility. He liked being alone. But having an heir meant he must have a wife first. And given the way he felt when he looked at her, he had chosen well. It was also good that Edwina didn't like crowds any better than he did. Still having someone, a lady—his wife—living with him might be a struggle at times.

Rick smiled as he thought of Edwina and how well she'd handled the day, the guests, and his mother. He liked the way she smiled at him and the way she looked for him in the crowd if they got separated. Yes, they should manage nicely together.

After Wyatt had married last year, it had been weeks before Fredericka had joined him in London to live together as man and wife. He finally adapted and adjusted well to being a husband. Rick assumed he would adjust too. In time.

After less than an hour, he gave up the pursuit of doing anything productive and headed up to his chambers.

Rick threw his coat on the bed and started removing his neckcloth. He looked over at the door that connected his room to Edwina's. No light was visible around the framing. He envisioned her lying across the bed surrounded by flickering candlelight, wearing a gossamer white gown with her golden-red hair spread invitingly across her pillow.

He undressed with rising anticipation. Not just the desire to be with a woman, he realized, but to be with Edwina. Did all men wait with such excitement as their brides readied themselves for the wedding night? Imagining Edwina feeling as he did in the next room made him want to go to her immediately. But he couldn't be a cad. He had to make sure he gave her all the time she needed to prepare for him, so he made no hurry to remove the last of his clothing.

Instead, he made himself comfortable in his slipper chair and sipped the brandy he'd brought with him. There was much about her that pleased him. She loved her sisters and wanted to take care of them. The fact they didn't want her help made her vulnerable. It was her misfortune that she was the one her father picked to carry out his dying wish, but he would now handle that for her.

He remembered the feel of her lips beneath his, honeyed and warm. The time he'd held her in his arms had left him wanting to be close to her again. Even now, thinking about her made his heart start beating faster and his muscles stir restlessly.

He hadn't paid a visit to his mistress since he'd met Edwina. He didn't know why. There could be several reasons, but none of them mattered anymore. His interest was no longer in women with practiced caresses and meaningless sighs.

The only woman he wanted to be with was his beautiful, challenging wife.

Until today, Rick thought the hardest thing any man could do was be responsible for the safety and financial condition of a dukedom. But not anymore. For any man, taking a wife to care for and protect for the rest of his life was the biggest and hardest thing he would ever commit to. It was a milestone most males crossed at some

SINCERELY, THE DUKE   185

point, and yet for all the massive responsibility of the life-altering event called marriage, Rick couldn't say he felt any different from before he said *I do*. Maybe that would come in time. Perhaps a change would become evident when Edwina was in the family way, or when he had a son and knew the title was secure under his lineage.

Throughout his ruminations about weddings, wives, and responsibility, Rick never forgot it was his wedding night. He was looking forward to sharing it with his duchess. He would be mindful of her innocence and take things slowly for her. It was the best way to enjoy the intimate pleasures with a woman anyway.

Mrs. Castleton had probably seen to it she knew a little in the ways of intimacy with a man. And then there was the universal, ethereal feeling called desire. It was the great educator that was the equalizer when a man and woman came together. By the way she looked at him and reacted to him, he was sure Edwina had felt desire for him. Now it was time to show her what to do with it.

Rick polished off the last of his brandy and finished removing his clothing. He turned out his lamp and started walking nude toward Edwina's door, but something stopped him just short of it. He was a gentleman when the occasion called for it and this one did. Edwina was not a well-seasoned mistress practiced in the art of looking at a man with scalding passion. Turning, he peered into the darkness of his room and, by the pale light from the window, spotted his nightshirt on the bed where it had been laid out for him. Grabbing it up, he tossed it over his head. No use in shocking her too much on their wedding night.

With his covering in place, he knocked lightly and then opened her door. The room was dark as Hades. Pitch black as an inner cave. Not even the glow of a lone glittering candle shed light in the room. The draperies had been shut so tightly there wasn't even a sliver of moonlight around the edges. He'd never had a reason to go into the rooms set aside for the lady of the house and had no idea where the bed was. He listened, but the only sound he heard was his own labored breathing.

What the devil was going on? He tensed as he felt a prickling at the back of his neck, telling him something wasn't right. Had he waited so long she had fallen asleep? Had she fled the room?

"Edwina?" he asked softly.

"Yes," came the cautious reply.

His muscles relaxed. For an instant he hadn't been sure she was there. It looked as if the place had been closed as tight as a tomb.

"I can't see," he responded in a low voice, wishing he hadn't turned out the lamp in his room. That would have thrown a little brightness into the room. "Where are you?"

"On the bed," she answered.

Of course. But where the hell was it? He couldn't see a blasted thing. Was it straight ahead or to the right or left?

"Should I be somewhere else?" she asked in a tentative voice.

"No, no." He stepped farther into the room, hoping his eyes would quickly adjust to the darkness. There weren't even any embers glowing from the fireplace. "Why is it so dark in here?"

"I thought I was supposed to turn out the lamp."

Maybe that's what she'd been told to do, but he'd see it didn't happen again. He couldn't see his hand when he held it right in front of his face. Part of the joy of lying with a woman was being able to see her beautiful body as he touched it.

"I'm going to relight the lamp." As soon as he could find the damn thing.

He headed in what he assumed was the general direction of the bed and . . . *thunk.* "Bloody hell," he whispered on a tight wince and a grunt as his big toe throbbed with shooting pain.

"What is it? Is something wrong?"

"Nothing," he managed to say and then swore under his breath like a season-hardened dockworker who'd missed his shore leave. "I'm all right." He'd stubbed his toe on the end of the iron foot of the bed. And it hurt like hell, but at least he'd found the bed.

Hobbling along the side of it, he glided his hand over the coverings until he felt the pillows at the headboard, and then reached for the nightstand. After a few seconds of fumbling with the lamp he managed to light it. Precious, golden glow spilled into the room.

When he turned toward Edwina he blinked. The provocative fantasy lady he'd imagined propped against satin pillows in a silky nightgown was nowhere to be seen. Neither was his wife. It took him several seconds to find her buried under a stack of covers. All he saw was a pair of wide-open eyes staring at him from the far side of the bed. Edwina held the dark covers pulled up and over her nose. A brown mobcap covered her beautiful hair and the wide band of lace trimming it came down to rest just below her eyebrows.

Rick's heart pumped at an erratic beat. He had never seen so little of a woman.

He searched his mind for what to say. "Are you cold?" he asked, feeling a little impatient with the way he found her and because his seductive dream had been shattered.

"No," she answered quietly, her eyes looking blankly at him. "It's very warm under here."

Tightly as she was covered up, there was no doubt about that. He'd heard of ladies who were exceptionally prim and frightened on their wedding night but as strong as Edwina was, he hadn't expected her to be that way. Was she frightened of him, or what they were about to do?

"You need to let go of the covers so I can pull them down and join you on the bed."

"All right," she answered, but hesitated before her fingers relaxed. She slowly drew the bedding down her face and stopped just under her chin.

"I'll help you," he offered quietly, trying to adjust from what he'd imagined to what was happening.

Rick bent over the bed and pulled the bedcovers and linens all the way down to her knees. She dropped her arms to her sides and lay still as a board. He blinked, and blinked, and blinked again. He had no idea what she was wearing. It looked like a brown feed sack. The long sleeves covered most of her fingers and the neckline rose almost to her chin.

He'd never seen anything like it except winter coats—possibly a burial shroud or prison garb. Nothing could have prepared him for the way his bride appeared in the drab color and ridiculous mobcap covering her gorgeous hair.

"What the devil do you have on?" he asked, tamping down the prickle of irritation at realizing she obviously hadn't been anticipating the same kind of wedding night he had. He'd been almost desperate to see her and obviously she'd been desperate to hide from him.

The fact his toe continued to throb didn't help his attitude.

"It's a nightshift. This is the thickest one I have. In winter, it gets cold in York."

Yes, well, she wasn't in York, and it wasn't ever going to get cold enough for her to wear that thing again. Whenever he got it off her, it was going straight into the fire.

Slowly, Rick lowered his weight onto the edge of the bed, being careful with his toe, and stretched his lean body beside her, resting on his elbow facing her. The sounds of shifting weight upon the mattress and rustling bedsheets tightened his lower body and filled him with an urgent sense of intimacy he couldn't wait to explore with her. Yet, as impatient as he was, he knew he had to take this night slow. Very slow.

Light spilled over his shoulder and he could clearly see the rise and fall of her chest. Her breath was deep and fast. Was she that frightened of him? The corners of her eyes twitched, yet her face seemed frozen as she watched him. He needed to do something to calm her.

He didn't touch her but could feel the nervous heat of her body next to him. The contact was warm, inviting, and instantly arousing. For a long moment, he stared into her eyes and let his gaze drift down her face, neck, and linger over the slight swell of breasts barely showing beneath the brown wool before sweeping back up to her lovely face again.

Astonishment flickered in her wary expression, but there was no panic. A good sign.

"Do you usually sleep in bonnets?" He reached over and gently brushed the lace of her mobcap away from her forehead and folded it back over the crown.

Her eyes watched his movement as she nodded.

"I think your hair is beautiful and would like to look at it. Do you mind if I take off your nightcap? It's not freezing in London tonight. I don't think you're going to need it." At her consent, he gently freed her hair from the offending covering. He dropped it to the floor, assuring himself it would go the way of the gown she wore.

Rick ran his fingertips down her cheek and smiled. The stiffness left her face and she twitched a bit of a smile too. He was beginning to see a little humor in the way she'd prepared for her wedding night.

He'd always felt he knew women, their likes, and dislikes. Granted, it had taken him a long time to garner all the knowledge. Apparently, he had more to learn.

"Did Mrs. Castleton suggest you wear this particular gown tonight?"

"No. She wouldn't tell me anything about the wedding night. She said it was a very private affair and couldn't speak of it. My maid was helpful. She said it didn't matter what I wore because I wouldn't be needing it for very long."

He smiled and kissed the tip of her nose, hoping the playful buss would further relax her. "That is usually the case."

Her eyes glistened as she moistened her lips and swallowed hard. "I didn't want to get cold while I waited for you."

No chance of that.

He chuckled lightly. He wanted to get her out of the *thing* as fast as he could, but the trepidation he sensed inside her and the worried expression on her face stopped him. For all her confidence and boldness when she talked to him, she suddenly seemed fragile and much younger. Especially compared to all the women he'd been with before.

Tender emotions for what she must be feeling stirred inside him. Didn't she know he would be gentle with her? In a soft tone, he said, "I'm not going to hurt you, Edwina."

She stirred a little under the covers. "I've heard the marriage bed can be unpleasant and painful . . ." she began, but then broke off her words.

"No, it's not." What was he saying? He didn't know anything about virgins. *Nothing.* He was used to a woman who knew exactly what to do, when and how to do it.

Edwina's expression was suddenly completely unreadable as she regarded him with stony silence.

"I mean, maybe for some ladies," he amended. "The first or second time might be uncomfortable, but that will go away. I will be gentle."

"All right." She inhaled deeply. "I'm ready to do my wifely duty."

Hell's teeth, he scoffed silently. Those words were like splashing ice-cold water in his face. *Wifely duty.* That wasn't what he expected to hear, and he wanted no part in such an act. Ladies clearly needed better teachers than their maids when it came to the wedding night. But then he remembered she hadn't had a mother to school her while growing up.

It wasn't that he expected Edwina to be as receptive as his mistresses and welcome him into her bed with a come-hither smile and arms open wide. Though that would have been nice. He had hoped to see interest, if not eagerness, in what was happening between them. But for now, he would deny his primal desire to treat her as if she'd been through this many times before and was eager for all the pleasures that waited for her.

The shock on her face after he'd kissed her at his home flashed through his mind. Was she remembering that?

He'd explained why he'd behaved so aggressively. She should know by now he could be a gentleman when the occasion warranted it, and this one definitely did. And too, she'd seemed responsive to him later at her home when she had to know he'd wanted to kiss her.

No doubt it was his own damned fault she was trussed up like an elderly spinster on the coldest night of the year. She'd wanted a longer betrothal to have time to get to know him. Maybe he should have waited. He could have slowly wooed her with kisses and tender caresses. If not for the fevers.

Truth be told, if not for the recurring fever he wouldn't even be married to her.

All he needed to do was stir up her passion. For him. That should relax her, ease her fear, and take away the tension that was holding her so stiff she could hardly move. He had felt her desire for him when he was at her house and so close to kissing her. He'd seen it in her eyes and felt it in the way she'd looked at him as if she'd wanted to throw herself into his arms and kiss him. He could still remember how much he'd wanted her to do just that.

Rick lowered his head and let his lips graze softly across hers with the merest amount of pressure. To him, the contact was sweet, enticing, and undemanding. Gentle though it was, it sent a quick, hard throb of pulsating heat directly to his manhood, causing an unexpected rush of intense desire to shudder through him, no matter that she didn't respond as he'd anticipated.

She kept her hands down by her sides and clutched tightly at her gown. A slight moan whispered past his ears. Her full lips parted slightly. They were beautifully shaped and made for kisses that satisfied all the way to a man's soul.

He hadn't expected the kiss to be so powerful, or to feel such satisfaction, particularly since she was doing nothing to participate. That small detail didn't keep him from wanting to abandon his reserve and show her just how quickly she'd made him want her, but fearing he'd frighten her more, he refrained.

Doing his best to shut down his own desire to see and touch what was hidden beneath the hideous piece of clothing, he lifted his hand and skimmed the back of his fingers down her soft cheek again, brushing aside a wispy strand of hair that hadn't been caught back. She didn't flinch from his touch but made soft sounds in her throat; her legs stirred restlessly as her upper body tensed and tightened more.

Rick continued his seduction, slanting his lips temptingly over hers, seeking more of a response from her that didn't come. Determined to succeed, he kissed her tenderly, slowly while the pads of his fingers traveled caressingly up and down her neck, along her shoulder, and across her chest until he realized her heart was racing faster than his, but not with desire.

Hellfire and damnation, he muttered to himself.

He'd never had to work so hard to get a woman interested in him. The way it was looking, he'd have better luck getting the queen to serve him tea. His body urged him to take her swiftly and just get the first time over with so she would know tomorrow morning everything would be all right. But he couldn't be brutish. He wanted to introduce her to the unending delights of physical passion.

When he lifted his mouth an inch or two above hers, he asked, "Did you get all your information about tonight from your maid?"

"Yes," she whispered and then took a long, heavy breath and closed her eyes for a moment before responding. "She said I was to be still and let you do whatever you wanted to do, and you would tell me when you were finished."

Rick grunted at the ill-chosen words from her maid. Why in the hell had the woman told her something like that? "What I wanted to do? When *I'm* finished?" He pressed his hand to his chest in frustration. "It's not *me*, Edwina. It's supposed to be *us*. You and I are in this together."

"Are you angry at me?"

"No." Annoyed. Frustrated, but not angry. Rick set his mouth in a grim line, plopped onto his back, and laid his head against the pillow, struggling to master his emotions. Damnation, he wanted her, but not this way. From the very first time he'd been with a woman they had welcomed him eagerly, seductively into their arms.

Edwina was innocent, trusting, and she had to come willingly to him. For her to do that, he had to take his time when all he wanted to do was rip the prison gown from her body and cover every inch of her with kisses and caresses. That wouldn't happen tonight. She was too entranced from whatever rubbish her maid told her the wedding night would be like.

Instead, he took in gulping breaths and tried to stifle his rising impatience. He could go to any number of women and they would receive him. But the truth remained that he had no desire to see a paid woman. He only wanted his wife.

Passion was inside her. He had felt it. Desired it. But he was going to have to take his time wooing her to make her aware of it and enjoy it. He wanted their coming together to be as good for her as it would be for him. A strange calm came over him and he willed himself to be patient. To give her the time she needed to be comfortable with him beside her. In the end she would be worth the wait.

Yet, he couldn't forget he needed an heir. The sooner the better. He'd have to be patient for that too and hope the fevers stayed away as they had today at the wedding. He couldn't start thinking every headache would turn into something more serious.

When he rose on his arm, he looked at the soft, beautiful lines of her profile. She appeared a little more relaxed, and he smiled. "I want you to forget everything your maid told you. Put it out of your mind and don't ask her any more questions."

"But it is my dut—"

He pressed his finger to her lips, smiled again, and then caressed her cheek with his cupped hand as he saw her eyes were glistening again. He didn't want her upset. Slowly, he removed his finger and lowered his lips to hers, lightly brushing across them with a kiss. At first, she remained still as if she didn't know what to do other than lay there without moving.

Rick continued the tender, languid kissing until her lips relaxed a little beneath his. He felt her body soften. Moments later she opened her mouth a little as his lips continued to move seductively back and forth over hers.

When he raised his head, he narrowed his eyes as if to question her in good humor. "My touch is gentle, is it not?"

Her expression relaxed and she gave him a shy smile, but her hands still clutched her nightshift with all her strength.

Rick shook his head and chuckled lightly. She was so beautiful as she lay there with her hair shimmering against the pillow. Something about how he felt and what he felt for her changed inside him. He didn't know what it was or why it happened. Only that it had, and it made him want to understand her more than he did.

"Good. I'll keep it that way."

She nodded and smiled.

Instinctively, Rick kissed her the same way again. Unhurried, slow, soft. Sometimes letting his lips hover just above hers as he moistened his before kissing her again. Gradually, he let his hand slip down her chest to cover her breast. The firm swell of it excited him and he deepened the kiss. She opened her mouth and his tongue brushed the inner surface of her lips and tongue. Through the scratchy fabric beneath his hand, he could feel her trembling. The more he kissed her the more her body tensed and the longer she held her breath.

Soft sounds came from her throat. He answered by whispering her name against her lips. Eager to feel her skin, he skimmed his hand down to her waist to pull up the nightshift so he could feel her inner thigh, but her hand quickly caught hold of his. He stilled.

Rick raised his head and looked at her. Her eyes were closed tight and it didn't look as if anything could have pried them open. Her lips were moving as if she were talking to someone but there was no sound. What was she doing?

"Are you praying?" he asked.

Her long lashes popped up in surprise. "Praying? Well . . . ah, no . . . no. Just whispering to myself."

Rick knew he'd lost the battle for tonight. He was glad for her innocence and should have known she would be a challenge. What he hadn't expected was that she would teach him something no one else had ever been able to teach him. Patience. It was going to be a hard lesson to learn. As a duke, one he never thought he'd have to learn, but he was determined to do it.

Her hair fell across her shoulders as he envisioned it would the first day they met. Only there was no bare ivory skin for him to see and she lay as still as a marble statue.

He wanted her to be his and not just a mother for his son. He needed that, but he wanted Edwina. As foreign as the idea was to him since she was already his wife, he would court her to make her willingly his.

"We aren't going to consummate our marriage tonight, Edwina," he said softly.

"What?" She rose to her side and propped up on her arm as she looked at him with confusion. "Did I do something wrong?"

"No, no." He smiled softly and tilted her chin up so she couldn't avoid his eyes. "We're going to take this a little slower than I anticipated so you can get used to me. To us. Being together in bed. Kissing. Touching. Freely enjoying each other."

She shook her head. "But I want to—"

Rick placed his finger against her lips again. "We will come together. I promise. When we do, I want you to have the same heated desire for me that I have for you. I don't want you worried about what is going to happen between us. I am not a patient man by nature, but I'm willing to wait until you want me without fear, Edwina." He kissed her lips softly, briefly. "I will woo you with soft words, kind things to make you happy. If it takes endurance to make that that happen, I will do it."

Remembering the pounding headache he had earlier in the day, he hoped it would be soon. Every twinge and ache brought thoughts of the burning fever. He had a very desirable wife who pleased him. Now he needed an heir. Maybe it would happen soon for him as it had for his cousin. Rick picked up Edwina's hand and kissed it before he turned and moved out of the bed. Pain shot through his injured toe as he hobbled back into his room.

CHAPTER 16

THE ART OF BEING A FINE GENTLEMAN
SIR DUDLEY SAMSON PEMBERTON FINE

*There are times when there is nothing
for a gentleman to do but wait, and he must
learn how to do it well.*

Only one thing was expected of Edwina, and she had failed. Miserably. She didn't possess a great deal of knowledge about intimacy but enough to understand she couldn't get in the family way without coupling.

And that hadn't happened last night. Why? She'd done everything her maid said was required of her. Except drink the tonic Henrietta prepared. Perhaps she should have. She'd remained still as a board as instructed, except for a few trembles and clutching the covers in her fists. She hadn't participated in any way with the delicious kisses and tingling caressing that had her wanting to writhe in passionate spasms. She kept murmuring silently to herself, "Don't enjoy it. Don't enjoy it," until she thought she was going to scream out loud. No wonder Henrietta had said it would be painful and she needed a tonic. Not responding to her husband's gentle, seeking touch and the most tender kisses she could ever imagine was the most agonizing feeling she'd ever experienced.

Still, she'd felt wretched and on the verge of tears last

night after the duke left her and throughout the morning. She hated crying as much as she hated the thought
she'd disappointed Rick and was glad she hadn't given in
to the tears. At least not yet. If she couldn't fulfill her
part of their arrangement, she couldn't expect Stonerick
to honor his. And that would mean she'd disappointed her
father too. Edwina didn't know which ache caused her the
greater misery.

Edwina sat by the window in her bedchamber, holding a cup of cold tea. Occasionally, she would take a sip.
She should have gone belowstairs long ago, but she hadn't
garnered the courage to do so. It might be ridiculous, but
she couldn't help feeling everyone in the house would
know she hadn't pleased the duke last night.

She didn't want to face them. And there was the possibility he could still be home. It would be worse facing
him. Through their connecting doorway, she'd heard him
moving about, talking softly to his valet earlier, but his
rooms had grown silent long ago.

Glum as she felt, her thoughts returned to the one
thing that made her feel better: remembering the sweet
thrilling kisses and caresses her husband gave her last
night. Though she'd experienced one erotic sensation after
the other, she'd had to deny how they were making her
feel. Still, she had wanted to lose herself in the sensual
world he was taking her to and it had been a huge struggle to maintain her wits and not reach up, encircle his
neck, and pull him closer, tighter, and participate with
abandon in the glorious, mounting pleasure.

But that would have been even more disastrous. Henrietta had insisted she must close her eyes, lie completely
still, and wait until the coupling was over. If she'd acted
as if she'd enjoyed anything he did to her, he would consider her a wanton woman of the evening who'd been

with a man before. The thought of that had given Edwina chills. She couldn't have him thinking her a loose woman. She had promised him she was pure. And she was, but it had been so difficult to remain motionless when the duke's touch had all her senses so attuned to him, she was ready to give in and let him think what he would about her.

Perhaps she was a wanton anyway because she had enjoyed every caress, every kiss, and every sensation that streaked through her like lightning. Her body still tingled, the taste of him lingered in her mouth. She had wanted to give in to the burning passion she was feeling for him and take the consequences of what he thought about her later. And she almost had a couple of times. She'd refused to fool herself and pretend she hadn't enjoyed his touch and kisses. She had. Her cheeks still heated whenever she thought about how deeply they'd touched her and made her feel special to him. Perhaps that was the reason she was supposed to drink the tonic her maid had mixed for her. If she had, maybe she wouldn't have been so affected by his touch.

She moaned softly in disillusionment as she looked out the window at the gray sky. She wondered if a storm was brewing. The air looked heavy with impending moisture. In the distance, treetops gently swayed in the wind. And she swayed with misery too. Rick had been gentle and giving last night. She wanted to lie with him again and openly enjoy his kisses without fear he'd think her blemished.

She needed to do something, but what? Her sisters wouldn't know how to help and his mother was already suspect of her appropriateness for her son all because of her hair and eye color.

When it was decided she would attend the Season, all

she'd really wanted was a husband who would be nice to her and good to her sisters. But the duke was making her feel and want so much more than she'd ever expected. She didn't know what to make of all that she was feeling.

A knock sounded on the door that led into the corridor, not the one connected to Rick's rooms. Thankfully. "Come in," she called.

Swinging the door open, the duke strode inside. Edwina didn't know if her heartbeat fluttered, skipped, or stopped altogether for a second. She took in the sight of his tall frame, handsome as ever, dressed in well-fitted buckskin-colored trousers stuffed into below-the-knee boots, but she noticed a slight hitch to his gait. His matching dark-blue velvet coat and waistcoat trimmed with burnished buttons seemed to make his blue eyes sparkle.

Her husband was looking her over carefully too as he entered. A concerned frown wrinkled his brow and tightened his mouth. Her chest heaved softly. Just being in the room with him kept her heartbeat erratic.

Hurrying to place the tea on the tray and stand up, the cup rattled in the saucer, which caused her to almost knock over the cream pitcher when trying to right the cup. When she straightened and looked at him her heart felt as if it fell to her feet. She knew she wanted to give this man a son more than she wanted anything else in the world.

"Your Grace."

His troubled gaze was fixed on her face. "Edwina, are you feeling all right?"

"Yes," she answered with as much bravery as she could muster considering the rapid pound of her pulse and pool of thick breath lingering in her throat. "I'm good," she answered, knowing it wasn't really the truth.

"I was worried. It's midafternoon. Palmer said you hadn't been out of your rooms today."

"No, I . . . well." She looked around, searching for a reason that might be halfway true. "I was finishing my tea."

He kept rapt attention on her face, and she hoped he could see how sorry she was to have failed him.

"Did you sleep well?" he asked.

Of course not!

"Adequately." She brushed her hands nervously down the sides of her camel-colored dress and shifted her weight. "And you?"

He walked farther into the room and stopped in front of her. Edwina watched his features closely, fearful of what he might say.

"I've had better nights."

She had no doubt. Probably many. That left her feeling even more disconcerted about what he may possibly be feeling about how she'd bungled their wedding night. Her eyes wanted to glisten again so she looked away from him to gain control of the disappointment in herself. She had put the duke's title and her father's wish for her sisters in jeopardy.

"I didn't sleep well either," she admitted sadly, turning back to face him. "The truth is, I expected more from myself than I was able to give last night."

He shrugged. "We both had expectations. It's over. By morning, I had come to some decisions."

Her hands slowly curled into fists at her sides and her spine stiffened. For a moment, she felt as if the walls were closing in on her. Was their arrangement off? Would he annul the marriage and seek another? She wouldn't stop him if that's what he wished, but . . . strange as it felt to think it, she knew it would break her heart.

"About what?" she asked in a whisper.

"Since you aren't unwell and you feel good, you need to finish your tea and get yourself belowstairs."

Edwina stared at him. Stunned. Her breath swooshed out of her lungs. The first day they'd met, she'd learned he was abrupt, even abrasive at times in how shortly he spoke, but that comment seemed beyond the pale even for her disaster in the marriage bed.

It was true. He was sending her away because she hadn't met his expectations last night. "Well, yes of course, I will." She clasped her hands together but couldn't seem to move her feet. "I'll leave the house right away."

His brows rose and eyes narrowed in a confusing frown. "What the devil? Leave?" He ran a hand through his hair and huffed a grunt. "Why would I want that when your sisters will be arriving soon?"

Another prickle of fear shimmied over her. "I didn't invite them to come today. Did they seek your permission?"

"What kind of man do you think I am?" he asked irritably. "This is your home. They wouldn't need my permission to come over. I went to see them and your aunt this morning. I told them they are to move out of the leased house today and come live with us. I've sent footmen over to pick up their luggage. You have a lot to do to get them ready for the ball tonight."

Edwina's shoulders lightened. He wanted her to stay. And her sisters too? Edwina couldn't utter a single word for a few moments. "They are coming to live here with us?"

The duke's frown softened. "I made the decision without asking you because I think it's best."

She tried to calm her racing pulse. "I don't know what to say because I don't know why you did this."

He sighed in resignation. "For you, Edwina."

She blinked at his surprising words.

Stonerick made another frustrated swipe through his hair. "I think—I *hope* it will help you to be more comfortable if they are here with you. I know you are close to them."

"We always have been," she said softly.

He came to stand before her. "I should have suggested it the day they arrived, but it didn't cross my mind."

It took every ounce of Edwina's courage, but she took a hesitant step toward him. "I'm grateful for this offer, but I don't think you realize what it might be like to have four ladies in the house with you when you aren't used to having even one. My sisters will not be like your servants who move quietly around the house without notice."

His chuckle was an easy, natural sound. Then, he inhaled deeply, and in a reassuring tone and with a tender expression, he said, "I lived through my school days at Eton and Oxford with hundreds of boys. I'll adjust. The house is big enough we shouldn't be stumbling over each other. I'm away most of the day and sometimes into the night. I'll be away at times with my sporting club. Having them with you is the right thing to do. Your aunt and sisters shouldn't be living in that small house when there is plenty of room here." He gave her a small smile. "We are family now. Your sisters are my sisters. I'll treat them that way and take care of them."

What he'd said and done was a precious gift. All she could say was, "Thank you, Your Grace, for asking them."

The skin around the edges of his eyes crinkled in quiet amusement. "Always call me Rick, Edwina."

She nodded, feeling a nervous jitter fluttering in her chest.

"Besides, it won't be for long, right? Our goal is to have them married or betrothed by the end of the Season."

"Yes." Encouragement and something deeper soared inside her. He had said *our* goal. "It is."

"I'm also not convinced your aunt is capable of handling all that will be required of your sisters during the Season and while they are being courted. After she has settled in, I'll have my apothecary give her a tonic to make her stronger."

For all his brash impatience, he really cared about people. "Thank you. That would be wonderful of you and wonderful for her."

"I'll have a better chance of getting your sisters married if they are living here where we can keep an eye on them when gentlemen call or pick them up for rides in the park. It will be beneficial to you and me. I told them to make plans to leave immediately so they would have plenty of time to prepare for the ball tonight."

Edwina was overwhelmed with emotion again. She felt on the verge of tears again, but for a different reason. "I'm . . . I don't know what to say. I'm so grateful you still want to help them find husbands when they are being difficult."

He gave her that curious expression she was getting used to, reached out and took hold of her hand and kissed the backs of her fingers. "Why would you think I changed my mind?"

Refusing to let her courage fail her, she managed to keep her gaze on his and speak the truth. "I didn't fulfill my part of our arrangement last night."

He moved in closer to her. She felt the fine cotton of his neckcloth as he held her hand to his chest. "Perhaps I didn't fulfill mine either."

Something in his tone touched deep inside her.

Without thinking, she broke her hand free of his grasp, threw her arms around his neck, and kissed his cheek three times. One for each triplet. Realizing what she'd done, behaving so brazenly and not like a lady, not like a pure bride, she slowly leaned back and looked into his eyes.

"I hope it was all right I kissed you." She started sliding her arms from around his neck, but his hands came up and took hold of her wrists. He pushed her hands back up to his nape and held them there.

His eyes searched her face. "Why wouldn't it be all right to kiss your husband?"

"I want to do what is proper and don't want you to think I'm a wanton or ruined lady because I enjoy your kisses."

"What?" He laughed as his hands circled her waist, lifted her off the floor, and swung her around once before setting her on her feet again. "A wanton if you enjoy my kisses? Where did you get that idea? Is it something else your maid told you?"

Edwina nodded. "She said you would think I'd been with a man before if I acted as if I enjoyed your touch."

He frowned. "Where would she have gotten an idea like that? Edwina, I know the difference between a lady and a lady of the evening. I will never confuse you with another. I want you to always respond to me."

He caught her up against his chest as his lips came down on hers with firm pressure. She swallowed a small shivery gasp and closed her eyes as his lips molded solidly to hers. Without knowing why or how her mouth relaxed from the tightness, she joined the kiss. It was as if she knew exactly what to expect and began to kiss him back.

Edwina melted against him. The strength behind his

hold was exhilarating. It was heavenly to be surrounded by such muscular arms, and having his lips moving so sensuously over hers, her whole body tingled. She stroked and tangled her fingers in the back of his hair, loving how the strands felt between her fingers.

A languid warmth stole through her bones and she felt as if she were light as air. His mouth moved against hers with an ardor that soothed, yet excited her as their kisses ebbed and flowed from short to long and soft to passionate. His hands slipped down her back and followed the curve of her waist to her hips before returning to her back again. Spirals of wonderful sensations curled tightly in her abdomen and then seemed to shoot throughout her body as she surrendered to the stirrings of passion his kisses awakened within her.

Edwina relaxed and concentrated on the pleasure soaring and building inside her. She enjoyed every gasp, moan, and breath that fell from his mouth into hers. They kissed long, deep, and savoringly. All her senses welcomed him—the woodsy soap, the luxurious feel of his velvet coat beneath her hands, and the taste of his warm mouth upon hers.

His lips left hers and he kissed her cheek, under her eye, and on down to the corner of her mouth and chin. Chills of pleasure made her tremble when his lips nuzzled her neck and around to the sensitive spot behind her ear before returning and melting to the contours of hers once more. She felt as if he treasured what he was doing and how he was making her feel.

When at last he drew his head away, she opened her eyes to gaze into his. Matching his raspy, uneven breaths, she said, "I like the way you are kissing me."

"I'm glad I finally got it right."

Edwina grew tentative for a moment and moistened

her lips before asking, "When kisses make me feel so wonderful, why is the act of . . . of intimacy painful?"

His arms tightened around her. "I don't know what your maid told you but the pain lasts only a short time. Some ladies never experience discomfort at all. I will show you when you are ready." He kissed her cheek, forehead, and then the tip of her nose.

"I want to give you a son, Rick," she said earnestly.

"I'm glad," he whispered in between kisses. "There *is* something else you can do for me."

"Yes, I will."

He looked into her eyes. "Have your maid burn the nightgown you wore last night and anything that resembles it. The nightcaps too."

She gave him a curious stare. "That's ridiculous. They are in good condition and warm."

He reached up and smoothed the hair above her ear. "You will never need them again. I will keep you warm. Give them to your maid to dispose of however she wants and never listen to anything she has to say again."

Edwina studied what he said. Henrietta certainly hadn't helped her on her wedding night. Maybe it was time to try doing it her husband's way. "I don't believe I will be asking her for any more advice."

Rick smiled and bent his head to hers and sought her mouth once again. The kiss was long and generous. Their tongues swirled, played, and enticed. Edwina skimmed her hands along the width of his shoulders and down the breadth of his back. She loved the feel of the firm muscles of his arms hidden under the velvet while she explored his broad chest and followed the buttons of his waistcoat to his tapered waist, and then around his lean hips, leaving no doubt there was a fine cut of a man beneath his clothing.

Her searching caused him to tremble and his arms to tighten around her more possessively, pressing her breasts against the firmness of his powerful chest as if he were trying to bind her to him.

Pleasure twirled and soared through her. She had never experienced anything so wonderful as being held tightly in Rick's arms and kissing him.

While they kissed, Rick's hand slipped down her chest to her breast. He palmed it, gently squeezed, and felt its weight. The thrill of his touch was shattering to her senses. His lips left hers and glided across her cheek, over her chin, and to the soft, sweet skin behind her ear again.

Edwina was pleased by his tenderness and her desire for him but worry strayed back into her mind. Rick had been so good to her but she still had not accomplished what she needed to do for him. That weight was still on her shoulders. Perhaps tonight she would have another chance.

CHAPTER 17

THE ART OF BEING A FINE GENTLEMAN
SIR DUDLEY SAMSON PEMBERTON FINE

*One of the first things a gentleman should do when
approaching a lady is learn how to read her expression,
so he can react appropriately.*

After a whirlwind of activity to get her aunt and sisters
settled into their rooms and preparing for the first ball
of the Season, Edwina headed belowstairs to wait for
them. She didn't know if it was excitement or worry that
had spurred her to dress so quickly. Probably both. She
wanted their first ball to be enchanting for all of them.

The duke's rooms were silent as she left her chambers,
so she assumed he was already in the drawing room, but
it was empty when she entered. She considered checking the book room for him, but instead placed her velvet
wrap and reticule on a chair and looked around the lovely
and quite lavishly decorated room, realizing she hadn't
seen it before. The first day she arrived at the duke's
house, Palmer had never invited her into the drawing
room to wait for the duke. Later, she and Rick spoke only
in the vestibule and book room. At the wedding, all the
furniture had been removed to accommodate the many
guests. Now that it was put back together, she saw the

lovely chairs with plump flower-print cushions, blue-and-ivory-striped settees trimmed with beautiful woodwork, and highly polished tables with vases and figurines of varying sizes and shapes sitting atop them.

Running her hand along the crest of a small sofa, she walked over to the secretary, imagining the duke sitting there while he wrote his proposal to her. She smiled to herself and thought, *Or perhaps he had been at his mother's house when it was written since the seal had been hers.*

Edwina fingered the tickle soft feather of the quill, and then the raised gold lettering on the duke's official stationery. She examined a pair of spectacles and wondered if the duke used them when writing or reading his correspondence. She tried to see him in her mind wearing them and laughed softly. Without thinking, she opened a drawer to look inside and simply stared for a moment. *Ten Black Cat Superstitions and More Shocking Facts* stared back at her. Slowly, she reached inside and took out not one, but two books. *The Truth and Dangers about Folklore, Myths, and Superstitions.*

Dangers? Oh, my. What did that mean?

Her hand trembled as a knot of tension grew in her stomach. Had Rick been reading these? Instinctively, she thumbed through one of the books reading the chapter titles. Her eyes caught sight of *Be Careful of Red Hair and* before she slammed the book shut. Was her husband, the man who kissed her so intently she wanted it to go on forever, reading these? He had to be. For what other reason would they be in his desk drawer?

Edwina didn't know if she was feeling hurt, anger, or disbelief he hadn't been truthful with her about his thoughts and beliefs concerning superstitions. He had said he had no leanings toward shallow, obscure notions, but obviously he was curious and didn't want her to know. "There you are." Rick walked into the drawing room, stopped, and smiled at her with appreciation flowing from his expression. "I thought I heard you leaving your room. You're dressed early." His eyes seemed to glow warmth at her. "You are beautiful in that shade of pale yellow."

Edwina swallowed hard as a sense of despair gathered in her chest. He was truly too handsome for words. Every time she saw him her breathing increased. She wanted to be near him, to touch him, smell his scent, and feel his warmth. He was so gentle and understanding last night she realized she wanted to be a part of his life, but could she? Glancing back to the books in her hands, her heart started pounding.

Unable to respond to his compliment, she held up the books and said, "You told me you didn't believe in these."

He gave her a perplexed shrug. "Books? No, I must have been talking about poetry, which I have no fondness for."

His lackadaisical attitude toward something so important surprised her. She struggled to say, "Not poetry or just any book, Your Grace. These books."

"Wait." Rick frowned tightly and started toward her as if suddenly realizing something was wrong. "What do you have there?" Taking them from her, he glanced at the titles. "Damnation," he whispered, anger hardening his eyes. "Do you think these are mine?" he challenged her. "That I was reading them?"

"This is your house," she managed to say in a tone she hoped didn't reveal the accusation she was feeling.

"That doesn't make them mine," he assured her. "I don't read rubbish like this and you shouldn't either."

"Me?" His comment provoked her sense of vulnerability and she stepped back. "I don't have to read it. I lived it. My father hid us away because of it."

"That he isolated you just because of red hair and green eyes was extreme." Rick said irritably. "And foolish."

Edwina gasped in outrage. No one ever said anything unkind about her father. "Foolish? How dare you? He was protecting us."

"You should never be hidden, Edwina."

"He didn't want—" She stopped abruptly. It probably did sound foolish to Rick because he didn't know it wasn't just because of their coloring. It was because they were triplets. "My father did what he thought was best for us."

"You wouldn't even know about these outdated ideas if you hadn't read it or if your father hadn't told you. I don't give a damn about other people's philosophies or positions, and I don't want you to either."

Rick sounded outraged and sincere. His words were logical, but she couldn't shake the uneasiness finding the books incited in her.

"Where did you get them?" Rick asked.

She looked down at the open drawer of the secretary.

Rick cleared his throat and let out a desperate huff. "I've never seen them before. There were over one hundred people in this house for the wedding. I don't know who put—" He swore another oath under his breath and winced. "But I have a good idea it was my mother who left them here."

Remembering that he told her his mother thought women with red hair and green eyes could read minds, Edwina said, "She almost dropped her champagne glass when she met my sisters."

"I thought she was going to faint. I understand my mother and know she means no real harm. She continues to feel she is protecting me as if I were still a small boy." He quickly opened the front cover of one of the books and there written in beautiful bold script was *This book belongs to the Duke of Stonerick.*

Rick blinked. Edwina felt as if the knot in her stomach started growing tentacles. They spread throughout her body and squeezed her tighter with each labored breath.

The silence seemed to stretch uncomfortably long before she lifted her gaze back to his and asked, "Were you lying to me about your inclinations?"

"What?" His eyes stayed steady on hers. "No, no, Edwina," he said vehemently. "Don't ever think that." He walked over and threw the books into the fireplace. They caught in the low flames with a *swoosh.*

He strode back to her and immediately swept her into his arms and held her tightly against his chest. He gazed deeply, earnestly into her eyes. "Listen to me. There have been two other Stonerick dukes in this house before me. Those books could have been my father's or his father's, but they are not mine."

The tension that had been choking her started relaxing. Her hands softened on his quilted white waistcoat and pressed against the fine linen of his neckcloth.

"I don't know how they came to be in my desk and it doesn't matter. What matters is that you trust me about my feelings on this."

His eyes were as clear as a summer day. Her breath was short and shallow. A sudden pain pricked her heart. Maybe this was the time to tell him the whole truth of her past. Maybe she could trust him to understand and actually believe they were as normal as any young lady. She opened her mouth to reveal everything to him, but his lips softly smothered her words with a kiss that vanished all thoughts from her mind except him.

Edwina's eyes closed as Rick's tongue tangled with hers. His arms tightened warm and strong around her. The passion that ignited between them was swift and undeniable. His palms molded over her hips, down to the curves of her bottom, and he drew her snugly to him as they kissed.

With nothing on her mind other than the amazing way Rick was making her feel, Edwina's hands roved over his back and shoulders, feeling the breadth and strength of him. His lips left moist kisses down her cheek, over her chin, and along the column of her neck and chest, and then up to cover her lips once more. Wrapped together in intimate passion, all seemed well with them, her sisters, and with the world.

"Do you like my kisses, Edwina?" he whispered huskily into her mouth.

"Yes." She liked them very much. They reminded her of the taste of honey, the scent of the woods, and the feel of sunshine on her face.

"Do they make you want more than kisses from me?"

Breathlessly she murmured another "Yes."

"And my caresses?" he asked with his lips still pressed against hers as he brought his hands around her waist and up her rib cage to her breasts to cup and fondle them with light pressure.

All her sense of feeling seemed to race to her breasts and burst with sensation. "Oh, yes, please. Yes."

But as she uttered the last word, his kisses stopped. His hands slid away from her body and he stepped back. Edwina's heart lurched, and she moistened her lips nervously as her chest heaved as if she'd been running. She focused enough to say, "Did I do something wrong?"

Rick smiled softly. "No. You did everything right."

That was hard to believe. "Then why did you stop kissing me, touching me?"

"Because I want you to know what it feels like to want me, Edwina." He caught her up to his chest again and looked deeply into her eyes, with mesmerizing detail. He bent his head and gave her a deep but short kiss. "I don't want you holding back or tamping down how I make you feel or what delights you. Enjoy and express it. I don't want you afraid of my touch, afraid to touch me. I want you to desire me with your whole being."

"I do," she managed to say past a tight throat.

She wanted his full attention right now. She reached up to wrap her arms around his neck, but Rick caught her arms and slowly took them back down to her sides. "I would love nothing better than continuing what we were doing, but it's time to get your sisters." He ran the tips of his fingers along her cheek and gave her a sweet smile. "We have a ball to attend."

CHAPTER 18

THE ART OF BEING A FINE GENTLEMAN
SIR DUDLEY SAMSON PEMBERTON FINE

*There will be times when a gentleman
has to be just a man.*

Edwina had no doubt the duke meant it when he said he wanted her to desire him. He had her senses careening out of control and her body still tingling as they started the short distance to the historic Great Hall Ballroom. Edwina and Rick sat forward in the carriage while Auntie, Eileen, and Elle were seated opposite as the horses clipped along at an easy pace.

The spacious coach was superbly finished in every detail. Its big wheels rolled over the hard-packed ground as smoothly as a sleigh would glide over freshly fallen snow. Deep-red velvet squabs were soft as goose-feathered pillows. Trimmed and framed with mahogany, the walls inside were overlaid with button-covered tufts of the same rich velvet. Matching draperies had been drawn away from the windows and held with gold-threaded tassels.

With her heartbeat starting to slow, Edwina wondered if she was as well-prepared and polished for their first ball as the duke's carriage.

Rick shifted his position on the seat beside her and

his arm grazed hers. Prickles of expectancy zinged deliciously over her, making her remember how enticing their kisses were just minutes ago. That set her heart to racing again. With flushed cheeks she glanced at Rick. He winked at her, assuring he had noticed the blush. But, along with the unmentionable emotions, that wasn't all she was experiencing. She felt great appreciation for the duke. Impatient as he was at times, he was kind to her and her sisters.

"What do you think Papa would say if he were sitting in this magnificent brougham with us?" Eleonora asked to no one in particular.

"He would say the same thing we are thinking," Eileen answered with a quirky smile. "How did Edwina manage to snare a duke when at most she hoped to catch the eye of a destitute poet who had a meager allowance but a soul kind enough to help take care of us?"

Rick glanced at Edwina with a wry grin. "A poet?"

She lifted her shoulders and sighed. "I was prepared to do whatever was necessary," she said honestly. "The viscount was adamant about washing his hands of us at the end of the Season."

"We don't want the truth, Edwina," Elle said, leaning forward. "We are far past that. We want something poetic and romantic about how the duke desired you above all others. Tell us how his hand casually brushed against yours. How his gaze searched for you across the distance in a room full of people and found you. Tell us how he makes you feel as if you are the only lady in the world who can make him happy."

"Elle, please," Eileen complained. "Enough of that kind of nonsense. I'm certain neither the duke nor Aunt Pauline want to be subjected to it either."

"Oh, I wouldn't mind hearing a bit more of it, dearie,"

Auntie said, perking up from her near dozing. "I thought that sounded quite nice, Eleonora. You should write it down and add it to your book."

That *was* very poetic of her sister, Edwina thought. Could it be that Elle was thinking about the possibility of love again even if she wasn't ready to admit it? Maybe this was the time to subtly mention the young gentleman Edwina saw eyeing Elle at the wedding. Edwina had wanted to talk to her about it before now, but with all that had happened between her and Rick since the wedding, she'd simply forgotten to do it.

"I'm sure all the gentlemen you saw or met at the wedding will be in attendance tonight, Elle. Perhaps there is one you are looking forward to seeing again."

Eleonora's brows rose slightly.

"I doubt that." Eileen gave a short laugh. "Most of them were the duke's mother's age and married."

"That's true, but not all of them," Edwina defended quickly, not wanting Eileen to dampen the bit of interest Elle was showing in a man.

The carriage rolled to a stop, leaving Edwina no time to continue her argument. The sound of music and hum of chatter and laughter were loud as they entered the grand, well-lit building. Edwina had read about the historic Grand Hall, but words couldn't possibly have prepared her for the lavishness. Shiny brass-and-crystal chandeliers lit the room while tall, wide mirrors hung on walls reflecting and scattering the candlelight. Everything shimmered as if gold and silver particles floated in the air, enhancing the glowing atmosphere.

The ceiling was painted a summer blue and framed by a wide stripe of gold. Puffs of white clouds and cherubs had been added to the scene and looked to be floating in the sky. Each small angel held a heart, harp, or bow. The heavenly scene was beautiful and whimsical.

Gilt-topped Corinthian columns enhanced the grandeur of the enormous room, each one decorated with streams of colorful ribbons and bows. Large urns filled with colorful flowers and different shades of ferns stood beside life-size statues of Greek gods and goddesses in every arched nook along the sides of the room.

The orchestra had assembled at the far end of a spacious dance floor, which was already swarming with beautiful ladies elaborately gowned in pastels and rich colors of gemstones. Every gentleman looked dapper, clad in black coats with tails, trousers, and waistcoats as white as their collars and neckcloths. They clapped, circled, and twirled to the lively quadrille as Edwina's mind tried to adjust to the outrageous ambiance and frenzied order of the room.

Edwina turned to Rick and realized he must have been watching her astonishment. His eyes sparkled with charm. Shyly, she said, "I guess you can tell I'm amazed by the elegance and splendor."

"Members of the ton expect extravagance, and the elite Society who maintains this place gives it to them."

Edwina glanced at her sisters and aunt. Their eyes were wide and expressions filled with awe. It was evident they were equally impressed by what was before them as they chatted together about the impressive room.

"I don't think we were prepared for the ballroom," Edwina added softly. "Just looking at the sketches in books, one's imagination can't comprehend how big and elaborate it is. Now that I'm here, I find I don't know what to do."

A soft, husky chuckle passed his attractive lips as he moved closer to her. In a low, slow, and enticing voice, he

said, "We are going to make sure your aunt is comfortable among the other widows and then we will line your
sisters up with dances to keep them occupied. You and I
are going to drink champagne." He bent close to her ear
and whispered, "I am going to touch you every chance I
get." He ran his thumb casually, unobtrusively across the
small space of bare skin on her arm between her capped
sleeve and long gloves.

Her stomach tightened.

He lowered his head even closer to hers, "And I'm
going to whisper how beautiful you are. How I can't wait
to get you home and make you mine."

She shivered, yet her skin heated. Yes, she wanted him
to do that.

"We're going to dance and I'm going to hold you so
close the gossips will be writing about how scandalous we
were in the tittle-tattle columns tomorrow."

The music stopped. The crowd clapped. Edwina
sucked in a deep breath. "You are no gentleman to say
things like that to me here and make me—"

"Feel guilty for knowing I want to kiss you right now?
That I desire you and no other lady in this room or anywhere else and that you desire me?"

Edwina smiled. What could she say? He spoke the
truth. Still, she was sure she shouldn't be feeling such sensations at a public event.

Rick gave her a knowing smile and turned to her
sisters. "Ladies, it's time we invade the ballroom. I see
Mr. David Culbreth and Mr. Oscar Mercy not far away.
Let's go meet them."

"Begging your pardon, Your Grace," Auntie said.
"Would it be all right if I excused myself?"

He nodded once. "We'll see you later in the evening."
He then whispered to Edwina, "I'm not going to be good

at pushing your sisters to get interested in the possibility of marriage, but I will get it done."

Rick led the three of them, one after the other, on a trail through the crush of people, bumping shoulders and nodding greetings until they made it to Mr. Mercy, where introductions were made. It was clear to Edwina the young man was delighted the duke had approached him. Edwina didn't see sparks of interest in Eleonora's or Eileen's eyes but there certainly was acute but nervous interest from Mr. Mercy. His eyes flitted from one sister to the other. To Edwina he seemed to be a happy person. He wasn't very tall or broad-shouldered but his smile was genuine and his dark-brown eyes seemed as gentle as a newborn puppy's.

Their chat had been brief when he said, "Miss Eileen, Miss Eleonora, I'd be pleased if you'd both save a dance for me this evening."

"I'm afraid I can't," Eileen responded immediately with a somewhat sad smile. "I'm having a slight problem with my ankle. Perhaps another evening."

He pressed his lips together and *tsk*ed. "I'm sorry to hear that, Miss Fine. I understand and hope you recover soon." He looked hopefully at Elle.

"Thank you for asking, Mr. Mercy, but I must decline a dance this evening as well. Another time."

As soon as the man excused himself, Edwina turned her perturbed face toward Rick. He nodded, so she looked at her sisters. "This is a ball. Why do you think Papa tutored us in dances from a quadrille to a cotillion and a waltz? You are dressed as fine as you will ever be. This is your night to show how beautiful and intelligent you are. You should have accepted a dance with Mr. Mercy."

"I find I can only think of Mr. Climperwell and how I would have enjoyed being here with him."

"That opportunity was taken from you," Edwina said, trying not to sound unsympathetic but fearing she might have. She looked at Eileen with the same determined fluster. "Your dream to visit and study with Mr. Herschel or his sister has not materialized either. It is time for you both to move on."

Eleonora looked away from Edwina and scanned the noisy, teeming room. Eileen stared solemnly at her.

As if knowing he couldn't add anything, Rick gave Edwina a quirk of his head and said, "This way. Mr. Culbreth is next."

The duke wasn't daunted by his mission. Suddenly, they were meeting one gentleman after another in the overly crowded and loud room. Edwina's exasperated words of encouragement hadn't helped. Over the course of an hour, her sisters gave the same excuse to every young man they met. Until the duke gave Edwina a weary smile and excused himself. So did Eileen, insisting she should check on Aunt Pauline.

Discouraged her sisters were not obliging or even cooperating a little, Edwina turned to ask Eleonora if she wanted to rest in the ladies' retiring room to get away from the music, chatter, and laughter, but stopped before speaking. Elle was looking with starry-eyed wonder at the tall, strapping young man from the wedding. He was looking the same way at her.

"Do you know that gentleman, Eleonora?" she asked.

"We met at the wedding and chatted for a while," her sister answered. "Not long because we hadn't been introduced and I was afraid I'd get caught talking with him."

Edwina had no idea who he was even though he had been at her wedding. He was almost as handsome as Rick. Perhaps as tall but not as wide-chested and maybe a couple of years younger. One thing was clear: He was definitely interested in her sister. For the second time. She watched his gaze as it swept up and down Elle's face as he smiled at her. Suddenly, he was making his way through the crowd and straight toward them.

"That was the right thing for you to do, Elle. Rules are not as lax here as they were in York. I think he might have left before introductions were made."

"He has such an attractive and confident swing to his shoulders." The dreamy-eyed look stayed on Elle's face. "And such a strong and daring look in his eyes."

Her sister had noticed a lot about the man if indeed it was only a short time they talked. The man didn't take his eyes off Elle or stop until he stood in front of them, bowed, and said, "Your Grace, please excuse my manners in approaching you. I don't know if you remember me, but we were introduced at your wedding. I am Mr. Matthew Malcolm."

Edwina's chin dipped and she pursed her lips. Society's rules were strict about introductions, and she didn't want to break any at her first ball, but she was sure they hadn't met. However, she was willing to give him the benefit of doubt since she was certain he had attended the wedding, and Elle was so interested she'd talked to him. "I met many people that day, Mr. Malcolm."

"I understand." He looked at Eleonora and then back to Edwina. "I was hoping you wouldn't mind introducing me to your sister. If I'm not being too forward."

Neither Elle nor Mr. Malcolm had taken the smiles off their faces since they saw each other from opposite sides of the room. She had to do the honors and proceeded to make their introduction official.

"Miss Eleonora, might I say you are the loveliest young lady here tonight." He quickly glanced at Edwina.

"With apologies, Your Grace, you both are the loveliest ladies here tonight."

Edwina smiled at his amended comment. It warmed Edwina's heart to see Elle engaged with a young man again, and one who was immediately taken with her too. This was the reason Edwina had come to the ball.

"A dance is starting soon, Your Grace. May I have permission to ask Miss Eleonora?"

Edwina nodded and, before she knew it, her sister was walking toward the dance floor with the young man. As they took their place in line, she watched as they continued to look at each other with such ease and talk as they waited for the music to begin.

"Why are you here by yourself?" Rick asked as he appeared at Edwina's side. His eyes lit with humor. "Both your sisters have deserted you already?"

"Yes," she admitted with an easy breath and feeling quite pleased. "As it happens, Eleonora is having her first dance."

"What?" He glanced toward the dancers. "I don't see them. With whom?"

Before she could answer, Rick's face twisted into a scowl and his whole body tensed.

"Why do you have such a grimace?" she asked. "I think this might have been love at first sight."

"No, hellfire, it wasn't," he murmured under his breath.

The low calm in his voice was cause for worry. "They were taken with each other from first sight. He seemed very sincere about everything he said."

"And I know why," Rick answered testily. "I'm sure he was delighted to ask her to dance. Why did you give her permission?"

"I didn't mind," she answered truthfully. "He asked, she accepted." Edwina caught sight of them again. They were laughing and having a wonderful time with the fast quadrille. What's more, with her so beautiful and him so handsome, they were perfectly matched. "What's wrong?"

Rick glared at her. "I don't want him anywhere near one of my sisters."

CHAPTER 19

THE ART OF BEING A FINE GENTLEMAN
SIR DUDLEY SAMSON PEMBERTON FINE

*It is always a man's duty,
under any circumstance,
to protect a lady.*

The music was loud and lively, and the room hot. Laughter and the constant roar of chatter from the packed crowd, and not yet having a dance with Edwina was making Rick irritable enough. Now he had to contend with Malcolm too. The man was proving to be a bad penny.

Rick swallowed the impulse to stomp over and usher Eleonora off the dance floor while telling the buck to never go near her again. Such an action wouldn't bother Rick, but it would humiliate Elle and, more importantly, Edwina. So, he stood still and fumed.

"Why isn't he suitable?" Edwina pressed curiously. "Is he a ne'er-do-well?"

"No," Rick said, keeping his aggravation in check. He assumed, because of the man's behavior at the shooting match, he merely wanted to dance with Eleonora because he knew it would rile Rick. "He's the younger son of Lord Derrybrooke, but acts as if he's the heir apparent."

Edwina shrugged a little. "That doesn't sound as if it

would be something to raise your ire. It's wonderful that someone of such prestige might have designs on Elle. Does he cheat with cards? Drink excessively on many occasions? Does he ruin the reputations of innocent young ladies?"

"Not that I'm aware of," Rick was forced to admit, but he had other vices. Like inviting Rick to enjoy his favorite tavern wench. "I heard he's recently back from his tour of Europe and hasn't been in London long."

"That could explain why he was a little forward and presumed we had been introduced at the wedding."

"Really, Edwina?" Rick interrupted with a low edge to his voice, staring at her in disbelief. "You let him get by with that arrogance? And allowed Eleonora to dance with him?"

"They had already chatted at the wedding and took an immediate liking to each other." She pinned him with an amused stare. "Do you really want to talk about someone breaking the rules of Society, Your Grace?"

"Yes," he said succinctly and without a hint of doubt.

"Then look at yourself first." Her chin lifted with a confident tilt. "You picked my name from a list, and your first kiss to me was definitely breaking the rules."

Maybe.

A boisterously talking man, who must have been moving his arms as he spoke, bumped Rick's shoulder, mumbled an apology, and went immediately back to his loud conversation. Rick touched Edwina's arm, and they moved closer to the wall and away from the people who were standing nearby.

"That was different, Edwina, and you know it. We were already betrothed and I was trying to help you get your sisters to London."

She gave him a satisfied smile. "Which you did."

Rick grunted. His beautiful wife didn't seem to be taking this seriously. "Mr. Malcolm is cocky, self-indulgent, and given to debauchery. He doesn't know how to win with honor or leave well enough alone." That was about as nice as Rick could make his objections. He wanted to add that the buck spent time in popular but unsavory gaming hells rather than gentlemen clubs, and with taproom wenches rather than more discriminating mistresses, as would most men with a generous allowance and a titled family member. If that wasn't enough, he was too damned young to consider marriage to anyone.

Edwina clasped her hands together in front of her and looked around the room for a brief time as if to gather her thoughts before speaking. "I have to admit those are not admirable qualities. My father wrote that bragging wasn't so bad in a young man. It takes time to mature and gain . . ."

The muscles in Rick's neck felt as if they were tied into a thousand knots. "This really isn't the time to mention your father to me, Edwina," he snapped. "I realize if he were here, he'd be handling Eleonora and Eileen differently from me."

Edwina seemed to consider her words again as she took a step back. "You're right," she answered calmly. "I only meant Mr. Malcolm seemed to be a gentleman who saw a young lady he caught a fancy for. He's not pursuing her yet. He is dancing with her—and in front of everyone, I might add."

Rick sucked in a calming breath. He simply didn't like the man and couldn't hide that fact. Some of his ill will toward Malcolm could have to do with the fact Rick missed the shot against him, causing the upstart to win, but it was more than that. Rick never boasted about his wins. When you were good, you didn't have to. Others would do it for you. He didn't like the noisy mass of people that seemed to be inching closer to them either.

"She's been denying dances all night. I turn my back for one minute, and she's twirling around with a restless buck who by no means is ready for marriage, but only to sow his seeds. It's irritating, Edwina. She needs to set her cap for a more settled gentleman, like Mr. Mercy."

"There was clearly no connection between her and Mr. Mercy and you know it." She paused, and then gave him a beautiful teasing smile. "Not like you and I had when we first met."

Rick's stomach tightened and reminded him how attracted he was to her before he even saw her face. The corners of his mouth eased up at the reminder. She was right. His voice softened as he said, "Now you are being unfair to use our situation against my argument."

"Perhaps." She took a satisfied breath. "While Mr. Malcolm might be a young man, how do you know he's not ready for marriage?"

"This isn't something you want to argue about with me, Edwina. I've heard him and his friends talk. I don't trust him to be the kind of gentleman he should be with her."

Edwina lowered her lashes, relaxed her shoulders, and sighed softly. Rick saw she was trying to hide her disappointment that he didn't have high expectations for Malcolm.

"Edwina, I am trying to do right by your sisters," he said in a softer tone. He stepped closer to her, realizing the natural flow of the crowd seemed to be advancing on them again. "I admit when you told me the stipulation of our getting married was that you wanted my help in finding your sisters husbands, it sounded like a chore I could do with my eyes closed. I have the money to plump their dowries and get the job accomplished. But now, I don't want to just do what is easy and convenient. I want what is best for them."

"I know and I am grateful," she admitted softly. "Since you're worried about his character and suitability, I'll quiz her about him when she finishes the second set."

"Don't do that," he said. "Wait until tomorrow. You don't want to ruin her night."

"Am I interrupting anything?"

At the sound of the dowager's voice, Rick turned to his mother and the two of them greeted her.

"Your timing is perfect, Maman," Rick said, happy to get the conversation away from Malcolm. "Do you know how two books on superstitions happened to be on my secretary in the drawing room?"

Her lashes fluttered innocently. "Is that where I left them? I wondered about that after I got home."

Her tone and expression were so guileless Rick turned to Edwina and smiled.

"I was borrowing them from your library, my dear. I knew you wouldn't mind." Her brows knitted closely together in concern. "You don't, do you?"

"No," was all he said, knowing the books were now ashes.

"I remembered your grandfather had a penchant for reading different kinds of books, so I plundered your shelves and found a couple that might interest me. I'll get them another time."

Rick glanced at Edwina again before looking over at his mother and saying, "I was just going to find out when the next waltz is to be played, Maman. I've promised my wife a dance. You don't mind chatting with her and keeping her company for a few minutes, do you?"

Alberta's brow rose gently. "The mother of my future grandson? I should hope not. I look forward to getting to know the duchess. Go, we'll wait here for you."

Rick forged a path through the people without stopping to speak to anyone. It was a duke's preference to choose whether a conversation was started. Right now, he wanted to ask about the next waltz and then get out of the crammed room for some fresh air.

After checking the time of the dance, Rick strode through the open double doors that led out to the back garden. Several couples stood close together in various parts of the lighted grounds. Having no desire to witness lovers whispering to each other, he walked past the aged Cupid fountain that centered the courtyard to where more people were taking advantage of being away from the overflowing ballroom.

If not for Edwina and her sisters, he would have already left the ball. Out of respect for Society, and his mother, he attended the affairs he was invited to, but seldom stayed long. Crowds always pulled in memories he'd tried to rein in long ago when he was a child. He'd see the servants crowding him—three, four, five and more at a time. Asking him, *"What do you want to eat? Sweet confections? Sliced apricots? What do you want to do? Ride a horse? Roam the woods? Where do you want to go? Skating on the frozen pond?"*

No, no. He just wanted them to go away and leave him alone. Their voices would get louder, their bodies closer, and their words would mingle together as they fought to be heard and be the one to find out what he wanted. Rick would keep backing up until his head and elbows were against the wall and he had nowhere to go. That is when he would lose his patience, push through the lot of them, and rush outside so he could breathe.

Rick stopped walking and pulled a hand restlessly through his hair a couple of times. The chill of the night air suited him. A half-moon lit the sky. His chest felt tight so he drew in one long breath after the other. Tension in his muscles subsided and Edwina came easily to his mind.

That was no surprise. She had dominated his thoughts since he'd met her. Even more so now that she was his wife. Still in name only, but not for long. Now that he knew the reason for her actions was a maid who was very wrong in her advice.

Rick didn't like arguing with Edwina. Not about superstitions, not about her sisters, and certainly not about Malcolm. Why couldn't she just accept what he said about the man and let that be the end of it? He remembered how she'd stood her ground with Palmer that day in the vestibule and smiled. It wasn't her nature to simply accept someone's word about anything. That was another one of her traits he wanted his son to have.

In the distance, he saw a lady standing alone, gazing up at the few stars that could be seen. He didn't see anyone with her. A lady shouldn't be out alone. He headed her way to see if anything was wrong, and as he got closer, realized it was Eileen.

He picked up his pace, hurried over, and asked, "Eileen, is something the matter?"

"No," she answered innocently.

"Then what the devil are you doing out here?"

She met his worry with a smile. "It's the clearest night we've had since I've been here. I'm enjoying the heavens. Do you mind?"

"Yes," he grumbled on an exasperated breath. "You can't wander around out here on your own."

She laughed softly. "Which would you rather, Your

Grace? For me to be out here by myself or be out here with a gentleman?"

"Either one will ruin your reputation," he argued. "Get yourself inside."

Crossing her arms over her chest in defiance, she asked, "Did Edwina or Aunt Pauline send you looking for me?"

"No, though one of them should be wondering where you are. How long have you been out here?"

"Not long." She looked toward the brightly lit Great Hall. "It is hot, stuffy, and filled with people I prefer not to meet. They are excited about dancing, fashion, and what others are wearing or saying. I am not interested in any of those things." She looked at him imploringly. "Can I stay out here now that you are with me?"

He scoffed. "I am not a chaperone."

"And I am not a Society lady. Tonight proves this kind of life is not for me." She waved her hand toward the lighted building. "Edwina will be happy in this life. Elle will do fine too. I would rather be out here even if I can't see as many stars or constellations as I could see in York. Papa's old telescope is of no use with all the lights."

"The Stonerick estate would be a good place for you to visit and watch the stars. Most any man you marry would have either an estate in the country or have access to one by a family member."

"I want to visit Mr. Frederick Herschel's Observatory House in Slough and look through his telescope." She shrugged and looked away for a moment. "I've written him letters. Not that he has replied to any of them. I always hope that one day he will."

"I've read about his discoveries, but we can have that discussion another time. You need to get inside. Perhaps you should search for gentlemen in the ballroom as carefully as you search the stars."

He started to steer her back toward the ball but only took a few steps before she stopped and turned to him. "As a duke, you have more privileges than most. Have you ever met Mr. Herschel?"

Rick shook his head as he stopped too. "His life is far different from mine."

Eileen smiled. "Do you ever imagine what it must be like to see the end of the sky?"

Rick grunted a laugh as he shook his head and tried to be tolerant of her lofty aspirations.

"I can't envision how big the stars might be," she continued. "Mr. Herschel has discovered, studied, and plotted many of them. His sister helps with documenting his research as well as making discoveries on her own. I want to talk with her and perhaps assist with her notes. I have a nice hand and I'm quite fast."

"An admirable goal, but she probably has all the help she needs from many qualified people."

"How will I know if I don't ask?" she whispered, sounding almost encouraged. "I wish you had met him so you could make an introduction for me. He's written many articles." She pressed her lips together for a moment. "I haven't read any of the more recent ones. When Papa fell ill, he wasn't where he could get the interest to find copies for me."

Rick felt a pang of sadness for her. She aspired to do something far different from what her father or Edwina envisioned for her, and he wondered if a young lady should be forced to marry if she didn't want to. That seemed restrictive considering they were nearly twenty years into the new century. Nevertheless, he couldn't allow her thirst for knowledge to direct her to unsafe places that would damage her reputation or place her in danger. Under his household and protection there were certain rules all ladies had to follow.

Hearing voices nearby, Rick looked behind him. As if from nowhere, he saw Mr. and Mrs. Everly Smith walking toward them.

Hell's gate! First Malcolm and now this. What was going to happen next? He didn't need to be seen in the darkest area of the garden with his wife's sister. He should have made her go back inside immediately instead of listening to her woes.

"The couple coming toward us will expect me to acknowledge them but I don't have to stop and speak. Just act natural and smile at them as we pass."

"Yes, of course. I don't want there to be a scandal about being out here. Especially with you."

He swallowed down his frustration. "It's you I'm worried about, Eileen. Not me."

They started walking and as they met the couple, he nodded and said, "Good evening, Mrs. Smith. Mr. Smith."

"Good evening Stonerick, Duchess," the man spoke first and then the lady mirrored his words.

A few steps past the couple, Rick heard a suppressed childish giggle.

"What are you doing?" he asked irritably. "This is not a humorous situation you are in."

"Of course, it is." She laughed softly again. "They thought I was Edwina and called me Duchess."

"I heard," he mumbled.

When they made it back to the Cupid fountain, Rick stopped. "Make your way back inside from here. I'll come in a little later."

She smiled and, for the first time, Rick realized it really wasn't like Edwina's smile at all. Eileen's was more cunning in a determined way. In fact, he was learning all three of the sisters were very different.

"Thank you for listening to me about Mr. Herschel and his sister."

Rick was not going to get drawn into another conversation with her and have someone else see them together. She had been mistaken for Edwina once, but he wouldn't press his luck.

"No more talk, Eileen. No more wandering off anywhere without one of your sisters or your aunt by your side. Don't stand here, go."

Rick watched Eileen turn and stomp off toward the open doorway of the ballroom. No wonder Lord Quintingham wanted to wash his hands of three young ladies of marriageable age. Getting them married wasn't going to be as easy as he thought. One seemed to be taken with a reckless blade, the other worried about not being able to see the stars, and his wife was still not his wife.

He didn't understand either of the sisters. But he was beginning to understand why Edwina had been chosen to take charge of them. Her father must not have trusted the other two to do it.

Edwina had a goal and it hadn't wavered. She was fighting hard to attain it. A worthy goal for a younger sister to take on. He admired her for that and should tell her. And maybe he shouldn't have been so rigid about Malcolm. He could understand why Eleonora would be more attracted to the strapping youth with a cocky smile than the older, settled Mr. Mercy.

But Rick hadn't reached his goal either. He had a wife he wanted but not an heir on the way. He had wooed Edwina today, but he had also argued with her. He smiled to himself. Wooing was much better. His words might have sounded like anger, but he hoped it was annoyance she heard in his tone. No matter. He intended to forget Edwina's sisters' issues and continue pursuing his wife.

He watched Eileen disappear inside and headed toward the ballroom himself. It was time to dance with his wife. When he was about to step inside, Malcolm came out and they almost bumped into each other.

They both stepped back. Malcolm quickly bowed. "My apologies, Your Grace."

Rick had wondered what else was going to happen tonight. Now he knew. The bad penny. "None needed Mr. Malcolm, however you can do me a favor and not go near my sister again." Rick turned to continue inside.

"Asking your pardon, Your Grace. I've already asked if I could call on her tomorrow for a ride in the park and she agreed."

Rick turned around slowly. The buck's voice had a slight tremble. His cocky smile was gone and in its place was a sober expression. Rick was happy to see the over-confident attitude he had on the day of their shooting match was gone, but he hadn't expected him to appear lacking courage.

"But I don't give my permission and I am her guardian."

His Adam's apple bobbed as he clearly swallowed hard. "Her sister, the duchess, agreed she could go as well."

What was Edwina thinking? After all Rick told her about this man, she gave permission for a romp around the park?

"She is the most beautiful young lady I've ever seen, Your Grace. I watched her at the wedding and tonight."

Rick took a step toward him. "You watched her?"

Malcolm's expression brightened and he held up his hands in a show of submission. "Not in a wicked way, Your Grace. I'm quite taken with her. I would never do anything to disrespect her."

Another stride took Rick toe to toe with the blade. "We are clear on that last statement. I am the one who has say as to whom she courts, Malcolm. You are young, wild, and not ready to settle down."

"I'm not denying I have fun with my friends after a shooting match and when we are about Town, but I would never mistreat a lady."

Rick gave him a critical eye. The buck seemed sincere, but then Rick remembered the ribald invitation to join him at the tavern.

"I am looking for her husband."

Malcolm jerked back a little, and quickly said, "Then I would like to be considered. I knew she was the lady for me the moment I saw her at your house. I'll court her properly and earn your respect."

"You can dance with her at parties and balls but there will be no rides in the park. I'll tell her in the morning that you won't be calling on her tomorrow."

Rick turned away. He had to talk to Edwina. And she had to decide if she wanted *him* to find her sisters husbands or whether *she* wanted to do it. It wasn't working with the two of them sharing the duty.

The music wasn't any softer as he entered but the crowd had thinned and the roar had settled to more of a hum. Edwina was with his mother. Only now her two sisters, Hurst, Wyatt, and Fredericka had joined them. Obviously, it wasn't the time for a talk with Edwina about who was in charge of making matches for her sisters. He wanted to woo her, not anger her.

As he approached everyone he watched the way Wyatt and Fredericka were interacting with each other. He could probably use a little friendly advice about wives from his friend. From the loving way Wyatt looked at Fredericka, it didn't appear he'd ever had a cross word with her.

Rick spoke to everyone before positioning himself close enough to Edwina that his arm brushed against hers. She was quiet and beautiful as she gave him an appreciative glance.

"So nice of you to join us, Your Grace," his mother offered in her usual formal manner. "I was just saying there's a lady in my new group, the Insightful Ladies of London Society, who is a stargazer and knows all about the alignment of planets. I'd be happy for Miss Fine to be my guest at a future meeting."

"That is not what I study, Your Grace," Eileen offered politely.

His mother looked confused for a moment. "Oh, but I thought you said you studied the stars."

"And planets, but for scientific reasons," she answered.

"We are still quite busy getting settled in London," Edwina added, stepping gently into the conversation.

"When your sisters are more settled, Edwina, perhaps I can be of help," Fredericka offered. "I'll be happy to ask among my friends if they know of a group that might be suitable for your sister."

"That would be wonderful," Edwina answered.

Rick was about to tell Edwina it was time for their dance when the Countess of Middleton walked up beside his mother.

"Your Graces, please excuse me for interrupting."

As the lady curtsied and exchanged greetings with

everyone, Rick took the opportunity to speak in a low voice to Edwina. "I've decided you are quite stunning when you are upset with me."

She stared at him with a softness that made his whole body respond with desire. "Only when I'm perturbed by your unreasonableness?"

He chuckled softly. "I stand corrected. I should have said you are always the most beautiful lady I have ever seen."

A wispy laugh passed Edwina's beautiful lips. "You are handsome all the time too, Your Grace—angry, impatient, or sweet."

He gave her a wry expression. "Sweet? I don't think so. I've never been called sweet and it's not in my nature."

She smiled at him and Rick felt as if his heart had turned over in his chest as she said, "You have been sweet to me several times."

It pleased Rick that she easily forgave him for being unpleasant earlier.

"I think you owe me a dance," she said softly.

Before he could respond, Lady Middleton looked specifically at Edwina and said, "Please excuse me, Duchess, but I'm hoping I might have a word with you."

Edwina gave Rick a tentative grin before giving the woman her attention. "Yes, of course."

"Something has been puzzling me since we were introduced at the wedding. When I saw the three of you together again tonight, I figured out what it was and thought this is the perfect time to ask."

Rick felt Edwina stiffen beside him. She remained still and quiet, waiting for the countess to proceed. That gave him pause. Something was wrong. For some reason, Edwina was instantly wary of this lady, and he didn't know why. Whatever it was didn't matter; his primal urge to protect his wife rose in him. He instinctively moved closer to her.

"The way you and your sisters favor and appear the same age brought to my mind a rumor I heard about twenty years ago of a lady who gave birth to three babes and then fled London. Of course, it was so fantastical none of us believed it and I haven't even thought about it in years. Looking at the three of you with your distinctive coloring and eyes—" she paused and gave a faltered laugh. "I felt I must ask if the rumor might indeed have been true and you three could possibly be the triplets I heard about so long ago?"

Rick heard his mother gasp softly, but he didn't take his eyes off Edwina's tight expression of friendliness. He felt a shiver of apprehension wash over her as what the countess said sunk in.

Triplets?

It couldn't be. No. It wasn't possible. Was it? But it would explain why they looked so much alike. And the same age too. Rick's throat tightened and his mind clogged with questions he had no answers to. He felt as if an iron weight had fallen on his chest and he couldn't lift it off. She turned and met his gaze.

It was true. He saw it in her eyes. And she had kept it from him. Deception hit him like a sucker punch to the nose.

Edwina kept her composure though her eyes were deeply troubled. She swallowed hard, and he knew she was struggling over what her answer to the countess and to him would be. She had the same fragile vulnerability he'd seen when she waited to hear if his proposal was genuine or a fraud. That was when he realized she wasn't as brave as she'd pretended to be. Something in her past had affected her deeply. Now he believed he knew what it was.

His gut tightened as he tried to sort out exactly what he was feeling for her.

One thing he knew for sure, it was fine if Edwina felt defenseless with him, but hell no, he wasn't going to allow this meddler or anyone else to make her feel that way. Edwina had kept this a secret from him for a reason, and he wanted to know why. But his priority was to protect her. He couldn't let her admit anything to this lady.

"I can answer that for you, Countess," Rick said calmly, leaning his shoulder closer to Edwina's so she could feel him. "They are sisters. Miss Eileen Fine is the oldest. Next is Miss Eleonora, and the duchess is the youngest. They do favor. I can see where you might have hoped for a different outcome to *your* gossip."

The lady's brows rose as she made a coughing sound. "Oh, well, yes, of course," she sputtered as she smiled at him. "I didn't mean to imply the rumor was true. No, no. I only mentioned it in humor."

"I don't think they look much alike," Wyatt said in an offhanded manner as he stared at the countess. "Miss Fine has freckles." He quickly looked at Eileen and flashed a worried grin. "But lovely freckles."

Rick sent Wyatt a thankful glance.

"Imagine what a story that would have been had it been true," Fredericka added with a light laugh. "Triplets born and all lived. It would have made all the newsprints and people would still be talking about it to this day if it had been true."

"Gossip never really dies, does it?" Hurst stepped up to offer his support too. "It simply lurks in the dark shadows of human minds and waits for a possibility to shine again. But perhaps this is one we can put to rest for good, Countess. And never hear of it again."

Rick looked at Edwina, but she was looking at his mother. He knew what she was thinking because of her superstitious leanings. *The others are supporting me but will his mother?* Rick wasn't worried. His mother always protected the title. She would never allow scandal to touch her family. Especially the mother of the next heir to the title. However, Edwina didn't know that.

"I should think so," his mother offered with the most indignation he'd seen or heard from her in years. "I don't know what to think when favoring one's sisters has become so unfashionable as to be open for gossip or ridicule, Lady Middleton. Perhaps the French started it. They adore creating new fashions and I suppose sisters looking alike is a new one."

Rick approved of his mother's answer. He knew her well. She hadn't made up her mind whether she believed what the countess had said, but that didn't matter. The countess had committed an unpardonable breach of manners the dowager would never forgive or forget. She had passed on gossip about the dowager's family.

The countess looked from Rick to the other two dukes and then to the dowager with a strained expression. "Yes, of course," she acquiesced without any trouble. "I can clearly see now that Miss Fine does look older. Excuse me for only wanting to engage in simple conversation, Your Graces. Not gossip."

Returning his attention to Edwina, her expression told him the rumor was fact. Astounding as it was, Edwina was one born of three? Why had she hidden it from him and not told him before they married? She had to know it was something he'd want to know when considering a wife—the mother of his heir.

He couldn't wait to find out, but for now they were all united. He would leave his mother to handle the countess. Rick smiled at Edwina as he took her hand and led her toward the dance floor.

CHAPTER 20

THE ART OF BEING A FINE GENTLEMAN
SIR DUDLEY SAMSON PEMBERTON FINE

*If a gentleman feels he has been misled by a lady,
no matter the circumstance or offense,
he must always accept the occurrence as unintentional.*

It had been a miserable ride home from the ball. Everyone inside the carriage had been quiet as it rolled along the empty streets. Rick sat still beside Edwina. Eileen looked out one window and Eleonora the other. Aunt Pauline spent the time dozing between the two of them and was unaware the secret of the triplets had been let out into the open only to be quickly swept back into the abyss of darkness again by the duke, his mother, and his friends.

Now as they stood in the vestibule removing their wraps and scarves, Auntie was the only one who chatted away about how much she enjoyed the evening of renewing acquaintances with old friends and watching the dancing. Edwina couldn't stop glancing at Rick and caught him eyeing her pensively too.

How could she have ever imagined he would hear the truth at a ball? She felt undeserving of Rick's immediate defense of her and her sisters. And then to have his friends and mother stand up for them too had almost brought her to tears in front of everyone. When confronted, she was ready to admit the truth to him, the countess, all of them, and get the burden off her shoulders and put behind her. She couldn't have foreseen Rick denying the truth before she could confirm it. Once he'd done that, she couldn't contradict him in front of her accuser. She had to let his answer stand.

Nonetheless, there was no doubt she read in his face that he knew the truth.

Ever since the countess had walked away from them, and through the tense waltz with Rick, Edwina had been fighting the threat of panic that wanted to overtake her. Quite smartly, Eleonora had claimed she'd once again overindulged in too much champagne, which Edwina knew she hadn't, and asked if they might hurry home. The duke agreed to call for the carriage.

"Are we going to talk about what happened tonight?" Eileen whispered to Edwina in a low voice.

"Not now," Edwina answered just as softly. "I need to talk to the duke first." Although he had stood up for her without foreknowledge or questions, she was sure he was going to have plenty to say to her privately.

The girls and Auntie said their good nights, and Edwina shored up her courage and turned to the duke. "I know you have a lot of questions."

"I'll see you upstairs in a few minutes," he said in an even tone, avoiding eye contact with her.

Anxiety filled her. "Of course," she answered softly, wondering how long he might want to avoid the conversation. "I'll be waiting."

Edwina hurried up to her chambers where Henrietta waited to help her out of her stays before retiring to her own room. After donning the sleeveless white nightshift the duke had asked her to wear, Edwina walked over to her dressing table and eased down on the stool. The fire had been banked and the room was chilled. Lamps burned on the dressing and bedside tables, but they added no warmth to the air.

She knew Rick wanted answers. Which she was willing to give, but could he understand the simplicity of them? They weren't complicated, filled with details, or even mysterious. Now that it had come to this, she wished he'd been the one to ask her if they were triplets so she could have told him when they were alone. It wasn't fair he had to hear it from someone else and in front of other people, but once spilled on a table, milk couldn't be returned to the cup.

Edwina was attracted to him from their first conversation. It might not have been a fleeting spark of love at first sight for her, but certainly attraction and longing desire, which she didn't even know existed until meeting the duke. She had never experienced the wanting to be held so close and kissed by a man until Rick. Perhaps there was never the time, or the man, but one thing was sure: She didn't want to lose him.

With a trembling hand, she started tugging the brush through her hair. She hadn't slept without a nightcap for many years but doing so was an easy thing to do for Rick when he'd done so much for her. Thinking a braid would be the best way to contain her long curls, she set about lacing three separate strands together as she mulled over the thoughts of how the conversation with Rick would start. Anger was a good bet even though she hadn't seen it in his expression or heard it in his voice. Confusion was a possibility. Disappointment. Perhaps all three. Condemnation, accusations, and much more.

There had always been the chance this would happen

but now it was real. The ramifications, whatever they may be, felt like a devastating blow to her chest.

A soft knock sounded on the door between their rooms and it opened immediately. Edwina's stomach jerked and tightened. With an uptick in her already racing heart, she quickly finished tying the ribbon at the bottom of her plait, rose, and turned to face him.

Stripped down to his white linen shirt, opened down the front, and tucked into the waistband of his well-fitted black trousers, she stared at him with awe. With his broad shoulders, tapered waist, and muscular thighs, he had to be the most powerfully built man who lived. Even in bare feet with hair that looked mussed, he appeared as strong as all the mighty warriors she had ever read about.

When their gazes met across the room, she wondered if she had the strength to fight for him. He looked at her with such questioning eyes she wasn't sure. Her greatest fear wasn't how he would react to her revealing news but that she would lose him, and that he would never take her to his bed as his wife. She wanted the chance to feel his kisses and touch without having to repress and deny all the wonderful stirrings in her body. She wanted to lie in bed with him and respond to his every touch, and more than anything, she wanted to give him a strong, healthy son.

All the different feelings she'd had for him since they'd met now made sense—how his kisses made her feel, and why she was eager to see him and spend time with him even when he was grumpy. Could it be that she was falling in love with him the way a wife should love her husband? All of him. His irritability and impatience, his kindness, and his caressing touch. Everything. Light from his room shined brightly into hers. There would be no hiding from him tonight. Edwina had to face Rick with the decision she, her father, and sisters made long ago, and accept the consequences of keeping silent about the truth.

Would he ask her and her sisters to leave the house, banish them to a small cottage on one of his estates, or—worst of all—file for an annulment on grounds the marriage hadn't been consummated? That was a very real possibility she couldn't bear to contemplate.

Inhaling a deep breath, she continued to meet his steady blue gaze, but didn't know what to make of his expression. There was no anger or disappointment in his features as she had expected. He didn't even seem perplexed. He looked resolute. That made her shiver more than the chill in the room.

Staring at him, knowing how she felt about him, an unwavering strength came over her and settled in her bones. No matter how he chose to deal with this information, she had to match him and remain resolute too.

Quietly, he said, "Why didn't you trust me with the truth of your birth?"

Trust?

Edwina's heart skipped a beat. Maybe two or three. Of all the things she'd thought he might say or ask, that wasn't one of them. It wasn't an emotion she'd thought about when considering her birth.

"It wasn't that I didn't trust you."

"Really?" He walked farther into the room and stopped near the foot of her bed where she could clearly see him. He lifted his hands in exasperation and then dropped them to his sides. "Explain that to me, Edwina."

"I trusted you with the proposal letter you sent to me." She felt her voice growing stronger. "I handed it to you.

You could have thrown it in the fire. My claim would have vanished quickly and no one would have ever been the wiser."

He nodded. "Yet, you didn't trust me with this."

"My father . . ." Rick's eyes narrowed tightly and he flinched when she mentioned her father. She hesitated, cleared her throat, and continued. "It was Papa's instructions that it wouldn't be talked about among us or with anyone else. To his knowledge, there was no written record of triplets ever living to adulthood that he could find. No one assumes we are triplets because it's never happened before. He told us not to lie if ever we were asked about it but to never offer the information to anyone, and to live as all young ladies do."

Rick nodded and looked around the room before settling his troubled gaze on her again. "Are you sure that was supposed to include prospective husbands?" he asked callously.

"Quite sure," she added, feeling a bit of ire at his tone, though she knew it was justified. "Anyone. Everyone. It should never be mentioned."

He grunted a laugh and shook his head painfully slow before his gaze locked on hers once again.

"I find that almost irrational."

Her father was not an irrational man, but she chose not to have that argument on top of the current one. "Perhaps," she decided to agree, sadly, but what was her father to do other than what he thought was best to try to keep his daughters safe? "After so many years of shielding us from most of society, it was his desire that we be treated as any other young lady with sisters. While growing up he didn't want us to suffer from extreme cruelties that might happen if anyone knew about the rarity of our birth. I know you are angry with me, but I stand by what I did."

He scoffed another half laugh as his eyes stayed on her face. "I don't know what I'm feeling right now, but anger is certainly part of it. That first day we met I kept having feelings of suspicion about you. I felt you were hiding something."

She winced at the honesty of his words.

"I sensed there was more to you than what you were saying or I was seeing. I allowed my infatuation with you and other things that were weighing on my mind to keep me from delving into what was bothering me. There was an innocent boldness about you that overruled my misgivings. And all the time my first reaction to you was correct. You were hiding something from me—by omission, if nothing else."

His words wounded her again. Could he stay married to a wife he couldn't trust? Would he truly consider annulment?

"No," she said firmly, and with much trepidation. She moved away from the dressing area to step closer to him. She wrapped her hands around her chilled upper arms. "I did not hide the truth of my birth from you. Hiding and not telling if asked are two different things."

He shifted his stance and placed his hands on his hips. "I'm not believing that right now, Edwina."

"It's true," she insisted.

"Call it whatever you wish. You hid it by omission."

"I simply withheld the details of our birth."

Frustration etched his handsome features. He touched his chest with his thumb. "Whichever word you chose, don't you think that was something I'd like to know before I agreed to marry you?"

His words stung as if hundreds of bees had swarmed her. It hurt that he was right, but she couldn't let his question stand without answer.

She exhaled a choppy breath and moved restlessly. "I was under no obligation to tell you anything about an occurrence as private as a lady giving birth. I told you we are sisters, Rick," she said passionately, wanting him to understand what she was feeling then and now. "One born after the other only minutes apart rather than years. Nothing of what I have ever said to you is untrue."

"But that doesn't answer my first question!" he exclaimed with a rising voice. His eyes gleamed as he brushed a hand through his rich brown hair and paced at the foot of her bed as if he were a haunted man. "I can't understand why you didn't trust me with this information."

Edwina flinched at his show of emotion. She believed she had angered him before but never this badly. That didn't mean she could back down from what she'd done or how she had handled it.

"If I had, it would be the same as if I were admitting we aren't normal. That we are different . . . abnormal, or oddities to the rest of the world. And we are not. Furthermore, I daresay you have never questioned the birth of any other lady."

"I've never had a reason to," he contested earnestly. "I had a right to know this."

"No, you didn't," she answered just as firmly. "Papa said some people would consider us curiosities and freaks of nature. We would be teased, shunned, or forced to think we should have our hair combed the same way, dress the identical way, and be on display in traveling shows for people to pay to see us and laugh—"

"Stop, Edwina." He spoke quickly, heavily as he came from around the foot of the bed toward her.

His body tensed with outrage as he stopped near her. She thought he might grab hold of her. Her chest heaved and so did his. Had he really raised his voice that loudly to her?

"You don't know what you are saying." He ground out every word with an incredulous stare. "Most people don't think that way anymore. We have entered the nineteenth century and more people are civilized and being educated."

Her passion was as steamed as his and she was in no mind to give mercy. "Have you not been to a May Day Fair or carnival in the past few years? There are always sideshows—"

"Don't say more about that, Edwina," he said angrily. "Not one word. I don't want to hear such madness from you. You are not an oddity."

Her breathing eased and so did his.

"Your mother believes in superstitions and almost fainted when the countess asked about the rumor of triplets," she reminded him, shoring up her strength.

"She only gasped. Your aunt has almost fainted twice since I've known her. It's what some ladies do."

"You are educated," she insisted fervently. "You have read the accounts of history and know how people have behaved toward those they perceived as different from them no matter what that difference might be."

"I am *well educated*, Edwina," he said in an intensely low voice, which seemed to be filled with warning. "That is not the point. What others think or don't is not important to me now or ever—*you* are. This has to do with trust. As your intended, as your husband, I had the right to know. You should have trusted me."

Edwina felt the prickle of her eyes watering but blinked the sensation away. She would not let him see tears. "You wouldn't have married me," she admitted honestly. "You would have gone to the next lady on your list."

The lines around his eyes, the breadth of his forehead and his mouth wrinkled into a tight frown. "You don't know that and neither do I."

Her words had stunned him and he had hesitated before answering. That was a telltale sign her words were true. He wouldn't have taken the chance on her if he had known.

"I do know. You want an heir."

"Of course I want an heir! That's why I married you." His words were loud, honest, and desperate.

She flinched.

"But that's not all. After I talked with you that first day, Edwina, I didn't want to marry anyone but you." His expression and tone were softer. "I have always been willing to take my chances with you, but you didn't trust me enough to tell me something of great importance about your past. I've always had trouble trusting people and I don't know if I can trust you are telling me everything now."

The strength of his words tore at her heart. Being a duke, he probably did wonder who he could trust. She couldn't refute that and even understood it but had to defend herself. "I know," she said in a softer tone too. "Yet, I'm sure you haven't told me everything about your life either. All the details about how you were born, what you have done. There are probably things in your life you might not want to tell me unless I specifically asked."

He was visibly upset but quiet. His eyes took on a faraway sheen and she knew in that moment there *were* things about himself he couldn't tell her. Things she might like to know—would consider it her right to know. So, they both had ghosts in their pasts that they would have rather stay buried.

"No one could be expected to tell everything and you know that," he answered, his anger seeming to ebb.

Edwina went on, knowing she had to strengthen her

claim. "I am told wealthy peers always have mistresses. I assume you have one. Is that something you should have told me?"

"That is completely different, Edwina," he defended, sounding and looking calmer than just moments before. "Gentlemen don't talk about things like that with ladies."

"But you think I am to discuss privy things ladies discuss with you," she answered, hoping she sounded stronger than she felt.

He remained quiet. The pensive expression returned to his face, and she felt her accusation to be true.

"My father said—" She stopped and rubbed her hands together restlessly in front of her again. "I know you don't like for me to mention him, and I realize I do it far too often."

He shook his head again and inhaled deeply. "I don't understand this great love, admiration, and unyielding devotion you have for him. My father died before I was old enough to know him. I have little knowledge of what a father is supposed to be, or how one loves a father as deeply as you loved yours."

"And I don't understand those feelings," she countered softly. "My mother died before I could know her, but I love her. At times, I imagine I remember her touch and voice and that causes me to sense her presence watching over me. Sometimes I talk to her and it comforts me. Because of those feelings, I can appreciate the devotion I sense you have for your mother."

"That is because you are a better, more forgiving person than I am, Edwina."

His words pierced her heart; her legs weakened. Knowing what his comment meant, anguish exploded inside her. He was not going to pardon her for the injustice he perceived she'd done to him. He was telling her she would have forgiven him, but he couldn't do the same for her.

All hope was gone. The weight of sorrow pressing against her chest was overwhelming. She had expected his reaction should he ever find out but hadn't expected *her* reaction and how deeply it would hurt. How could she have known she would have such deep feelings for him, or that the pain of losing him would be so great even though she had never been truly his?

It took moments to accomplish, but with her inner will, she pushed a breathy sigh from her lungs, and swallowed the lump choking her. "No matter. I can take care of myself and my sisters. I will inform the viscount's solicitor not to enforce anything written in the marriage contract and I will not contest the annulment. You owe me nothing. My aunt has a small allowance and a cottage where we—"

In two strides he reached her.

CHAPTER 21

*There are times when a gentleman's actions
should speak louder than his words.*

Edwina gasped as Rick caught her around the waist with
both arms and pulled her tightly to his chest. She heard
and felt every rapid breath he took. To brace herself, her
hands landed on his upper shoulders.

His gaze bore fiercely into hers. "What in the devil
are you talking about, Edwina? You, your sisters, and aunt
are *my* responsibility. You belong here with me. Don't ever
speak such rubbish again."

"Then don't give me reason to," she answered, glaring
back at him.

If his body had not been so warm and instantly soothing, she would have pushed him away and demanded he
leave the room. But, for however long she was in his
arms, she wanted to feel the security and draw from the
courage it afforded. Her anger didn't change how she felt
about him or how his staunch response gave her hope.

Still, she said, "I can't stay here with you and feel welcome in your home."

"Our home, Edwina," he snapped quickly. "This is
your home."

Conviction filled her heart and tension ached in her chest. "You believe I am untrustworthy."

His arms immediately tightened. "You hid the fact you were a triplet."

"I didn't reveal it," she insisted hotly once again. "I will never agree I hid it from you," she retorted as fiercely as he had spoken. "Look at me, Rick. Look at my sisters. It was in plain sight for you to see and ask if you had been curious enough about us, as was Lady Middleton, to do so."

It was easy to see in his features that he was studying the validity of her comment. His eyes gleamed with indecision. She wanted it to inspire hope, but fear forced her to keep it at bay.

"Why did you support me if you thought I had hidden the truth from you?"

He leaned his head back and searched her face as if he couldn't believe she had said that. "I would never leave you defenseless or open to suspicion and ridicule. No one comes after my family with gossip or innuendo and gets away with it. I will always defend and protect you, Edwina."

The passion with which he spoke and his words touched her with the warmth of tenderness and renewed hope. She wanted to slip her arms around his neck, lay her cheek on his chest, and press her body against his, but couldn't. She wanted to fix this rip between them but didn't know if it was possible.

"I do hope I can gain your trust, but I must tell you that if I were somehow afforded the opportunity to do our first meeting all over again, I wouldn't change how I handled the truth. My oath to Papa was at stake."

With his gaze fixed on hers, arms locked securely around her, his face slowly relaxed its tense expression.

Edwina felt the heaving of his chest subside and his breathing slow to a natural pace. As if following his lead, she calmed too. His chin dipped a little but she wasn't sure whether he was giving a nod of surrender or mere acknowledgment of acceptance.

Either would satisfy her. It was clear she'd wounded him and any measure of forgiveness he gave would be appreciated.

"All right." He spoke softly. "As you indicated a couple of minutes ago, sometimes there is only a scant difference in the meaning of words and how people perceive and understand them."

Neither of them moved. She remained in the pulsating comfort of being pressed close to him, and, unexpectedly, he gave a tender smile. She took it as the possibility of his forgiveness for whatever error in judgment he deemed she'd made, and the hope they might move forward.

She hadn't wanted to hurt or anger him or ignore his rights to know everything about her. Most of all, she didn't want to cause him any more pain. As she looked into his eyes, she wanted him to be happy with her. She wanted him to desire her with the same intensity he had when they kissed before the ball, and with the same desire she wanted him. That might not ever be possible.

"No matter what happens between us, I want you to know how much it meant to me for you, your mother, and friends to stand up for me tonight. I will always cherish that."

He lowered his head, taking his nose to where it nearly touched hers. "You don't understand yet, do you?" His gaze held tightly on hers and he kept his voice low. "It doesn't matter if you were born of one, two, three, or ten. You are mine. That's not going to change. You are normal. That's not going to change. You are the most desirable woman I have ever met." He kissed her softly, briefly, and then added huskily, "And that's not going to change."

The warm, moist, and fleeting brush of his lips against hers caused a hiccup of breath to stall in her chest. His words were balm to her soul and thrilling to her body. He would never know how desperately she needed to hear them and feel the touch of his lips against hers. Her heart swelled with tenderness. Without effort or fear, she leaned into him and his arms tightened in response.

A seductive aura swirled about them. "You are still angry with me," she whispered.

His gaze stayed unwaveringly on hers, his lips close to hers. "I'll get over it."

"Tonight?" she asked, knowing she didn't want to go to bed with animosity between them.

"Probably."

Hope gathered in her chest once more, making her breath short and deep.

His shoulder twitched. So did his lips as his gaze softly caressed her face.

"Yes. I will," he offered.

She smiled softly.

"I already have."

Relief shuddered through her. After their fierce argument, he was wooing her a little at a time with his charm and she was drinking every drop of it.

He let go of her and moved his hands to the upper part of her bare arms, where he caressed and warmed her chilled skin as if he held a luxuriant velvet.

"I like your nightwear. It's the kind I was expecting you to be in on our wedding night." He reached around to her back and pulled her braid over her shoulders, laying it gently on her chest.

Her breathing increased. "What are you doing?"

"Releasing your hair from the binding."

Taking his time, he untied the bow and let the ribbon flutter to the floor. The movement of his hands delving into the strands of her plait were slow, deliberate, and utterly intimate. She felt the weight of her hair on her shoulders and down her back as he separated the lengths.

"You are beautiful, Edwina, and I want you. Never let anything I might say make you think otherwise. I am not always careful with my words or how I say them. I learned early in life that a duke is often expected to be eccentric in some way. With me, that sometimes translates into impatience, intolerance, or offense."

His simple honesty endeared him to her heart and love for him opened and blossomed inside her.

"I am not perfect," she answered shyly. "Far from it."

A wrinkle formed between his brows briefly. "You are, for me." He spread the last of her hair over her shoulders.

"I have unattractive traits and other things I need to overcome."

Like conquering her fear of the marriage bed and being in the family way. She wanted to do that tonight.

"Why did you unbraid my hair?"

"I want to tangle my fingers in it while I make love to you. Tonight. You need to know that from this day forward you are mine, Edwina."

"Yes," she whispered. "I do need to know that."

Rick pulled his shirt from the waistband of his trousers, yanked it over his head, and tossed it away. From the glow of light shining from his room into hers, she saw him clearly. Her breath quickened and her body trembled. Edwina had never seen a man's bare chest, other than in paintings or statues. He looked every bit as muscular, strong, and beautiful as men chiseled out of stone.

He started unfastening his trousers. Edwina tensed. "Henrietta said we should always turn out all the lights," she said hurriedly, lowering her eyes to the floor, thinking she was going to see something she shouldn't see, married or not.

Placing fingertips under her chin, he said huskily, "Edwina, look at me."

Lifting her lashes, she stared into his beautiful blue eyes. Fear and excitement warred inside her. She knew there would be pain and the possibility of life-altering consequences. She must put those fears aside and give herself up to the way Rick made her feel when he held and kissed her and embrace the unexpected fact she was falling in love with her husband.

Quirking his head to the side, he asked, "What did I tell you about your maid?"

"Forget everything she said and never listen to her again," she whispered.

Rick's arms circled her again. Pulling her gently against him, he placed his lips near her ear. A low, attractive chuckle whispered past his lips. "Do that for me and hear only my voice whispering to you tonight."

Snuggling into the warmth of his bare chest, she answered, "Yes, make me forget everything she said."

"It starts with you not being afraid to look at me and not being afraid for me to feast my eyes on you. We'll go slow."

A tremor of expectancy shivered through her. "All right."

Rick stepped back and held his arms out. An easy, attractive smile formed on his lips and her stomach tightened. "Look at me and touch me wherever you wish."

Edwina reached out and placed her hand at the base of his warm neck. With an open palm she made a path along the smooth width of his muscular shoulders and chest before skimming down his rippled ribs to the open flap of his trousers. The amazement and stimulating wonder of how firm he felt caused fluttering in her chest, abdomen, and elsewhere. She gave herself over to the undeniably pleasurable sensations of looking at him, touching him.

Rick moaned with pleasure at her caresses and gave her a searing kiss. Without forethought she lifted her arms and wound them around his neck. Edwina melted against him as their tongues swirled in each other's mouths.

With unhurried movements, he untied the ribbon of her nightgown and brushed it off one shoulder. Bending his head, he kissed down the column of her neck to her chest and lingered over the swell of her breasts before kissing his way up her tingling skin. He covered her mouth with his in a long, gentle, sweet kiss as his hands tangled in the length of her hair.

Passion seared hot and their kisses turned fervent. His hands palmed her breasts and the excitement of his touch was thrilling. Thousands of sensations blossomed inside her all at once, causing her to reel as shivers of pleasure tingled down to her abdomen and lower to settle between her legs.

In one fluid motion, he hooked his arm under her legs, picked her up, and gently laid her on the bed. With her heart beating faster than it ever had, she trembled, but not from fear—from the wonderful feeling of anticipation.

Rick sat on the edge of the bed and slid his trousers off before stretching his nude lean body beside her.

He drew her into his embrace.

"Now, it's your turn."

Edwina needed no other encouragement. In his arms, she was safe. She took hold of her nightgown and started pulling it up her legs. Rick smiled and helped her ease the garment up her body, over her head, and toss it.

When they lay bare together, her cool soft breasts pressed against his warm solid chest. Edwina gasped at the intimacy and could have never imagined the heady experience of skin on skin. His confident hands moved across her shoulders all the way down her back and over her buttocks.

"Your body is as beautiful as your face, Edwina," he whispered, his hand tracing the line of her shoulder down her arm to the plane of her hip and back again. "I knew it would be."

"You are beautiful too and you look magnificently strong."

He chuckled lightly. "If you think so, touch me and let me know."

That was an easy request to fulfill. With eager hands she explored down the length of his chest, his midriff, his lean and narrow hips. The sensation was wondrous, evoking unimaginable excitement and delight as they took turns getting to know each other.

Rick knew exactly when to take over and make her fully his.

He made love to her with a slow tenderness that over-whelmed her as they became one. His movements, kisses, and caresses were a slow, sensual giving of indescribable pleasure. She gave herself up to the exquisite feelings spiraling through her body. Waves of sensations collected in her womanly core, robbing her of breath before fading into pleasant, languid ripples of immense satisfaction. Moments later, Rick joined her in the heavenly climax.

He whispered her name over and over before saying on a gasp of breath, "That is what loving is supposed to feel like."

They lay on their backs not moving. Edwina finally understood what happened on the wedding night and was breathless with awe.

After a time, their breathing slowed and the last tremors of sensation ebbed into feelings of contentment.

Rick turned to her and asked, "Did I hurt you?"

She lifted herself onto her elbow and looked him. "Not at all." With gentle strokes, she brushed his hair away from his forehead and stared at him in amazement. "Why would my maid have told me there would be excruciating pain? All I felt was immense pleasure. I should have trusted you."

Amusement danced in his expression. "Did you just say you should have trusted me?"

Edwina smiled sheepishly and cleared her throat. "I might have misspoken," she said teasingly before lowering her head to kiss the corner of his mouth.

He rose on his forearm and leaned over her. "You don't ever have to be frightened of anything again." He placed a soft kiss on her lips.

"I don't know that's true," she said, feeling more concern than she wanted to after such a glorious experience. "The countess has probably spread the rumor she heard to half the ton by now."

"She hasn't said a word, nor will she," he said, winding a strand of her hair around his finger.

"You sound so sure." Edwina was not.

"I saw the look on her face when she realized who she was talking to and what she was saying to my wife in front of me, my mother, two other dukes, and another duchess. All of them defended you. She will keep the rumor to herself, or else she knows she will have ostracized herself from all of Society."

Knowing his assurance would be tested if she should have more than one babe, she asked, "Do you think I am with child now?"

He chuckled softly. "I doubt it. It usually takes many times." His eyes narrowed. "You are all right with that, aren't you?"

"Very," she answered, feeling a blush rise to her cheeks.

Their coming together had been perfect and she hadn't wanted it to end. Still, she had worries. She laid her hand over his heart. "What will you do if I have triplets?"

His gaze swept up and down her face as if he were searching for something he'd lost. With the back of his palm, he slowly, softly caressed her cheek. "It's very rare. Do you have reason to think you might?"

"I've had much anxiety over the prospect. My father always said I was more like my mother than either of my sisters. What will you do if I have three sons at one time?"

He shrugged and brushed her hair away from her shoulders. "I suppose I'd have reason to be quite boastful. A man gaining three sons at once. I think that would impress even my mother." He smiled and so did Edwina. "And, of course, I'd have to leave it up to you to keep up with which of the three babes was the oldest and heir to the title."

Rick couldn't have said anything that would have pleased her more. Edwina pressed a soft kiss to his lips as he pulled her into his arms again.

CHAPTER 22

THE ART OF BEING A FINE GENTLEMAN
SIR DUDLEY SAMSON PEMBERTON FINE

It is essential for a gentleman to learn the art of answering a question without answering it at all.

Rick pushed the dull ache in his temples to the back of his mind as he stepped down from his carriage and headed for the stone pathway that led to his mother's house. A lot could be said about the marriage bed. All good things he found out. He hadn't expected kissing, touching, and becoming one with someone you had tender feelings for to be different from being with other women. He could never have imagined it would be more satisfying. Odd as it was to him, he was content in a way he never had been.

To his surprise, he had easily accepted Edwina snuggled close to him, sleeping with him all through the night and waking beside him each morning. He'd never wanted or needed that with any other woman. Giving and taking pleasure and then leaving was all he ever needed. With Edwina he wanted to linger in bed with her in the mornings and by the end of the day as her sisters were settling down for the evening, he was impatient for the nights and his time alone with her to begin. After the house was quiet, he felt as if he and Edwina were the only two people in the world. It reminded him of when he was a boy and would manage to slip away from his mother and the staff that was paid to constantly watch him.

However, bliss with his wife wasn't without misgivings. After the first ball a few nights ago, he'd had the perfect opportunity to tell her about his fevers. And many times since. He'd considered it when she'd suggested there were things in his past he had not told her. Yet, he hadn't uttered a word about the sickness. Mainly because he hoped he'd never have another one. Why try to explain something that might never happen again? Besides, Edwina had enough worries of her own and didn't need any of his. Whenever she became in the family way, he'd have his physician and a midwife check her often. They would know if she was carrying more than one babe. He just hoped they'd know what to do if she was.

Then there were days like today that made *him* worry, which was the reason he saw his physician before coming to his mother's house. He woke with a blasted headache again. That was troublesome.

The visit was futile. With no other signs of the fever, no chills one minute and sweats the next, the man suggested all he needed was a tonic of willow bark for the ache in his head. So far the mixture was working. Thankfully, his headache was better and he didn't feel any of the usual feverish symptoms.

Rick had received several messages from his mother, Wyatt, and Hurst during the past week and answered them all the same way. He would see them soon. He assumed they were eager to hear more about what Lady Middleton had said at the ball, but he'd come to a conclusion about that. They wouldn't hear any more from him or anyone else on that subject. The fear Edwina's father had instilled in her about how some people might react was still very real to her.

It was his responsibility to protect her. Rick didn't want the gossip talked about even among his best friends and mother. He would keep Edwina away from any talk of triplets, oddities, or anything else that might cause her pain. For that reason, he'd purposefully taken Edwina and her sisters to small dinner parties in the evenings and kept them away from the elaborate balls where they were certain to see his mother and his friends. Unfortunately, his plan hadn't kept Matthew Malcolm from seeing Eleonora. He seemed to make an appearance for a chat with her at almost every house they entered.

Rick handed his hat and gloves off to his mother's butler, Webster. "Where is she?" he asked.

"Waiting for you in the drawing room."

He nodded and made his way there. She was in her usual spot on the chair she considered the only comfortable one in the house.

"Good afternoon, Maman. I trust you are well?" He bent over and kissed her cheek.

"Five days, Stonerick?" she answered with no reprimand in her soft voice but no smile on her lips either. "Six, if you count this one."

He grinned. "How can you count today when it's not much more than half over?" She was miffed, as he expected. "I sent a note to say I'd be over soon."

"'Soon' means in an hour or two, not most of a week."

"I wanted to get here earlier, Maman, but I've had many things to do with Edwina and her sisters."

"Really?" She lifted her chin and questioned the legitimacy of his statement with her expression.

"Just because Edwina and I decided not to take a wedding journey until later in the year doesn't mean we don't want to spend as much time together as possible."

"That's nice, dear," she said a trifle too sweetly.

Rick turned to take his usual place on the plush velvet settee and saw a stack of books at the far end. Two titles caught his attention immediately. *An Introduction to Superstitions* and *The History of Superstitions*. That raised his ire. It didn't appear his mother was ready to give up her new venture, but he could keep Edwina away from it. "What's this?" He motioned toward the end of the settee.

"Books. You've been enjoying getting to know your bride while I have been dithering night and day wondering about the truth of your wife and her sisters' birth. Is it or is it not true they are triplets?"

"It's true they are sisters," he answered without hesitation and only mild firmness, considering how he was feeling at the moment. "All beautiful and very different from each other, I assure you. I've found out just how much since they've been living with us."

He would forego telling her the sisters were noisy, calling out to each other when they were in separate rooms, or when one was abovestairs and the other below. They seemed to stomp up the stairs rather than walk quietly as the servants were taught to do, and at times, he heard them giggling like little girls at play when they thought something funny. But moving them in had been the right thing to do for Edwina. She had loved having them near, so he'd put up with the disruption for her. And the hope they would both soon find a suitable man to marry and be living in their own homes.

Alberta leaned forward and peered into his eyes. "I will take up for your wife anytime necessary or her family if that might be needed too, Your Grace, but I have concerns about the title."

Rick blew out a laugh. "You always have."

"I always will," she answered with no excuses.

He knew, but his responsibility right now was to Edwina, and he had to make that clear to his mother. "She makes me happy." Rick looked at the books and then back to his mother. "I don't want to hear any more talk or discussion about superstitions, folklore, myths, or charting the skies in hopes of telling your future. I don't want to hear one word about the society you joined. I don't want to see any more books, pamphlets, or anything else left at my house or yours when I visit. What you do is your prerogative, but it won't be a part of my life."

She inhaled deeply and appeared to study over his words. "Is that your way of telling me you don't intend to look into the duchess' past to try to determine if what Lady Middleton heard might be true?"

His smile was sincere. "That's exactly what I'm telling you. Where, when, or how she was born doesn't matter to me."

"Well, I heard an insightful quote at the meeting the other day: 'Superstitions are only what we think, fear, or want to be true.'" She sniffed and then smiled. "Fate is what actually happens."

"My thoughts as well. You must decide if you want to believe the countess' gossip or dismiss it as I have done." He paused and looked directly into her eyes.

His mother absently fiddled with the cuff of her sleeve as she often did, and said, "You say you are happy."

"Immensely," he assured her with conviction. And he was. He wanted to live a long life with Edwina, yet the risk of another fever was never far from his mind. "She's the perfect wife for me."

The dowager absently drummed her fingertips on her lap. "Did I tell you I found out Miss Fine's name should have never been on the list that led to the proposal letter you sent her? My secretary admitted the error to me when we talked about the letter. She wasn't making her debut, only attending parties at Lord Quintingham's request."

"I knew. Edwina told me."

The dowager's finely arched brows lifted, and she said softly, "It's good to hear she's not hiding everything from you."

"Maman . . ." he said with a tinge of exasperation.

"I was only going to add that's what's called fate, Your Grace. The way you decided on her name and all the rest of what happened to bring her to your door." His mother relaxed for the first time since he entered the room. "I suppose I've had enough enlightening for now. I'll go ahead and tell Webster to dispose of the books I've collected. That's why I had gathered them all together. I don't think I need them anymore." A pleasing smile appeared quickly, and she looked at her cuff again before saying, "I'll expect you and the duchess for dinner on Sunday."

"We accept. I assume the invitation includes her sisters and her Aunt Pauline?"

His mother lifted her chin and shoulders a tad as her brows rose again too. "All three sisters at one time?"

Rick nodded slowly.

Alberta gave him a conciliatory soft breath of a chuckle. "Yes, of course. I'm intrigued by them, you know. And I guess if any of them can read my mind I best find it out sooner than later."

"Maman?" he said in a warning voice.

"Oh, don't worry, Your Grace. They are family, are

they not? And I will treat them as such as long as they give me no cause to do otherwise. Perhaps I'll invite a few friends to join us. Not as many as at the wedding and no one you would disapprove of, dearest. Young, handsome gentlemen such as the duchess' sisters would enjoy talking to. Perhaps Mr. Mercy and Mr. Malcolm."

Rick gave a rueful snort. *Malcolm?* Again. Rick couldn't get away from the man.

A few minutes later, Rick left his mother's house and drove his curricle down to White's. He walked in, taking off his hat and gloves and handing them off to the attendant. Midafternoon was usually the quietest time of day at the club but he heard billiard balls smacking in the gaming room and a smattering of conversations coming from the reading room.

Wyatt and Hurst were waiting for him at their usual table near the front window that faced St. James' Street. He knew what they wanted to know.

On his way to join them, he nodded to a couple of gentlemen he passed but took no time for polite conversation.

"Am I late?" Rick asked, pulling out a chair to join them at the table. Brandy had already been poured for the three of them but judging by the glasses, his friends had been waiting for him before taking their first drink.

"No," Hurst replied. "We just arrived."

His friends looked at each other as if they still hadn't decided what they wanted to say next, but Hurst swiped his hair away from his forehead with the back of his hand and came right to the point. "Is the rumor the countess heard about triplets true?"

Rick grimaced. "I have no idea about anything she might have heard twenty years ago, yesterday, or today. Nor do I care." He picked up his brandy and took a drink.

"That's good enough for me." Hurst lifted his glass.

"For me too," Wyatt agreed, adding the clink of his glass to their toast. "Why did it take you so long to meet and let us know?"

"I've been— Hell's teeth. Can't a man stay at home for a few days and enjoy his wife?"

"No further explanation needed on that either," Wyatt said with a grin. "We worried after the ball. Not knowing if the gossip caused you and Edwina trouble."

"No," Rick said, seeing no reason to say more about the matter. "I am doing my best to adjust to Edwina's sisters in the house. When I suggested they live with us, I had no idea how much trouble they would be."

"In what way?" Hurst asked, placing his drink on the table in front of him.

"Probably the same way I had to adjust to Fredericka's nieces and nephew living with us," Wyatt suggested. "A time of adjustment is needed."

"He's living with three beautiful young ladies," Hurst said, with a grin. "How much adjusting is there to do concerning that?"

"A lot," Rick grumbled good-naturedly. "None of them can play an adequate game of chess or cards in the evenings."

"That's probably because they talk constantly and don't study the game," Hurst suggested.

Wyatt nodded in agreement.

"During the day they squabble over embroidery thread, reading, and anything else they can think of," Rick complained with a bit of a grin. "Eleonora enjoys playing the pianoforte, which she does quite well, but feels the need to sing at the same time, and that is where the problem lies. I haven't found a room in the house yet where I can't hear her."

Wyatt and Hurst laughed. Rick sipped his brandy again, thinking it was good to be with his friends.

"We do have news that won't make you any happier than your sister-in-law's serenading," Wyatt offered as he moved his glass in a circle on the table.

"As long as the fever stays away, I can manage anything," he said, knowing he wanted a long life with Edwina.

Wyatt gave him a *we'll see* look, and said, "When we let it be known that the Brass Deck Club was looking for younger members, Matthew Malcolm applied for membership."

Rick tensed. "What the devil will that man do next? He should know I'm a founding member and wouldn't vote for him."

"Obviously he doesn't," Hurst murmured.

Rick expelled a short burst of breath. "When did this happen?"

"Today. Some of the team seem quite excited he's interested in joining. With you now married as well, the fear is that your participation will soon be less and less as with Wyatt. Malcolm is a damn good marksman. Has there been more to his machinations than what we saw from him at the shooting match?"

"He wants to court Eleonora. He asked her to go for a ride in the park with him, and I had to tell her no."

"Do you think he's doing this to get back at you for not letting him pursue your sister-in-law?" Wyatt asked, leaning his chair away from the table on its back two legs. "Or does he really want to be a part of the sporting team? And does he want to court Eleonora because you rejected his friendliness after the shooting match?"

"Could be all of that," Rick admitted without qualms. Hurst cleared his throat, causing Rick and Wyatt to look at him. "Wait. Neither of you should discount Miss Eleonora's beauty and charm," Hurst said. "Everything about her is inviting. Her voice is sweet, and her innocence shows in everything she says. And Eileen's intelligence is exceptional."

Wyatt and Rick looked at Hurst with interest.

"Do you have designs on either of them?" Wyatt asked.

"Me? No, no. I just don't want Rick to minimize the sisters' attributes—minus the singing, of course. I've heard talk among the bachelors. There's interest in both of them."

Hurst was right. Edwina's sisters were the loveliest young ladies on the marriage mart.

"What does Edwina think about Malcolm?" Hurst asked with a nonchalant quirk of his head.

Rick relaxed and his breathing slowed. All he had to do was think about his wife and he smiled. Strange as it was for him to admit, he had enjoyed the past few days with her. He loved watching how she watched over her sisters and her aunt. Suddenly, he was looking forward to getting back home to her after the card game with his friends.

"She thinks he's a nice young man," Rick said after taking another sip of his drink. "And I am sure he is around her and Eleonora."

"Well, you must admit Malcolm has some brass stones," Wyatt groused as he slowly let the front legs of his chair back onto the floor with a soft thud. "Thinking he can get into the Brass Deck Club without our vote. He knows we will side with you."

"We have several who are seeking membership," Hurst offered. "We'll assess them all when the time comes. Some are good enough to help us win; others, we'll have to pass over."

Rick took a deep breath as Wyatt motioned for another round of drinks. Rick had a lot of things he needed
to think on. There was no doubt Malcolm had a good
eye, steady hand, and keen concentration when it came
to competing. With his skill, he would be a good man
to have on the team, but would he be a good beau for
Eleonora?

CHAPTER 23

*A fine gentleman knows when it is time to give up
the search for that which he seeks but cannot find.*

Rick helped Edwina into the curricle and then climbed up and took the reins as she opened her dainty fringed parasol. This would be the first time they had a ride in the park without her sisters or aunt joining them. He clicked the ribbons a couple of times and the horses took off with a rattle of harness and roll of squeaking wheels on hard-packed ground.

Spring had finally arrived and it was the warmest and driest day London had seen in a week. The air felt fresh and smelled fragrant. Puffy white clouds slowly drifted across the blue sky. An abundance of rain the past week had the trees, shrubs, bushes, and flowers showing their vibrant colors.

Now that the Season had officially started, the park was buzzing with pedestrians and horse-and-carriage traffic when they entered. Carriages of different sizes and shapes, along with peddlers' carts and milk wagons, rolled along the worn paths and open spaces. The landscape was dotted with children playing, couples walking, and gentlemen on horseback.

Edwina had been quiet for their short drive to the entrance. Even when they had passed other people who were enjoying the sunny day. Her waves, nods, and calls of greetings were subdued to the gentlemen who doffed their hats and ladies who smiled and nodded.

Letting the horses choose their own lazy pace, Rick put both reins in one palm and picked up Edwina's gloved hand and kissed it.

She turned to him, tilted her head, and pursed her lips as if in deep thought before saying, "You do know showing affection in a public place is forbidden by the ton, do you not?"

"I do, and probably by most everyone else too. However, kissing a lady's hand is never out of place."

"Really?" she asked with a curious expression. "Not even in church?"

Rick laughed and kissed her hand again. "Perhaps you are right about that. But we aren't in church and I am feeling very devilish today."

Edwina twirled the handle of her parasol and the pale-green fringe danced around her. She gave him a spicy smile that tightened his lower body. He started to tell her how much he enjoyed being with her. At a party, home, or beside her on a carriage seat. It wasn't just that she made him happy. It was more than that, and for the first time he was wondering if it might be love.

Swallowing and shying away from that very probable idea, carrying on with their playful attitude, he gave Edwina a questioning grin. "I do believe you are inviting me to kiss you on your beautiful lips here in the open where anyone—including the people in the carriage that is about to pass us—could see."

"Absolutely not," she said deliberately and unconvincingly as she waved a greeting to the couple. "I was trying to think of a different way to tell you how happy I am. You've been kind and more than accommodating to Elle and Eileen. I wish they would appreciate your efforts more by trying harder to find someone to make them happy. I can't talk either one into going to Lord and Lady Windham's party tonight. Both say they are too tired."

"We've been out most every night for over a week. It's time we all take a rest from the parties and dinners."

Edwina sighed and looked out over the green park with its gentle green slopes, stands of trees dotted about the landscape, and people milling about. "Both seem quite popular with all the young gentlemen. Their attention is sought wherever we go. Yet, Elle only has eyes for Mr. Malcolm and Eileen has eyes for no one. How are we going to find them husbands by the end of the Season?"

Worse, how was he going to get them out of his house and into a house of their own if they couldn't make a match? Rick truly didn't understand why they weren't just happy they were no longer in the Netherlands of York.

He was at a loss what to do next. Despite less than favorable weather, in the time they had been living at his house, he and Edwina had twice taken them out on the Serpentine in a rowboat. They spent an afternoon in the landau enjoying a ride and picnic in the countryside. A few nights ago, they had been to Vauxhall Gardens to watch the varieties of acts performing there. Over the past few days Rick had bought Elle a half dozen books, and Eileen a new telescope and old copies of articles on astronomy she wanted to read. The truth of it was that he hadn't minded doing any of it. All of them were simple things to do that made Edwina happy.

That pleased him and all of it had helped him too. He was learning to be patient. He had no idea it could take someone more than three hours to pick out six books. There were other things he was learning: the meaning of obligation and being responsible for someone other than himself. He was discovering there was more to life than just doing and saying what was convenient and easy for him or the title. But all that said, Edwina was right. Little progress had been made.

He looked over at her and said, "I don't know what else I can do for them."

Edwina pursed her lips again for a second or two and sighed before saying, "You could be more considering of Mr. Matthew Malcolm. He is the only man Elle wants to be with. Why will you not allow him to call on her, but keep pushing her toward Mr. Mercy?"

That's not what he was expecting to hear. Or wanted to hear. Only a few days ago it was Hurst and Wyatt telling him the man wanted to join their sporting club, which he finally agreed to, so he had made allowances for the man. Rick guided the horses over to a budding tree and stopped underneath it.

He turned in the seat to face his wife. "He beat me in a shooting match." It wasn't as hard to admit to her as he thought it would be so he gave a quick grin. "The first man to win against me in years."

Edwina lowered her parasol, closed it, and laid it across her lap. "Is that what you have against him?" she asked, as she deliberately turned her knees so that they jutted up against his.

He lifted his brows at her bold move. "It's enough," he answered, thinking he was going to have to kiss her before they got home. It would be risky, but doable under the cover of the budding tree. While she seemed to ponder his answer, she slowly unfastened the first four buttons of her pelisse, rested both hands onto her knees, and leaned forward. It was unlike her to be so brazen but he loved getting a forbidden look at the swell of her breasts in the park as they talked. It was inviting and she was enticing.

"Did he cheat?"

"No," he answered, more interested in her and the delicious way she was making him feel than in their conversation about Malcolm.

"Have you challenged him to a rematch?"

Rick frowned and stretched his arm out on top of the seat back in a relaxed manner. "No."

Edwina lifted her chin, showing her slender neck and hollow of her throat.

"Then challenge him, beat him, and retake your title as the best shot in London."

"England," he corrected with a bit of a smile and arrogance to his tone.

Whether on purpose or in innocence, she folded her arms across her chest, lifting the swell of her breasts higher. "Correction noted and accepted."

However, he had to admit his beautiful wife had a good point about retaking his place at the top. Rick supposed he would always have a glimmer of resentment toward Malcolm. Not so much because the man won the match. Rick knew it was a fluke glint of sunlight. It was the blade's attitude afterward. Nevertheless, Rick believed he'd take Edwina up on her advice. Maybe if he allowed Malcolm to pursue Eleonora, she'd find out for herself she didn't like him any better than Rick did.

"Tell Elle that Malcolm can call on her."

Happiness lit up her eyes. "Thank you," she whispered softly. "I'll be sure to do that."

"And I'll tell Malcolm he better not break her heart or be caught visiting Mademoiselle Rivoire."

Edwina's arched brows furrowed. "Who?"

"Never mind," he said. "I'll have a chat with him about that before he comes over."

"I think that would be appropriate."

Rick wasn't so sure Malcolm would think so, but he had to understand that if he wanted to court a duke's sister, there were certain rules he had to obey.

"What do you say we cut our ride short, go home, and start dressing for tonight's party a little early? As soon as Elle hears Mr. Malcolm can call on her, I know she will want to go."

Rick chuckled huskily. "That's a good idea, but first, I must do this." He picked up her parasol, opened it, and placed the canopy facing out and the shaft held tightly between his knees. He pulled Edwina to him and kissed her soundly on the lips before letting his lips drift over to her ear. "You are tempting me, dear wife, to behave naughtily. I assume that's what you intended."

"I do admit I've been wanting you to kiss me all day, but to do it here is dangerous. Someone could see us."

"Hidden as we are, no one is close enough to see us right now," he whispered, brushing aside her concerns. "I will hear if anyone approaches."

His mouth opened once more and met hers with hunger. She yielded sweetly into his arms with soft gasps of pleasure. With urgent hands he skimmed lightly, teasingly over her breasts and kissed down the column of her neck to the hollow of her throat where his tongue tasted her warm skin.

"We could have everyone in the ton talking about our behavior before the day is over. This is very improper, Your Grace," she whispered.

"And delicious," he answered. "And satisfying."

The sounds of harness and carriage wheels approaching registered at the back of his mind. No matter the way Edwina was making him feel, Rick had to stop. Smiling, he eased away from her, picked up the umbrella from between his knees, and, leaving it open, handed it to her.

Edwina took in a deep solid breath, straightened her shoulders, and smoothed down her dress. "Thank you," she said with a pert expression. "I always knew there must be more than one use for a parasol."

The word *love* floated across his mind once again and he let the idea linger for a moment before chuckling as he picked up the reins.

CHAPTER 24

THE ART OF BEING A FINE GENTLEMAN
SIR DUDLEY SAMSON PEMBERTON FINE

*There comes a time in a gentleman's life
when there is no correct answer to a conflict.
A fine gentleman knows when that time has come.*

Something startled Rick awake. He didn't know what it was, but his inner sense told him all was not well. His head pounded and his breathing was heavy. Gritting his teeth against the pain, he quickly looked over at Edwina. In moonlight from the window, he saw her sleeping peacefully beside him. A second later, he realized his nightshirt was soaked.

Damnation! Did he have the fever again?

He put his hand to his forehead. It wasn't burning hot right now, but that didn't mean he wasn't fevered. He knew what would happen if it raged unchecked. Through the fog of just waking, he realized he needed to mix and drink some willow bark and the powders the apothecary made for him and hope it would stop further progression of the fever. The medicines were in the herb room off the kitchen where all remedies were kept. First, he had to get up without waking Edwina.

After easing off the bed, he was light-headed for a moment but the feeling cleared quickly. He made it to his room and quietly closed the door. He stepped into his trousers before walking barefoot belowstairs. As soon as he rounded the door to the kitchen, he sensed something was wrong and tensed.

A lone burning candle was on the edge of the table. Palmer would have a conniption if he knew someone had been so careless, but then he heard a sound. Rustling. Rifling? Though he'd grown up in the house, this wasn't an area he was familiar with, but he believed the noise came from inside the dry larder.

Someone was either getting an early start to their workday, or pilfering food. He didn't have time to worry about which. He only wanted to make the tonic and go back to bed in hopes of sleeping off the fever.

Rick started for the herb room at the same time someone rushed out of the larder. They almost collided. A woman gasped. She wore a long black cape with a hood pulled low. In her hands she held a basket stuffed with bread, cheese, and jars of cooked fruit.

He took a step forward and held his light toward her face.

She stood as if frozen for a moment before whispering, "Jumping Jupiter, Your Grace. You scared the daylights out of me. Lower that candle before you blind me."

Her face was unnaturally pale and her eyes searched behind him as if she expected someone else to walk in any second. "Eileen, what in the bloody hell are you doing down here in the middle of the night?" he asked as quietly as she had spoken. "Dressed like that?"

"At least I am covered. You are not properly clothed either."

Rick placed his light on the table, straightened his shoulders, and tucked the front tail of his shirt into his trousers. "I didn't expect to meet anyone," he groused. "What are you doing in here?"

Still watchful of the doorway behind him, she pulled the basket to her chest as if to protect herself from an assailant. "Nothing."

He leaned toward her and looked closely at her. "Are you a somnambulist? Uncover your head so I can determine what is wrong with you."

"I am not asleep," she said indignantly, shaking the hood from her head. "I'm very much awake and know what I'm doing."

Rick felt like hell. The last thing he wanted was to put up with this kind of behavior. A chill that had nothing to do with a fever trembled through him when he realized what her denial and actions meant.

The muscles at the back of his neck tensed. "Then what are you doing gathering food like a common footpad?"

"If you must know," she said in a reluctant tone, "I am leaving and going to Slough. Since Mr. Herschel has never answered any of my letters, I've decided to go to his door and hope he will see me."

"No, you aren't." Rick grunted. Along with feeling like hell, his wet shirt was making him cold and irritable. He had no patience for this kind of nonsense prattle or to figure out what madness she had cooked up in that exceptional brain of hers. "I'm not letting you do anything so foolish. Steal away in the middle of the night as if a schoolboy yearning for home? If the man didn't answer, he had a good reason. It means he doesn't have time to see you."

Eileen scowled.

"How the devil were you planning to get there?"

"Safely, I assure you. I've been giving this much thought since Papa passed. Being in London has just made my plan come sooner and easier than I expected when in York. I've checked the mail coach's schedule and how to get to where it is. I need to be there in exactly forty-five minutes to board. My maid is waiting by the back gate with our satchels packed, and I have enough food for us for several days." She looked down at the laden basket. "Unless you take it from me."

"What? No. No, I wouldn't take food from you, and no, I'm not letting you go anywhere."

"I have everything all thought out. I've been saving my pin money a long time," she continued. "There is enough for lodging and more food for at least a month or two. Longer if I'm frugal. The only thing I must do is get out of here before Edwina finds me and locks me in my room for the next thirty years."

"I am the one standing in your way, not your sister," he snapped, unable to understand why she couldn't find a way to be happy where she was and with the plans Edwina had for her. They were good plans. "I can't let you do this. You've been attending parties and dances this week, and from all I've seen enjoying yourself quite well. You even went for a ride in the park with your sister and Mr. Malcolm."

"I've been biding my time until I could get my plan in place."

The agony of how damned bad he was feeling swamped his senses. He needed brandy, willow bark, and whatever the other powder was the apothecary had given him. He looked around the tables. There were bowls, vegetables, even flowers, but there wasn't a bottle of brandy, wine, or port on any of them.

Eileen inhaled a deep breath. "After getting this far, if I don't leave tonight, I will tomorrow night. If not then, the next, or in a week. You and Edwina cannot keep watch over me twenty-four hours a day unless you lock me in my room."

"Of course we can," he grumbled, rubbing and squeezing the back of his neck, trying to ease the tension and the chill sweeping over him again. Evidently, this was more critical than he first thought. "I hope it won't come to that. I'll talk to Edwina and get her to see reason about how you feel and how unhappy you are. We'll arrange for you to do more of the things you enjoy."

"You cannot make my sister see reason," Eileen scoffed. "I have tried. She only sees her sworn oath to our father. I have no such oath and I don't want to live under the weight of hers any longer."

"You are the one not adhering to reasoning." He opened a cabinet and looked inside. "You can't run away simply because you are unhappy."

She dropped the arm holding the basket to her side and squared her shoulders. "I wrote Edwina a note and left it on the table in the vestibule. I don't think she will understand but maybe you can help her. Papa is gone. I can't live my life for him or for her any longer."

Of all nights for her to plan her escape. Why this night when his head was thundering and he was weary with fear the fever had returned? He wasn't fully alert.

"Go back to bed," he said and turned away from her and opened another cupboard, looking for brandy or claret or something to drink. Hell, he didn't know where it was. Palmer always kept it on a tray in the drawing room, book room, and his chambers.

"I'm not going back to my room, Your Grace. I am leaving. I know how to take care of myself and my maid. We will be fine."

The seriousness of Eileen's tone shuddered through him. Damnation, she reminded him of Edwina the first day he had seen her standing in the vestibule of his home telling Palmer she wouldn't take no for an answer.

"I'll think of something tomorrow, Eileen," he said, willing himself to be patient. "Just give me time and I will help you." He opened another cabinet. He was in no temper or disposition to continue to argue with her over practical solutions to her restless desire to find a new life.

Eileen walked closer and eyed him carefully. "Are you all right? You don't look well."

No. He wasn't. He was dazed, feverish and sweating as if it were a hot day in July. "I have a pounding head. I'm half asleep. I came down for something—a brandy— and I don't know where a damn thing is in the kitchen."

Eileen walked over to a freestanding cabinet, opened one of the doors, and took out a bottle of brandy. She handed it to him. He gave her a curious look.

"I don't know any more about a kitchen than you do," she offered to alleviate his fears of how she knew where it was. "I saw it when I was looking for food. I don't know where they keep the crystal, so I can't help you with a glass."

"That's all right," he said, pulling out the stopper. "I'll drink it out of the bottle." He took a stinging sip, hoping it would quickly help him to feel better. "Get yourself back up to bed."

"The only way you are keeping me here tonight is to throw me over your shoulder, carry me up the stairs, and lock me in my room while I am kicking, screaming, and waking the entire . . ." She paused.

"House," he finished for her and took another drink from the bottle.

"Neighborhood," she said. "Let me leave without trouble and help Edwina understand why I had to go."

"I am not good at trying to *make* her do anything."

She grabbed her basket with both hands again and said, "I'm leaving. It's up to you if you call to my sisters, grab hold to stop me, or let me go."

She turned and started walking toward the door.

Rick had no doubt if he stopped her she would try to leave again and again until she managed to escape. Her mind was set.

What should he do? What was right for his wife or what was right for her sister? A wave of dizziness caught him off guard and a sweltering heat felt as if it was consuming him. He simply had to do what seemed right to him.

Edwina would never agree for her sister to go and certainly not to aid her in doing so. He had already been up against his wife's oath to her father and lost. That was futile, as he feared trying to stop Eileen would be. He had no doubt she meant it when she said she'd try again.

"What the bloody hell? Eileen, get back here and put down the basket of food and come to the book room with me."

She stopped and turned back toward him. She held her mouth at an odd angle and her eyes squinted as if she faced the sun. Obviously, she thought he'd lost his mind. And maybe he had. His wife would surely think so.

"You want me to just quietly walk in there with you so you can lock me inside? That's not going to happen."

"I'm not going to lock you inside, although I should. I'm going to help you. If you are going to chase your dream, you are going with enough money to take care of yourself and not travel like a destitute drifter. And certainly not carrying your own food. I'll give you plenty until you return."

Her expression showed her doubt of his sincerity. "You give me your word?"

"Yes. For better or worse, I'm going to let you go. But you'll damn well have enough blunt in your pocket to take care of yourself. I'll also be sending a footman with you to make sure you are safe. While I'm at it, I might as well write a letter of introduction to Mr. Herschel for you. I have no idea if it will get you in the door since we are not acquainted, but if you meet with the man, or his sister, and talk with them, maybe you'll get this fool notion you have out of your mind, come back home, and be ready to find a husband and be a proper wife."

Her face softened, but her expression remained distrustful as she asked, "Are you really going to help me?"

"If it were any other night, I probably wouldn't. And don't forget to send a message to your sisters as soon as you get there so they will know you are safe."

"Thank you, Your Grace." She made her way as if to hug him but he held up his hand to stay her.

"Don't thank me for this." Rick took another drink from the bottle. "I know Edwina will *hate* me in the morning."

And that made him realize he loved her.

CHAPTER 25

THE ART OF BEING A FINE GENTLEMAN
SIR DUDLEY SAMSON PEMBERTON FINE

*It is not easy to be a fine gentleman,
but it is essential.*

Edwina didn't mind having her tea and toast brought to her bedchamber each morning, something that had never occurred when she was in York. In the duke's home, Palmer and the meticulous housekeeper liked to have everything done the proper way. Edwina was getting used to their more formal style and cooperating as best she could, especially since her first meeting with Palmer had been somewhat contentious. They were getting along well and she didn't want that to change, but she might modify her morning routine occasionally and join her husband downstairs.

Today, Edwina's tray remained untouched on the table in front of the window where she stood looking out.

She didn't know where Rick was. The door connecting to his room had been closed and quiet all morning. This was the first time he'd left before she'd awakened since sharing her bed. She'd missed that morning intimacy with him and tried not to feel bereft. He had probably forgotten to tell her about an early appointment. Maybe he had one of his early shooting or fencing matches that he was so fond of participating in.

Finally deciding she couldn't mope about it, she walked over to her breakfast tray to pour tea before it turned completely cold and noticed a note by the cup. Assuming it was from Rick telling her what he was doing, her spirits lifted, but just as quickly evaporated when she recognized Eileen's beautiful penmanship.

Why would her sister send a note when she lived in the same house? That was odd. She opened and read.

> I beg you not to be ill-tempered with me, Edwina, but understand I had to leave the security and comfort of your new home and life. You are happy and I'm delighted. Elle is adjusting more each day to life in London, but I am not. Therefore, as you read this, I am making my way to Mr. Herschel's Observatory. I have done my best to help you fulfill your vow to Papa, but marriage is not for me. I am sorry I can't do more but must fulfill my own dream. Please don't follow me. I promise to write.
>
> With love, dearest sister,
> Eileen

"No," Edwina whispered as her hands trembled. "She couldn't have done this. It can't be." Edwina's mind swirled with denial, but the weight pressing against her chest, obstructing her breathing was very real. Yes, Eileen had been unhappy in London, but she wouldn't run away. This must be a joke. Except, her sister was not the kind to enjoy a joke.

Fear paralyzed her for a moment. If Eileen said she

was running away, she was. Edwina bit down on her lip
and forced away the rising panic, trying to think of what
she should do first.

Find Rick. She dropped the letter onto the table and
rushed toward the door connecting her room and his
chambers. If his valet was there, he might know where
Rick was. She swung the door open to darkness. The
draperies were closed tight but sunlight from her room
spilled inside. Rick was sprawled on top of the bed side-
ways in a deep sleep. Her first thought was, *He is dressed
only in his trousers and shirt and with his feet bare?* A
prick of suspicion needled her. Had he left her bed after
she slept and gone somewhere? There was no time to concern herself with that.

"Rick," she called, hurrying over to him. "Rick, wake
up." She climbed onto the bed beside him and rested on
her knees. Leaning over him, she shook his shoulder. His
shirt felt wet, yet his body seemed warm. That was odd.
She called him a third time and he roused slowly, blink-
ing rapidly and holding his head.

His lashes fluttered up. "Edwina," he mumbled and
groaned as he rose on one elbow.

"I have a note from Eileen saying she's run away to
Slough to see Mr. Herschel. I don't know how long she's
been gone but I need your help to go after her."

He continued to hold the side of his head and hooded
his eyes with his lids as if the sunlight was torture. "What
time is it?"

"Midmorning." Anxious relief flooded her. "I'm glad
you are still here," she said gratefully. "We must go after
her. Quickly."

Rick sat up and swung his feet off the bed with a grunt.
He didn't look or act like his usual morning self. In fact,
he looked dreadful.

Fear rose up in her again. "Is something wrong? You don't look well." She scooted off the bed and looked at him more carefully. His damp hair lay limp across his forehead, his rumpled shirt hung off one shoulder. More uneasiness crept over her. They hadn't been together long but she'd never seen him in such a state.

"Nothing's wrong," he rasped, and tried to clear his throat as he rose and stood in front of her. "I'm fine. Eileen left you a note."

That's when she smelled the brandy and saw an empty bottle on the bedside table. "You've been overindulging in spirits?"

"I . . . had a headache," he mumbled as a shiver shook his shoulders.

Edwina huffed a frustrated breath. "You know brandy won't cure a headache!" she exclaimed, upset to find him in this condition and worse, on a morning she needed him so desperately. "You're dressed. Did you go somewhere after you left my bed?"

"Yes, I went—" He bent his head as if in pain and didn't finish his sentence.

The most wounding of possibilities popped into her mind. Her heart started beating so fast she wasn't sure she could breathe, but the words tumbled from her mouth before she could stop herself. "Did you leave my bed and go to your mistress?"

His head jerked as if she'd slapped him. He winced again. "Damnation, Edwina, what would make you ask that?"

"You've been drinking heavily." Her hands closed into fists at her side as her body went rigid with thoughts of where he might have been. "What should I think? Your shirt is damp, your face is flushed red, and you most definitely didn't have on your trousers when you were in bed with me."

His gaze focused and connected with hers. Anger filled his eyes. "I haven't been with a mistress since the day we met, Edwina. I no longer have one. This isn't something we need ever discuss again." He punctuated each word with emphasis.

Edwina's heartbeat and breathing slowed a little. "Thank you for telling me that," she answered, softly. "I'm pleased, but why did you drink so much?"

Rick ran his hand over his hair to the back of his head and cupped his neck. "I woke with a headache and went belowstairs for a . . . headache powder." He winced. "I know Eileen is gone because I caught her taking food from the larder."

"So, you stopped her."

"I tried." He shook his head as if trying to clear a foggy mind.

A gasp of surprise pushed from her lungs. "You saw her last night and didn't stop her?"

"She was determined to go. There was nothing I could say that changed her plan to leave."

"What?" Edwina's heartbeat raced again at the thought of her sister somewhere on the road in the dark and Rick letting her go. "Nothing? You must be three or four times stronger than she is."

"I would never put my hands on her to force her to do anything and you know that."

Edwina started trembling. "But she was running away? In the dark?"

"I tried to talk her out of it, but she was determined. I thought it best to let her leave and maybe she would realize it's not the life she wants."

"I can't believe you would do this to me," Edwina said

in a raised voice. "To her. You just stood by and let her walk out the door and into the night?"

"No, Edwina." His angry tone matched hers as he shivered again. "I helped her."

"What?" The lone word cracked with astonishment. "You aided her escape? How could you do that to me?"

Rick widened his stance and rested his hands on his hips. "I didn't do it to you, but to aid her. Her maid was already at the back gate with their satchels. Eileen knew where to catch the mail coach and what time it was leaving. It was all well planned, including taking food from the larder. So yes, I gave her money, wrote a letter of introduction to Mr. Herschel, and sent a footman to keep her safe and us notified."

For a moment, Edwina was so light-headed she couldn't breathe or speak. She couldn't move. Disbelief, anger, and betrayal swirled so quickly inside her it was too much to take in at first. "You did all that when you could have called for me to handle this. To stop her."

"You couldn't have stopped her," he said tiredly as he blinked against the bright sunlight streaming into the room from behind her. "Eileen's mind was made up long ago. She was going. If not last night, then another night. Another day or different week. She would keep trying until she made her escape. At least this way she is safe, has enough money to eat and find appropriate lodging befitting a duke's sister. It's what she wanted to do."

Edwina thought she might pound his chest. Instead, she whispered, "I don't care what she wants."

Rick shook his head. "You don't mean that, Edwina."

"I do," she said earnestly. Her heartbeat thrummed loudly in her chest and ears. Her shoulders were shaking. "I do mean it. I'm asking you to go with me to bring her back."

A muscle twitched at the side of his mouth. He swayed again on his feet. A light film of sweat had developed on his forehead. She'd never seen him in such a condition before. Rick looked positively ill. Her father had told her that too much drink could cause a good man to do bad things, and now she knew what he meant.

"I can't do that, Edwina," he said softly.

"You will help my sister but not me." She swallowed hard. "Very well. I will do it by myself," she whispered on a winded gasp of despair that hurt all the way to her soul. Her shoulders straightened. "You don't understand. Keeping my promise to my father means everything to me."

"Oh, no, Edwina," he answered on a broken, gusty chuckle. "I have always known how much that means to you. But you must recognize this: If she is old enough to marry, she is old enough to decide who she marries and when. I won't force your or your father's will on either of your sisters. It's unfair you want to keep a vow that affects someone else's life and happiness."

Edwina held back a sob and glared at him hurtfully, with more anger than she thought possible for her to feel.

He was making too much sense for her condition. She didn't want to hear it. Defying his claim, she argued, "She doesn't know what she wants, and doesn't know what's best for her. I do. Since you won't go after her, I will. If she can travel to Slough by herself, then so can I."

Edwina turned to walk away, but Rick caught her upper arm, stopping her as she entered her room. She whirled. "You will stop me but not her?"

"You are my wife." His voice flared. "She isn't. You will remain here."

"But she is your responsibility as much as I am. I trusted you to take care of her."

"Which is why I sent her with the things she needed to keep her safe."

Without thinking, she jerked her arm free from his grasp and blurted, "That does not fulfill your requirement to our arranged marriage."

"Yours has not been met yet either, Edwina," he answered sharply.

Edwina stiffened and so did Rick.

"I made no vow to your father," he continued in a raised voice. "From what I understand, neither did Eileen. I did what I thought was best."

"But it wasn't best for *me*. You don't understand. I must get them married for Papa because he gave me life."

"All fathers give their children life," he argued firmly.

"No, it was more than that. I was left to die." Her words were barely a whisper as she managed to swallow another sob.

Rick's eyes narrowed. "What?"

"Papa told me I was the smallest, youngest, and the one who kept gasping for each labored breath. The midwife and nurse urged him to lay me aside and leave me to die. They had to give their attention to Eileen and Eleonora. They had a good chance at life. But insisted I didn't." She felt that warning at the back of her eyes that preceded tears and blinked rapidly to forestall the onslaught that wanted to rush forward. "He told them I was as precious to him as the other two babes. By his strong will and exceptional knowledge, and by trying many different things, he kept me alive."

With compassion filling his expression, Rick moved closer to her. "How?"

"Papa hired extra servants to take care of us, paid them well, and swore them to secrecy." Edwina's throat tightened. "I couldn't suckle for days so they kept spooning drops of milk into my mouth every hour of every day until I started to thrive."

"Edwina," he whispered earnestly. "I'm glad he did. He worked a miracle." Rick's hand reached out as if he wanted to take her in his arms, but she stepped back. She didn't want his pity or comfort.

"Now do you understand why I must see that they are married? Papa saved my life and the only thing he ever asked of me was that I do what he had failed to do because of fear and see that all his daughters were accepted into Society and married to respectable gentlemen."

"You fulfilled much of it." Rick's voice and eyes softened. "All of you are accepted in Society. You are married. Possibly Elle one day."

"I always felt if I couldn't get them married the first Season they never would and it looks as if I will be right."

Weariness seemed to be dripping from Rick, and she thought he might have shivered again. She didn't know what kind of powder he had taken with the brandy but the two hadn't mixed well together. For an instant, the feelings of love she had for him surged inside her, and she wanted to brush her fingers across his brow and offer to comfort him. She wanted to bury her face in his chest, feel the strength of his arms so he could console her. If she were at the point she could listen. But she couldn't get past his betrayal of assisting Eileen, so she whispered, "I can't give up Papa's dream and my promise to him."

He slowly shook his head and peered deeply into her eyes. "And I can't help you, Edwina," he said as if finding it difficult to catch his breath. "You'll have to excuse me."

Something she didn't understand pricked at her intuitive feeling again. "Are you feeling all right?"

"I must get dressed for an appointment, and then I will be away for a few days."

"Away?" Her chest heaved with anxiety. That comment sent her mind reeling. "Days? I didn't know about this. And to leave now when I need you?"

"It came up suddenly," he said, in a low tired tone. "Probably best anyway. I need some time to think, Edwina. And quite frankly so do you."

Slowly, Rick turned and disappeared into his dressing room, shutting the door behind him.

CHAPTER 26

THE ART OF BEING A FINE GENTLEMAN
SIR DUDLEY SAMSON PEMBERTON FINE

*The art of becoming a fine gentleman doesn't happen
from reading just one book, but if you have finished
this one, consider you have a good start.*

Edwina missed Rick. Thoughts of him and her feelings
for him had consumed her. It had been four days since
he'd left the house and she hadn't heard from him. She'd
pressed Palmer on more than one occasion about the
duke's whereabouts. The butler couldn't have been tighter-
lipped if he were made from a hunk of iron. If he knew,
she didn't think threats of being thrown into a fiery furnace
could scare him into telling.

She nervously tightened the fingers of her gloves as
the carriage bumped, rattled, and rolled along to her next
stop. It was a short ride but would seem long, anxious as
she was. She straightened the skirt of her new dark-lilac
dress just to have something to do. Rick had said he'd love
to see her wearing this color. And he would today. If she
could find out where he was and go to him.

Edwina had had plenty of time for reflection on many
things. Not the least of which was the way Rick appeared
the morning after Eileen had run away. The way he looked
pained and his mannerisms continued to trouble her.

Something more than the aftereffects of too much brandy and headache powder had been wrong. For some reason, he hadn't wanted her to know what it was. It could have been because she was overwrought about what Eileen had done and that Rick had helped her. That had been difficult to comprehend and even harder to accept.

Now, with disquiet, she remembered the strain around his eyes, the tightness of his mouth, the unnatural flush on his face, and his unsteady feet. At the time, she hadn't paid much attention to how warm his body was when he'd been sleeping with no covers and wearing a damp shirt. His skin should have been cool to her touch.

Edwina had no familiarity with someone who'd over-indulged in spirits or headache tonics. Her father certainly never had. Too filled with her own hurts and anger with him, she'd made little note of his condition and the way he'd winced, thinking they too were the aftereffects of being jug-bitten.

Now she was worried. A fourth day wouldn't pass without her finding out where he was and what he was doing. Someone knew where he was. She was sure of that and wasn't going to stop searching until she found him.

Edwina had to make sure he was all right, ask him to forgive her for being so irrational about Eileen's heart-breaking decision to leave her family, and, most of all, she wanted Rick to know that she didn't hate him for what he'd done. She loved him. More than anything or anyone in the world. It was just that simple.

She had to find him.

With that in mind, the first stop had been to Wyatt and Fredericka's home, but that had been no help. They had taken Fredericka's nieces and nephew for a picnic in the park and the butler had no idea when they might return. She'd thought about waiting but decided it would do no good to sit in their drawing room for what could be hours. Scouring the park to find them would probably take just as long.

After a bit of contemplation, she was now bound for Hurst's house in the hope he was home and knew Rick's whereabouts. If that didn't work, she would be forced to her last and most dreaded resort. Rick's mother.

The possibility of that tightened Edwina's stomach into knots. Not that the dowager duchess had ever said an impolite word to her. Far from it. She was pleasant as the day was long. She would probably always look at Edwina with what appeared to be curious thoughts. That didn't bother Edwina, however the idea of the dowager learning she didn't know her husband's whereabouts did.

If left with no other choice, Edwina would humble herself and go to Rick's mother's door. She would do anything necessary to find him and make amends. If it wasn't too late.

The carriage hit a hole and jostled Edwina's musings back to the coach. Taking a deep breath, she leaned forward and looked out the window. Through the slice of space between two houses, she saw a small section of the sky. The color was a heavenly blue and reminded her of Rick's eyes. She remembered how she loved lying beside him and looking dreamily into them. That thought led her to think about how tenderly he caressed her cheeks, shoulders, and breasts. How his passionate kisses were filled with such desire for her that she was left with nothing but indescribable joy.

Reasoning out one's thoughts, perceptions, and wants, and then settling them in your own mind was not an instant but a journey. Her answers hadn't come easy the first day he was gone, nor on the second or third. The process of it all was wrenching.

At first, all the feelings of anger, betrayal, and distrust swirling inside her were raw and impossible to fathom, so she stayed numb and didn't try. Finally, she searched her feelings for her father and Eileen to find peace within herself and with both of them. The realization she'd done all she could to fulfill her vow to her father gave her the strength she needed to let go of the bindings she'd placed on her sisters.

Her love for Rick came first and foremost, and at the end of her emotional journey, she knew Rick was right to tell her it wasn't her responsibility to force her father's will on Elle and Eileen. That had been a difficult decision to come to.

The carriage rolled to a stop and minutes later Edwina was waiting for the Duke of Hurstbourne in the vestibule of his Mayfair home.

Thankfully, he was at home, but since she had no appointment, the butler had to see if the duke was available for a visit. She didn't know Hurst well. That didn't matter. She hadn't known Rick at all when she'd first knocked on his door.

"Edwina."

She rose and saw the powerfully built duke striding toward her. The short ends of his light-blond hair fluttered out to the sides as he walked. "This is a surprise."

To her astonishment, he didn't reach for her hand, but instead, took hold of her upper arms and planted a brotherly kiss on first one cheek, then the other before letting go and stepping back.

"I hope I'm not interrupting you." She smiled, grateful for his warm reception.

"Nothing of importance." His gaze searched hers curiously. "Is everything well with you and your sisters?"

Edwina thought she heard a tinge of concern in his

voice and that filled her with even more unease. "Yes, and Aunt Pauline too. I'm here about Rick. Do you mind chatting with me a few minutes?"

The bridge of his nose crinkled and she wasn't sure if it was because of curiosity or concern, but he said, "Not at all."

He brushed his long hair away from his forehead, as a distraction or habit she wasn't sure, but somehow, Edwina discerned Hurst knew exactly where Rick was. But how was she going to get him to tell her? Grabbing hold of his neckcloth and trying to force him sounded like a good idea but probably wouldn't work.

Instead as she was inclined to do, she clasped her hands together in front of her skirts, and on a hunch, she said, "He wasn't feeling well when he left home a few days ago. I've been worried about him."

"Let's go into the drawing room and sit down," Hurst suggested. "I'll have tea brought in."

She grew more anxious by the moment. "That's not necessary, but thank you." She moistened her lips and remained still as she said, "How is he? Better?"

The duke fell silent for a moment. He searched her eyes before saying, "Yes, he is. I wasn't aware you were told he'd been ill."

Edwina's pulse jumped. Her thoughts reeled at hearing her instincts had been right. How sick had Rick been? Why hadn't he wanted her to know? Why had he gone to great lengths to keep it from her? Yes, they were angry with each other about Eileen, but to keep his illness a secret and allow her to think he'd had too much to drink? Suddenly, the urge to demand Hurst tell her immediately where Rick was rose in her again. But she was reminded of something her father used to say: *"One could get more bees with honey than vinegar."* She had to be calmer and more civilized in her approach or risk him not telling her anything.

"I've been concerned about Rick, thinking every day I would hear from him." She paused, doing her best to come up with something sensible to say. "I heard from Eileen this morning. He was instrumental in helping her do something. I knew he would want to know she's settled."

"Would you like for me to tell him?"

A nervous flutter started in her chest as she did her best to remain composed. "I would rather do that myself, if you don't mind," she said, knowing her words sounded more like a plea. "That is why I'm here."

He studied her face as if searching for a destination on a map. "What makes you think he is staying with me?"

Edwina's stomach quaked with relief. She'd found him. "A wife's intuitive spirit led me here," she answered carefully, hoping that would be enough to sway the duke. If not, she was prepared to search the house until she found him. She wasn't leaving until she did.

Hurst brushed his hair again and smiled. "That reason's good enough for me. He's better. Stronger. The fever's passed."

Fever? Yes. That would explain so much.

"It's probably best if I don't ask him if he'll see you," Hurst said, kindly.

"No, no, no," she responded quickly, shaking her head and stepping toward him. "You must."

He chuckled lightly. "If I ask, he might say no. I don't think you want that." He motioned toward the stairs with his head. "At the top, turn right. Third door."

A gust of breath broke past her lips and before thinking

she grabbed him around his wide chest and hugged him quickly. "Thank you!" she whispered, before racing off.

Edwina quickly found the room and reached up to knock but halted in midair when she realized her hands were shaking and her knees were trembling. What would she do if he insisted she leave? She couldn't. Taking several deep breaths, she decided to handle that when the time came. Right now, she needed to see him.

Quietly, she opened the door and peeked inside. He was in a sitting position on the bed, leaning against pillows with his face turned away from the door. Tears pooled in her eyes as she walked closer to him. She would never be able to explain how happy she was to see him, and sleeping too peacefully to disturb. The redness and stress had left his face.

It didn't matter why he hadn't wanted her to know he was ill, or if he refused to forgive her for the things she said. Right now, she only wanted him to let her stay until he was completely well. Everything else could wait. While watching him, she removed her gloves, bonnet, and pelisse and laid them aside. She took the pins from her hair. Shaking it loose, she let it fall across her shoulders the way he loved to see it. Any small way she could please him was important.

Seeing him made the thought of losing him all the harder. She didn't want to live without him. When they married it was an arrangement. A means to an end that was the most important thing in her life. Now Rick was her everything and she loved him deeply.

She wanted to press her lips to his while he still slept in case he demanded she leave as soon as he awakened. Brushing that thought aside, she decided to ease onto the bed beside him for a moment and softly lay her head on his shoulder. She had done that before without waking him. The possibility she might never feel that soothing, wonderful feeling again wrenched her heart.

Edwina slipped out of her shoes, lifted the hem of her dress, and placed her knee on the bed. It creaked loud as a boom of thunder after a hot flash of lightning.

Rick's lashes flew up. "Edwina," he murmured, rising from the pillows. "What are you doing here?"

"Trying not to wake you." She smiled with all the love she was feeling though tension racked her body. She bent over him and placed her hands on his shoulders, gently pressing him back down. "Don't try to rise. Rest."

"I've been resting for days," he grumbled in the irritable voice she'd come to enjoy as he acquiesced. "I can't believe Hurst told you I was here."

"He didn't." By an act of will, she reluctantly drew her hands away from his shoulders. No need to push her luck when he hadn't instantly insisted she leave the room. Still, she kept the one knee on the bed. "I have been so worried about you. My heart led me to seek help from your friends and that led me here."

His eyes searched hers intently but he remained quiet.

"Why didn't you tell me that morning you were sick with fever and not from brandy?" she asked, wanting to understand.

"That's a simple answer. I had downed a fair amount of brandy as well." He looked away from her briefly before making eye contact again. "I didn't want you to know about the fever."

"A fever, Rick?" she asked softly, wanting to hold him close. "Not a contagious one. That doesn't sound so bad. And you've recovered now."

He sat up straighter in the bed, bringing his body

closer to hers. "Not just an isolated fever. Intermittent fevers, Edwina. This was the third."

A new rush of fear stabbed her. She hadn't read much about them but knew they could be deadly. "That can be serious. What can we do about them?"

"I'm doing all that can be done for now. I drink the tonics and wait for the chills, fever, head and body aches to pass."

"Why didn't you tell me?" she implored, leaning toward him, longing to wrap her arms around him. "Did you think I wouldn't understand?"

"I hoped I'd never have another one, and I didn't want to add to your burden. You were dealing with your own troubles, Edwina, and I know how deeply it hurt you for Eileen to leave. For me to have helped her. I'd given you enough heartache."

"I still would have wanted to know," she replied a little briskly, wounded by all that had been said between them last time they were together as well as the news of his illness.

"Would it have made any difference in how you felt at the time?"

"Yes, of course," she whispered earnestly.

His jaw tightened. "And I would have liked to know you were a triplet, Edwina. But you chose to hide that from me."

"My life wasn't in danger," she argued heatedly. "Yours was. Not only that, but you could have told me about the fevers when you found out I was a triplet. Why didn't you trust me?"

"Trust?" he said the word as if an oath and leaned toward her. "That is an odd question coming from you, Edwina. Perhaps it was the same reason you didn't trust me with your past?"

Her heart squeezed. Her anger dissipated as suddenly as it had flared. "You're right. I didn't. And after much thought, I am sorry I didn't. Maybe I should go. I didn't come here to argue or tire you. I only want you well."

He took hold of her wrist when she started to move her knee off the bed. "Why did you come?" he asked as his gaze swept over her face.

Should she be honest? A lump rose rapidly in her throat, and she couldn't seem to swallow it down. *Could* she be completely honest and trust him with the truth of her feelings? Looking into his beautiful eyes, she knew she had to take the chance. "I wanted you to know that no matter what you think or feel about me, I've fallen in love with you and want to live with you as your wife for the rest of my life." The heartfelt words poured from her soul. "I'm sorry for putting my father's wishes and my sisters' issues before you. I shouldn't have done that."

A smile brightened his expression and he nodded. "I'm sorry I helped Eileen without talking to you first, but I still would have helped her."

"I know," she answered with sincerity. Her lashes closed over her eyes for a moment before she spoke. "I am grateful you took steps to see she was safe."

"Edwina." He regarded her with deep concentration. "I told you I will always take care of you and your family. Not just because you are my wife, not just because you will be the mother of my heir, but because I love you. I've missed having you beside me."

"I wanted to hear those words," she whispered, grabbing hold of his hand, and kissing it as she squeezed tightly.

He pulled his hand away and his arms circled her, pulling her close as she crawled onto the creaking mattress and relaxed against him. Their lips met in a brief, tender kiss.

He brushed her hair away from the side of her face. "I've always had issues with trusting people. When I was a child, my mother never trusted me to be left on my own. In turn, it was difficult for me to trust anyone because I was constantly watched. Before I was ready to take over my duties as duke and all my inherited properties, my father's best friend and a trustee mismanaged my estates. The accountants didn't catch on to what they were doing until I pointed it out to them. In turn, I've never trusted anyone."

"Learning to trust each other is something we are going to have to do together," she said softly.

Rick hugged her tightly to him before setting his attention on her face once again. "No more hiding or omitting by either of us again. No distrusting each other about anything."

"I trust you, Rick. With my heart, my sisters, our children. Everything."

"You've probably already guessed the fever is the reason I wanted to marry so quickly. I need an heir."

Edwina let out a soft, easy breath as she nodded. "And I'm happy to oblige."

He moistened his lips and added, "You need to know there's always a chance the fever will rage so high the willow bark won't bring it down. I could have a fever I don't recover from."

"No," she whispered, denying the fear his words caused. "That won't happen. We promised each other in sickness and health. I will be with you if the fever returns again, and I will take care of you."

Placing his hands to each side of her face, he kissed

her gently. And then he kissed her again. Longer, sweeter than she could remember.

With all conviction, she was sure they were going to successfully weather this illness.

"Apothecaries, alchemists, and others are always coming up with new concoctions and combinations of herbs and plants," she reminded him. "Too, if it comes again, I will bathe you in water from a cold spring to bring the fever down." She ran her hand across his shoulder and down his arm as if washing him. She repeated the motion. "And again until the fever is gone." She moved her hands slowly down his ribs, to his waist and along the plane of his hip to his thigh and back up the same route. Edwina placed her lips just above his and whispered, "I love you with all my heart and I will not let a fever overtake you."

He tenderly touched her cheek. "You are my love, Edwina. No one else could have ever taught me the things you have or won the respect I have for you."

Rick's words thrilled her as he covered her mouth with his kiss. Taking his time, he kissed her lovingly, slowly. Softly and long. Sweetly and soothingly. She wanted to make love with him but for now would be happy to just be with him. It was a glorious feeling to feather her hands up his rippled ribs and across his muscular chest and shoulders.

They were quiet for a moment or two and she listened to his heart beating against her ear.

"I had a letter from Eileen this morning. She is well and wanted me to tell you that your letter of introduction succeeded in getting her an appointment to meet with Mr. Herschel."

"I'm glad dukes are good for something."

"You, my duke, are good for many things."

A chuckle rumbled in his chest. "Did you answer her?"

Edwina shook her head. "Not yet. I've been too worried about you."

"You'll have to tell her, you know," Rick said and raised her chin to look into her eyes.

Edwina tensed. "Tell her what?"

"That you are all right with her pursuing her dreams instead of her father's dreams."

"I won't lie to her," she said unequivocally. "You know that."

He nodded. "Then make it the truth. Settle this for the last time in your mind. The debt you had to your father was an honest one, but you've paid it now, Edwina. Your sisters are accepted in Society. As I have to settle in my mind I have recurrent fevers. We've done all we can do for both. The outcome is not up to us. Give up your burden and let her have happiness."

"Do you think she will be happy chasing after stars in the heavens rather than a husband?"

"It doesn't matter what I think. It's what she believes."

Edwina inhaled a deep breath. "I still want her to come back," she whispered.

"You probably always will, but don't try to force her. Look at me," he said, with the tips of his fingers under her chin. "I love you. Let my love be enough to make you happy."

Edwina reached over and kissed the side of his cheek near his ear and the crook of his neck. "Your love is enough. It always will be, and I don't want to ever disappoint you."

He hugged her closely. "You have not disappointed me, my love. I am a gruff beast at times, but you have taught me how to love, and to be careful what I say and how I say it. Most of all, you have taught me that we can trust each other."

Rick couldn't have said anything that pleased her more.

"I want to give you sons. As many as you want."

"But not all at one time," he said with a grin.

She laughed softly. "No. No. One at a—" From the corner of her eye, something caught her attention. Delight filled her. "You have a copy of my father's book."

"I read it while I didn't have the strength to do anything else."

"I don't know what to say other than I'm shocked and—"

"Happy?" He smiled.

"Yes, of course I am. Especially when you have been less than—"

"Glowing with my compliments of your father?"

She shrugged and said, "Yes."

"I have more admiration for him now that I know he saved your life after you were born. I'm indebted to him. However, in keeping with our promise not to hide or withhold all the truth from each other, I must reveal that Hurst had already bought the book. He brought it in here in case I wanted to look it over."

"It doesn't matter how you got it. Thank you for reading it. And, as long as we aren't going to hide anything from each other anymore . . ." She grinned. "I remember a conversation where you once said you'd never been attacked by two women at the same time. What exactly did you mean?"

Rick made an exaggerated sound of clearing his throat. "Yes, my darling wife. I seem to recall something about that, but perhaps I'll take a bit of advice from a man who wrote a book titled *The Art of Being A Fine Gentleman*."

Her eyes filled with delightful surprise. "And what is that?"

Rick grinned. "When talking to a lady, a fine gentleman knows when to speak and when to hold his tongue."

EPILOGUE

THE ART OF BEING A FINE GENTLEMAN
SIR DUDLEY SAMSON PEMBERTON FINE

At the end of the day or the end of this book,
being a fine gentleman doesn't start with
good manners. It starts with his heart.

"It looks like rain," Rick called from the back steps of their London townhome. "What are you doing out here?"

Edwina looked up from their son on her lap to see her husband coming down the steps toward them. She smiled and waved, thinking he was now more handsome than the first day she saw him. Five years hadn't changed him. Or her. Her heart still fluttered when she looked at him.

"Papa!" Emmeline squealed and ran over to him. Rick picked up his daughter and swung her around a few times before planting a kiss on her forehead and setting her back on her feet. That was enough attention for the active little girl who looked so much like him with light-brown hair and sparkling blue eyes. She skipped back over to her governess at the play area filled with a small wooden castle and cloth dolls.

"There's already a mist in the air. You may get wet." Rick bent over his son's head and kissed Edwina on the lips before making himself comfortable on the bench beside her.

She looked at him lovingly. "We have time. Emme doesn't want to go in yet. Who won?"

He shrugged arrogantly. "I did."

"Are you ever going to let Matthew win another shooting match with you?"

He seemed to think seriously about that before shaking his head and grinning. "Not in this century. Maybe in the next."

"It would help make Elle feel a little cheerier at times if you would be more cordial to him when we are with them. He's been in the family four years now."

"They spend Christmastide with us at Stonerick and dinner most Sundays with my mother. I tolerate Malcolm. That is enough." Rick chuckled and rubbed the top of his son's bonnet-covered head. "What's our little red-haired fellow doing? You can't get both fists in your mouth at one time," he said to his babe. "Sir Dudley Fine would never approve of a gentleman doing that." Rick tried to pull Stone's hands down but his son wasn't having any of that and started to fret.

"He's trying to help his teeth come through. Leave him alone and let him be about his work."

Rick immediately ceased and scrunched up his face. "The front of his shirt and sleeves are soaked."

"I will see he gets into dry clothing as soon as we go in," Edwina assured him patiently. "Your shooting was obviously excellent today. You are in a wonderful mood. How did you find your mother?"

"Happy as a lark on a sunny Sunday morning."

The dowager had always been polite toward Edwina and her family. But something in her had changed the day the heir to the title was born. Rick's mother had become warm, friendly, and a frequent visitor to their home to spend time with Stone.

"Speaking of family . . ." Rick pulled a letter out of his inside pocket. "Palmer said this had just arrived for you so I brought it out. It's from Eileen."

"Oh, wonderful. I haven't heard from her in a month." Edwina plopped Stone onto Rick's knee and took the letter out of his hand.

"Wait, no," he said, holding the baby stiffly around the chest as if he were afraid to touch him. "You know I am not good at this. I'd rather wait until he gets a little older to hold him."

Edwina smiled. "Nonsense. He'll be walking soon and following you everywhere. You learned how to be comfortable with Emmeline and you will with him too."

Stone made a sound or two as if to cry. Rick started bouncing his knee and soon his son found his mouth with his fists again. It didn't take much to make the little fellow happy.

"He's too thin," Rick suggested, touching around his son's chest area with his fingers. "I feel his ribs. Are you sure he's healthy?"

"Of course. Stop worrying. It will be twenty years before he's as tall, strong, and handsome as you."

Rick gave her a knowing smile and reached over to kiss her again.

"I do wish Eileen would write more often," Edwina complained.

"She is busy with writing her notes about the stars."

"I have many things to do too, but I manage to send her a short missive at least once a week with news of the family." Edwina broke open the seal. "Would you like for me to read out loud?"

"Why not?" he said, his knee continuing to bounce. "It will take my mind off the slobber that is running down my hands and soaking my trousers."

Edwina laughed and then read, "'My dearest Edwina, we have had many beautiful, clear nights this summer and have finished numerous calculations and charting of movements in the sky. My head is full of such luxurious moments of discovery too perfect to put into words. And so goes the way of my heart.'"

Edwina felt a chill run down her spine. She stopped and looked at Rick. "Heart?"

He shrugged. "Read on."

"'I would like for you and the duke to make a visit as soon as you can. There is a gentleman who recently started working with us and I want you to meet him.'"

Edwina jerked toward Rick again. "Did you hear that?"

"Of course, my darling," he said patiently. "Has she ever mentioned a gentleman to you before?"

"Never. And not her heart either. Not even at Stone's baptism." Edwina anxiously lowered her eyes back to the page, wanting to make sure it said what she thought it had.

"'I shan't tell you more for I fear you won't hurry to come to me if I reveal too much in a letter. But I can't wait for you to meet him. All my love to you, dearest sister, and everyone, Eileen.'"

"I don't know what to think," Edwina said while searching the letter for unwritten clues. "Rick, do you think this means she has fallen in love and is thinking of marriage?" Her heart pounded with the possibility of it being true.

"I don't know, my love, but you probably shouldn't get your hopes up about anything until you talk to Eileen."

"But I feel so anxious. She's never asked us to come visit her before. She's always come to stay with us."

"Only look at this as she wants us to visit and nothing more," he advised. "I don't want you to read too much into her words and be disappointed." The babe gurgled and squirmed. Rick started moving his knee again.

"But it is a good sign that she is actually thinking about something other than the heavens, and I do think we should make plans to visit her soon, don't you?"

"We'll visit," he answered, sounding completely uninterested in the conversation as he struggled to keep his son happy with both knees bouncing.

"Thank you." Edwina smiled at him sweetly. "When do you think we should leave?"

He looked at her and grinned. "Tomorrow. I'm as anxious as you to find out who this gentleman is."

"Oh, Rick!" She threw her arms around him and kissed him so fast it scared Stone and he started crying.

Rick tried to hand him over to Edwina and he cried harder. Emmeline ran over. "What's wrong with him? What did you do to him?"

"Nothing," Rick said, giving his little girl a smile while wiping his wet hands on his trousers. "He's fine."

Edwina called the governess over and told her to take the children inside. It was important to Edwina to spend time with Stone and Emme as her father had with her and her sisters, but time alone with Rick was even more important.

"Thank you for not wanting to wait to go see Eileen," she said as they settled back down onto the bench. "I do hope she's not teasing me."

Rick put his arm around her shoulder and scooted closer to her. "Why would she do that, my love? You've said yourself she's not the type to tease."

"True. It would be so wonderful if she finally married, completely fulfilling my father's wish."

"You already have," Rick said, picking up her hand and kissing it. "I think all he wanted was for the three of you to live and prosper out from under the sanctuary where you grew up. Too late in life he realized he should have never hidden you but rejoiced in your amazing birth and life."

Edwina felt her love for Rick overflowing. "I know you are right."

"And I like hearing you say that." Rick bent his head and kissed her lovingly.

"We should go in. I always worry the fever and chills might return if you get caught in the rain."

Rick frowned. "It's been almost five years since my last episode, my darling. We've been told the Peruvian bark tonic has been very effective in curing the fevers, and I believe it has cured mine."

Edwina wound her arms around his neck and smiled. "I don't want to take any chances. I love you too much."

"And I love you," he whispered, and pressed his lips to hers.

Edwina thrilled to his touch.

AUTHOR'S NOTES

Dear Readers,

I hope you have enjoyed *Sincerely, The Duke*, the second book in my series Say I Do. It was a delight to write Rick and Edwina's story and watch their love for each other grow.

I suspect most, if not all of you, quickly concluded that Rick's recurring fever was malaria, though it wasn't given that name until after the Regency in 1829. This periodic fever has been around since ancient times, but in 1820 two French chemists, Pierre Joseph Pelletier and Joseph Caventou, isolated quinine from cinchona bark, also known by several other names, including Peruvian bark. The powder was highly effective and became the preferred treatment of choice for reducing the recurrence of intermittent fevers.

When it came to Eileen's study of the heavens, I took literary license with Frederick William Herschel and his sister, Caroline, and gave Edwina's sister, Eileen, employment with them. Herschel is well known and acclaimed for his forty-foot telescope, constructed between 1785 and 1789 at Observatory House in Slough,

England. He's credited with many discoveries, including the planet Uranus, before his death in 1822. Caroline not only aided her brother in his studies but made many discoveries on her own and became the world's first professional female astronomer.

I also took literary license when it came to the birth of triplets living to adulthood during the Regency, a time when it was still rare for twins to do so. Since there is no proof it didn't happen, and it made a wonderful addition to my story, I decided to make Edwina born of three.

Red hair and green eyes are one of the rarest combinations. Some statistics I read said less than one percent of the world's population had this coloring. It seemed all agreed red hair and blue eyes are the rarest.

If you missed the first book in this series, *Yours Truly, The Duke*, you can order it at your favorite bookstore or e-retailer. And don't forget to watch for publication dates for the third book, *Love, The Duke*.

Hearing from readers is always a pleasure. You can email me at ameliagreyauthor@gmail.com, follow me on Facebook at facebook.com/AmeliaGreyBooks, or visit my website at ameliagrey.com.

Happy reading!
Amelia Grey